Second
Chances

ELIZA LENTZSKI

DEDICATION

To C

CONTENTS

Other works by Eliza Lentzski

Diary of a Human

Love, Lust, & Other Mistakes

Date Night

Winter Jacket (May 2013)

PART 1: JUNIOR YEAR

CHAPTER ONE

Reagan Murphy looked up at the Broadway stage before returning her gaze to the notebook in which she'd been frantically scribbling for the past hour. She hated this assignment, hated that her professor was making her pick apart one of her all-time favorite Broadway musicals, and hated that yet another Saturday night of her Junior year was passing her by. If she had to spend the evening this way, she wanted the freedom to sit and soak in the ambiance of the historic theater and move her lips along with the familiar songs – not write notes for an assignment she felt was blasphemous.

Taking her attention away from the action on stage, she looked around at the faces of the theater patrons seated in her section. One of her greatest pleasures in attending theatrical performances, particularly those with which she was familiar, was looking at other people's faces and watching their reaction to poignant scenes and songs. Under the blanket of theater darkness she could anonymously observe the myriad of emotions playing across different people's faces. She loved catching the most unexpected reactions from otherwise stereotypical-looking people. The embarrassment or keen interest in a heavy love scene. The tears and anguish of a heartbreak and star-crossed lovers. The joy and laughter in a well-timed comedic scene.

Tonight, almost everyone in her surrounding section was older than her. One of the perks of going to her school was the discounted and sometimes free tickets to Broadway and Off-Broadway productions that she normally wouldn't be able to afford as a jobless college student. Her eyebrows furrowed together when she noticed a cluster of girls about her age a few rows back just off to her right. She wondered how they could have afforded the same orchestra pit seats. She inspected their faces more closely. Maybe they went to school with her and had taken advantage of the reduced-priced tickets. She scanned the row of unfamiliar faces until her gaze stopped on one. A young woman – a blonde with high, chiseled cheekbones. She almost looked like...

The girl, as if sensing Reagan's stare, flicked her eyes away from the stage and made eye contact with her. Reagan immediately looked away and retrained her eyes on the center stage and pretended to be watching the show.

There was no way that could be her. *It would be an* impossible *coincidence.*

After another painful minute, Reagan once again hazarded a glance in the direction of the far too familiar-looking girl. The woman in question was still staring at her. Reagan sucked in a sharp breath when she lifted an eyebrow at her.

"No. No. No. This can't be happening. She *can't be happening.* She *can't be here,"* Reagan mentally panicked. Her chest constricted *"It's dark,"* she tried to reason with herself. *"It's just a girl that looks similar. A trick of light."*

She looked again. The other woman was still looking in her direction. When their eyes met again, Reagan could just make out how one corner of the woman's mouth curled up into a peculiar smile.

She tore her eyes away again and forced herself to pay attention to what was happening on stage. But as much as she wanted to, she just couldn't concentrate. She gripped tightly to her armrests. Her palms were sweating. She needed to escape, but she couldn't. It would be terribly rude to get up in the middle of a performance. Plus, she needed to pay attention. This was homework. This was for a grade.

"Focus, Reagan," she chastised herself. She slumped down in her chair and forced herself to keep her eyes turned toward the stage, counting down the minutes until the final curtain call.

When the house lights finally turned on, flooding the theater, Reagan leapt from her seat. She wasn't going to take any chances in case the girl she had seen was in fact who she feared it was. She hastily grabbed her winter jacket from where she'd draped it over the back of her chair and made her way toward the nearest aisle exit. She was forced to stop, however, when she reached a family of four slowly gathering their personal items. She spun on her heels to exit in the other direction, but spotted an elderly couple in her direct path unhurriedly standing and stretching out ancient limbs.

She cursed under her breath. She was stuck.

"Don't think you get to run away without saying hi to me, Murphy."

Oh no.

Reagan slowly turned in the direction of the frighteningly familiar voice. There, standing in the aisle nearest her, was the last person she ever expected to see again. She found herself speechless. It wasn't a feeling to which she was accustomed.

"Should I be offended?" The blonde woman's lips twisted into a familiar smirk. "You look like you've just seen a ghost."

Reagan blinked hard a few times and shook her head, hoping the movement would rattle her brain back into commission. "N-no," she uncharacteristically stuttered. "I'm just surprised to see you here is all."

A perfectly manicured eyebrow lifted on an unlined forehead. "I'm not allowed to enjoy one of the top Broadway shows of the season?" the other woman mused.

"Of course you are. I just thought you were in Rhode Island. At Brown," Reagan stated, still clearly confused as to why Allison Hoge, the girl who had personally made her high school years a living hell, was standing in front of her. In New York City.

Allison nodded. "I am. I'm just here for the weekend with some friends," she observed with a casual shrug. She glanced behind her shoulder at a group of similarly aged girls who appeared to be waiting for her.

Reagan glanced in the direction of the group. Three young women, each in tailored wool jackets and designer scarves, impatiently shouldered their nearly matching, oversized designer purses. They looked exactly like the type of people with whom the Ivy-League-College Allison Hoge would be friends, she mentally observed.

"Well it was, uh, nice to see you," Reagan nodded. She clutched her notebook to her chest, feeling oddly like the high school version of herself under Allison's intense gaze. "I hope you enjoy your weekend. New York's a great city."

Allison's hazel eyes narrowed perceptibly. "Are you giving me the brush off, Murphy?"

"No, I just didn't want to keep you from your friends any longer," Reagan hastily explained.

Allison regarded the shorter woman for a moment. She seemed to be struggling with something before making up her mind. "I'm heading back to my campus in the morning," she said. "We should get brunch before I have to catch my train."

"Why?" Reagan reflexively fired back without really thinking.

"Is it so hard to believe that maybe I'm curious to know how you've been doing?" Allison rolled her eyes.

"Honestly, yes. It is." Reagan stood a little taller, emboldened by her words.

"Just have brunch with me," Allison sighed. She absentmindedly raked her fingers through her corn-silk hair. She had been meaning to cut it, but there never seemed to be any time. "We could meet at Pershing Square at 11am. You know where that is?"

Reagan nodded. "It's across from Grand Central Station."

"Right," Allison confirmed. She glanced once more at her impatient friends when she heard one them clearing her throat to get her attention. The girl, a tall redhead with long, wavy locks and an upturned nose, tapped at her wristwatch. "I've got to go," she said hastily. "I'll see you tomorrow." Without waiting for a response from Reagan, she spun on her heels and started to follow her friends out of the now-nearly empty theater.

Reagan stood, dumbfounded, her brain unable or unwilling to process what had just happened. She couldn't help but feel like she'd been blindsided. She hadn't seen Allison Hoge since graduation, over three years ago. But they hadn't been friends in high school, so that wasn't so surprising. What did surprise her was not only Allison's unexpected appearance, but also the fact that she wanted to have brunch the following morning.

It had to be a trick, she reasoned to herself. It had to be a trap.

And she really needed a drink.

"Hey, Murphy!"

Reagan jerked to attention when she heard the familiar voice calling to her. She saw Allison standing near the rear exit. The house lights illuminated her beautiful features. "Yes?" she called back.

Allison's lips twisted into a wry grin. "Don't stand me up tomorrow."

Reagan tried to smile back, but it felt more like a grimace. She waved weakly and then dropped her arm, immediately feeling ridiculous. She half expected a bucket of pig's blood to spill over her or a shower of rotten eggs to cascade from the balcony seats above; instead, she watched Allison disappear out of sight, leaving her physically unscathed.

Mentally, however, was another story altogether. Reagan took a few more moments to gather her thoughts, and then she finally pulled on her jacket to prepare for the New York winter night.

+++++

Reagan unlocked her dorm room door and was instantly greeted by the sound of her roommate's loud music. Ashley, a music performance major, looked up from her laptop and smiled when she saw Reagan enter their shared space. She turned down the volume on her laptop's speakers.

"How was the play?"

Reagan shrugged out of her jacket and hung it on a set of hooks near the door. "It was good," she acknowledged, pulling off her scarf. "It would have been even better if I had gone for fun though and not as an assignment for my script writing course."

Although an art and graphic design major, she'd originally signed up for the course thinking it would be an easy A. She loved to write and she loved movies and plays. The class, however, was turning out to be more work than some of her major field classes.

"Guess you'll just have to go see it again when the semester is over," Ashley suggested. "I'll go with," she volunteered. "I've been wanting to see that show since the semester started."

Reagan sat at her desk and opened her laptop. "Definitely," she agreed. "Let's get tickets for after Finals Week. We can celebrate the end of another successful semester."

Ashley grinned. "Awesome. I'll get some tickets right now." Her fingers flew across the keys of her computer. "What are you up to the rest of the night? Want to find a party?"

Reagan made a disgruntled noise. "I've got to finish this assignment while the thoughts are still fresh in my head."

"Aw, can't that wait until tomorrow?" Ashley pouted, looking up from her computer screen. "It's the weekend!"

Reagan opened a word document. "I know, I know," she sighed. She closed her eyes and pinched at the bridge of her nose. "But I might have plans in the morning," she grumbled reluctantly.

"Might?"

"Yeah, might. Maybe. I don't know. I probably shouldn't even go," Reagan worried out loud.

Ashley chuckled at her roommate's dramatics. Although she was the performance major, Reagan had a particular talent for turning her real life into a Broadway show. "Are you going to tell me what's up or are you going to insist on being vague and make me pull it out of you?"

"Tonight at the play I ran into someone I knew from high school."

"From Michigan? Wow," Ashley remarked. "Small world, huh?"

Reagan nodded, momentarily thoughtful. "And she wants to meet up for brunch in the morning."

Ashley's eyebrows scrunched together in confusion. "But you don't know if you're going to go? Why not?" she pressed. "You love food."

Reagan stuck her tongue out at her roommate. "You're lucky I have a healthy relationship with my body," she quipped.

"Whatever, Skinny," Ashley breezed. "Now tell me, why are you on the fence about meeting up with an old friend?"

"Because we weren't exactly friends in school. In fact," Reagan said, sucking in a deep breath, "we kind of hated each other."

"Oooh," Ashley cooed. She sat up straighter in bed, suddenly more interested. "Even better. Did she get fat?" she asked excitedly. "I love it when they get fat."

Reagan laughed. "God, no. She looked as perfect as ever."

"Well it's not like you let yourself go after high school, right?" Ashley pragmatically noted.

Reagan shook her head.

"And you're successful in a highly competitive arts program, living in the capital of awesomeness, right?" her roommate added.

Reagan chuckled. "Yeah, I guess so."

"So? Why wouldn't you want to go? Show Miss Thang how awesome you are," Ashley crowed. "I bet it pales in comparison to whatever she's been up to lately. You can make her insides *rot* with jealousy."

"She goes to an Ivy League school."

Ashley's face drooped. "Oh. Well. You're still pretty great."

Reagan laughed and threw a balled up piece of paper at her friend. "Remind me why I *volunteered* to be your roommate?"

Ashley easily deflected the tossed projectile. Reagan was a lot of things, but naturally athletic wasn't on that list. "Oh, don't kid yourself, Prez. You know I'm fabulous."

Reagan rolled her eyes at the nickname. As soon as the two had met their freshman year, Ashley had insisted calling her 'President,' and now shortened the nickname even more so. The name always drew odd looks from people who didn't know them. "Uh huh," Reagan said drolly. "I'll keep reminding myself that tomorrow morning when I'm sitting across the table from my arch-nemesis."

"So does that mean you're going?" Ashley clapped excitedly. She bounced on the bed a little.

"Maybe I should send you along instead," Reagan snorted. "You seem more excited than me."

Ashley hopped off her bed. "You should be excited, too," she exclaimed. "How many times does the universe give us second chances and do-overs?"

"You think that's what this is?"

Ashley stood in front of Reagan's open closet and tapped her fingers against her lips in thought. "Maybe," she murmured. "But at the very least it's your opportunity to outshine her."

Reagan stood up to stand next to her roommate. "What are you looking at?"

Ashley reached into the closet and pulled out a top. She held it in front of Reagan's torso. "Your clothes. What's this girl's name?"

Reagan eyeballed her roommate suspiciously.

Ashley let out an exasperated sigh. "Come on, Prez. I'm not going to Facebook stalk her."

"Allison," Reagan finally answered. "Allison Hoge."

Ashley reached back into the closet and pulled out a few more tops. "Well, then," she declared dramatically, "let's find you the perfect outfit. Watch out, Allison Hoge, because here comes Reagan Murphy."

+++++

CHAPTER TWO

Reagan checked the time on her cell phone and released a shaky breath. 10:59am. One minute until the time Allison had instructed they meet up at the New York diner. She'd actually arrived half an hour early – she had a habit of being early for everything – but hadn't actually gone inside the restaurant. She didn't want to appear too eager to meet up again with her high school foil, so she'd hovered outside until she arrived. The only problem with her plan, however, was that she *hadn't* seen Allison arrive yet. And her fear that the invite had been just the latest joke in the long line of cruel pranks that was their relationship had reared its paranoid head.

Despite her gut feeling that Allison had no intention of showing up, Reagan entered the mom and pop diner promptly at 11am. She briefly glanced around the small restaurant, looking for a familiar shade of blonde hair. She stood on her tiptoes and craned her neck to garner a better view, but amongst the sea of faces, she couldn't find the specific one she sought.

"Can I help you?" a curly haired hostess chirped pleasantly.

"Hi, yes," Reagan greeted. "I'm meeting up with a…" She faltered on the word *friend*. "I'm meeting up with someone," she settled for, "but I don't think she's here yet. I'll just wait here, if that's okay."

"I'd suggest getting a table and waiting there," the hostess proposed. "Things are slow right now, but it'll pick up soon for the lunch crowd."

Reagan visibly winced. She hadn't wanted to commit to a table in the likelihood that Allison failed to show up. But luckily she'd had the foresight to bring along some homework. If and when Allison didn't show, at least she wouldn't be stuck at a table by herself with nothing to do.

After some hesitation, Reagan nodded. "Table for two."

The hostess grabbed two laminated menus and guided her to the center of the diner and stopped in front of a vacant table for two. "Coffee?" she asked.

Reagan nodded and slipped out of her puffy-down jacket. "Yes, thank you. And a water too, please."

The hostess left her side, and Reagan carefully draped her jacket over the back of her chair. She deliberated between the two chairs and finally settled on the seat that afforded her a clear view of the front entrance. She could see when and if Allison ever decided to show up. And as a bonus, her high school tormentor wouldn't be able to sneak up on her.

She took a moment to scan over the breakfast menu. She'd planned on looking at it online that morning to mentally prepare for the lack of vegan options. But she'd run out of time when she'd spent an agonizing amount of time coordination an outfit that would show off her New York fashionability, but also not look like she was trying too hard. In the end, she'd paired a scoop neck top with a pair of dark skinny jeans that tucked into faux leather boots.

A light breeze caressed her face when the front door swung open. She glanced up from the menu and frowned. Unless Allison had had a sex change and had grown a foot taller, she wasn't the person who'd just walked into the busy restaurant.

Reagan closed her eyes and sighed. Her entire body felt tense as though waiting for a snowball to smack her in the face. She opened her eyes when she heard the telltale clink of porcelain. A waitress stood near her elbow and poured her a cup of steaming, black coffee.

"You ready to order?" the woman asked around a wad of pink bubble gum.

Reagan tried not to wrinkle her nose. She'd always thought chewing gum was a nasty habit; it only made a person look like a cow chewing cud. "I-I'm waiting on someone," she stated.

The waitresses nodded curtly and walked away without another word.

Reagan set her menu flat on the table and rubbed at her temples. As much as she'd wanted to believe that things were different, nearly three years removed from high school, Allison still hadn't shown up.

As soon as those negative thoughts passed through her brain, the front door opened again. The sun was bright that day and everyone near the front of the diner was backlit, making it hard to see distinct faces. Reagan squinted her eyes and stared hard at the entrance. If she'd been drinking her coffee, she no doubt would have spit it all over when her gaze finally settled on an all-too familiar blonde.

She watched as Allison shook her head to dislodge a few snowflakes that clung to her corn-silk tresses. It had begun to lightly snow while Reagan waited inside. Allison patted at her clothes and smiled graciously at the hostess who continued to hover at the front of the restaurant. Reagan had the strangest urge to duck beneath her table when she realized Allison's hazel eyes had begun scanning the intimately small diner.

When that penetrating gaze finally rested on her, Reagan thought she observed the slightest flicker of surprise pass over Allison's delicate features. But as quickly as the unexpected emotion appeared, it was replaced with a cool, polite smile as the diner hostess led her back to the table for two.

Reagan allowed herself a bold moment to regard the girl from her past as she walked toward her table. Although she'd seen Allison the previous night, she'd been too frazzled to actually *look* at her. Her porcelain skin was as flawless as ever and the crisp winter weather had pulled an attractive blush to her chiseled cheekbones. Her blonde hair wetly shimmered from the combination of light snow and sunrays streaming in through the front plate glass windows. She stopped in front of the table and pulled off the Burberry-print scarf wrapped around her neck and slid out of her fitted wool trench coat. She looked every bit as polished as Reagan remembered.

"I didn't think you'd actually show up," Allison said softly, speaking for the first time. She draped her winter jacket on the back of the free chair.

Reagan stiffened. "Well, if you didn't want me to come, you shouldn't have invited me. I would have been just fine not seeing you again."

"For Gods sake, Murphy. Calm down." Allison straightened her shoulders and readjusted the fit of her three-quarter-length cardigan.

"No, Allison. I will not *calm down.*" Reagan rose from her seat as she felt years of pent-up anger and frustrations begin to boil over. "You can't just come barging into *my* city and start bossing me around like we're back in high school."

"Reagan, please sit down." Allison nervously looked around the diner to see if anyone was watching them. Reagan was being overly dramatic, but it didn't appear to faze the locals. They were probably used to these kinds of outbursts, but that didn't mean Allison wasn't rattled. She dropped her tone low. "I'm sorry," she said in a soothing burr. "That came out wrong. I'm happy you decided to come."

Reagan stared hard at the girl across the table, inspecting her visage for signs of deceit. Finding nothing there, however, she reluctantly sat back down.

The rigidness of Allison's body gave way as she sat down as well. She said nothing and instead picked up her menu. "Am I going to offend you if I order eggs and bacon?"

Reagan raised a questioning eyebrow.

Allison looked over the top of her menu. "I assume you're still vegan," she clarified.

"I'm surprised you remembered. But don't not do something on account of me," Reagan said. The ice in her tone sounded foreign to her ears.

Allison carefully set her menu down and pressed her lips together. "What's with this attitude? You didn't have to come here today," she pointed out. "Why are you here if you're just going to insist on being rude?"

Reagan dropped her gaze to the tabletop. Someone had carved initials into the wood and she traced the light lines with her fingertips. "I came because I wanted to show you that I've changed since high school." She looked back up, hazarding a glance at the girl seated across from her. The heat in those hazel eyes never failed to be intimidating.

"Well, you're not the only one who's different," Allison murmured.

Reagan released a long breath that she wasn't even aware she'd been holding. "I'm sorry," she apologized. "I don't know where this attitude is coming from."

The intensity in Allison's eyes softened. "Don't apologize. Your anger is completely justified. I was..." Her voice nearly cracked. She paused, swallowed, and composed herself with a small smile. "I was *horrible* to you in high school."

She reached across the table to grab onto Reagan's hand. The brunette was taken aback by the unexpected gesture, and when Allison's fingers brushed against her knuckles, she jerked her hand back, knocking over a plastic water glass. Both women scrambled to their feet as the glass spilled its contents across the small table.

"Well at least it wasn't the coffee," Allison softly chuckled.

Reagan cursed under her breath and hastily grabbed a handful of paper napkins from the tin dispenser on the table. She felt hot tears spring to the corners of her eyes. She'd wanted so much to impress this girl from her past, but so far she'd only been rude and clumsy.

"Reagan," Allison sighed as she continued to uselessly throw more and more napkins at the mess. The napkins were made from a thin, cheap material and only became saturated with the water. "Reagan," she repeated, but her voice somehow wasn't reaching her ears.

Finally, Allison grabbed Reagan's wrists and physically stopped her flailing. Reagan's head snapped up. Her gaze showed her surprise from another unexpected Allison Hoge touch.

"Leave it," Allison softly urged. She released her grip and reached for the wallet inside her jacket liner. She pulled a few bills from the wallet and tossed them on the table.

Reagan looked up questioningly.

"There wasn't anything on the menu you could eat," Allison said flatly. She almost sounded bored. "I'm assuming you've got a favorite vegan brunch place?" Her eyebrows rose expectantly.

Reagan nodded and chewed on her lower lip. "But it's in Brooklyn," she noted, finding her voice again, "and you have a train to catch."

Allison grabbed her jacket and scarf and pulled them on. "There'll be other trains." She rolled her eyes with impatience. "Hurry up and put on your jacket, Murphy. I'm hungry."

Reagan held her arm in the air and flagged down one of the first taxicabs rolling down the street. She checked over her shoulder to be sure Allison was still behind her and then opened the back passenger-side door to slide into the backseat. The material of her pants caught momentarily on the vinyl bench seat and Allison, following immediately behind her, knocked into her as she'd expected Reagan to have been on the other side of the backseat by then.

"Sorry," Allison muttered uncomfortably.

"No, it was my fault," Reagan countered as she put her seatbelt on. She smiled politely at the taxi driver and told him the Brooklyn address of their brunch destination. The driver responded with something unintelligible. She didn't bother asking him to repeat himself, however. When she'd first moved to the city she always asked the driver to repeat what he or she said, but most of the time it turned out they were talking to someone on the phone, the Bluetooth gadget hidden from plain view.

Outside the yellow taxicab, New York City bustled by. Inside the vehicle, however, the passengers were quiet. A news talk radio station chattered in the background, creating white noise.

"How do you like your school?" Allison asked when the silence had become unbearable. She hated small talk, but she hated uncomfortable silence even more.

"It's great, actually," Reagan said, a natural smile tugging at the corners of her mouth. For all the grumbling she had done about last night's homework assignment, she actually really loved NYU. She'd enjoyed the majority of the classes she'd taken, she loved her major field of study, and she'd met people who she could see being life-long friends. "Probably the best decision I ever made."

"Those boots were a good decision, too," Allison noted, nodding at the footwear in question.

Reagan looked down at her legs, startled to be on the receiving end of what felt like a genuine compliment. "Oh, uh, thanks," she stumbled.

A few awkward, silent minutes later, their cab stopped in front of the brunch location. Reagan reached for her bag, but stopped when she felt Allison's cool fingers brush against the top of her wrist.

"I've got this," Allison said, already pulling her wallet out of her bag.

"No, you're visiting," Reagan protested. She dug around her oversized bag in search of her wallet. "You're already paying for your train ticket," she noted, futilely looking for the small wallet floating somewhere in the chaos of her bag's contents, "and if it weren't for my specialized eating habits, we could have gotten something at the other place. I should take care of this."

"Stop trying to be so noble," Allison said more forcefully. She handed her credit card to the taxi driver. "My dad pays for my bills," she stated flippantly. "Let him take care of this."

+++++

The restaurant was sparsely populated, which wasn't unusual for a late Sunday morning. It was one of the reasons Reagan preferred the Brooklyn spot to a restaurant closer to where she lived. If they'd eaten in Manhattan, near her residence hall, they would have had to battle tourists and Gossip Girls for a tiny table at a too-crowded and over-priced eatery. Here in the outer boroughs, however, she could breathe a little easier.

The hostess sat them at a table for two near the front of the restaurant and left them with waters and menus.

Allison opened the paper menu and scanned her options. "So what's good here?"

"Pretty much everything," Reagan noted. She opened the menu as well and scanned down the listings. She didn't really need to look; she'd been to the popular vegan spot numerous times with her friends from school. But she looked anyway to give her something to do. With her hands clinging to the paper menu, she felt stable. She desperately wanted to avoid spilling anything else in Allison's presence if she could help it.

"I always go for the tofu scramble, but I don't know how you feel about tofu, so maybe you should stay away from that. I'd hate for your entire morning to be ruined by a sub-par breakfast if tofu's not your thing," she noted. "There's some faux meat products you might like as a side," she observed, still looking at the menu's options. "I'm told they actually taste like the real thing even though they're made out of soy and tempeh. I wouldn't know if they really taste like real meat though. It's been quite a while since I've eaten real bacon or sausage." She was conscious of her word vomit, but once she started, it was hard to stop. "This is one of the completely vegan brunch spots I like to frequent, but I also enjoy organic restaurants with vegan options. As long as it's socially conscious meat, I'm not so offended by its presence on the menu." She ended her ramble and bit down on her lower lip as if only that motion was keeping the verbal garbage at bay.

Allison pursed her lips, looking amused, rather than annoyed by Reagan's enthusiasm. She hadn't needed to take a breath at all during her food monologue. "You haven't changed," she observed with a thoughtful smile. "Still as eager and passionate as always."

Reagan flushed and looked back down at the menu to avoid Allison's inspecting gaze.

"I take that back." Allison's voice floated into her ears. "You're wearing a shocking lack of neon colors and kitten sweaters," she smirked.

"Neon is making a comeback," Reagan huffed. "Besides, you try being raised by a single dad and see how *your* fashion sense turns out."

Allison frowned at the casualness with which Reagan referred to her parental situation, but she mentally shook those thoughts away. If Reagan wasn't going to be bothered by it, she wouldn't allow herself to be upset either.

A tall man in dark skinny jeans and a maroon t-shirt with a deep v-neck cut walked up to their table. "You guys ready to order?" he asked, pushing his square-framed glasses up higher on his nose.

Allison looked up from her menu and smiled, showing two rows of perfectly white, even teeth. "I'll have the eggless omelet with fake cheese, real mushrooms, real spinach, and a side of fake bacon. Oh, and some real orange juice if you have it." She carefully placed the menu back down on the table and folded her hands on her lap.

The waiter's heavy eyebrows furrowed together. He obviously couldn't tell if this girl was mocking the vegan menu or not. But she had ordered with such calm authority, he could only nod and scribble down her request on his hand-held pad of paper.

Allison had always exuded a casual confidence that put Reagan on edge. She had possessed a calculated maturity beyond her years even when she was belittling Reagan in high school or persuading a football player to shove the brunette into a locker. It had never felt fair that while others struggled mightily in adolescence, Allison Hoge looked like she knew the secrets of not just survival, but of *thriving* during the typically traumatizing years.

"And for you?" he asked, turning to Reagan.

"Tofu scramble and coffee."

The waiter continued to write for what felt like longer than their order warranted before nodding and walking off towards the kitchen. Before long, their food appeared on the table. Reagan hadn't realized how hungry she'd actually become in the late morning until the waiter had brought them their food, and she eagerly dug into her breakfast.

"How's your dad?"

Reagan paused at the question and finished chewing. She was thankful for the extra time. She couldn't tell if Allison was genuinely curious or just making polite conversation. She wiped at her mouth with a napkin. "He's fine," she said. She took a small sip of her water. "He misses me. Naturally."

Allison chuckled at the response and continued to cut her eggless omelet into uniform bites.

"He's taken up some new hobbies," Reagan continued. "Staying busy, I guess." She eyeballed the girl seated across the table. "And your parents?"

Allison shrugged delicately beneath her light cardigan. "They're fine." She picked up her fork and stabbed a carefully measured bite.

Reagan waited for Allison to elaborate, but nothing came.

The rest of the meal was filled with similar awkward silences. Reagan found herself looking everywhere except across the table. They finished their meal civilly, and before too long the waiter had returned with the check. Once again, as she had done in the cab, Allison circumvented Reagan's attempts to pay for anything.

"Well this was..." Reagan searched for a neutral word, "interesting." She looked up when their waiter returned with Allison's credit card. "And thank you for brunch. You really didn't need to do pay though. Again."

Reagan watched Allison scribble down an overly generous tip at the bottom of the paper bill. "You don't need to thank me. Thank Rodger Hoge."

"Well I guess as soon as we're finished here," Reagan quipped, "I'll be sending him a fruit basket."

Allison stared across the table with a bemused look sketched on her features. "I can never tell when you're being serious."

Reagan shook her head. "I say ridiculous things when I'm

nervous."

Allison's pink lips twisted coyly. "You must be nervous a lot."

"Only around you," Reagan countered.

Allison cocked her head to the side, but said nothing for a long, awkward moment. Reagan hated the silence. She always felt the need to fill empty spaces; it was a compulsion of hers. Instead of giving in this time, however, she silently counted in her head.

Allison grabbed the pen from inside the bill folder. Her head tilted down toward the table and she wrote down a series of numbers on a white napkin.

"What's that?"

Allison carefully set the pen back on the table. "My cell number." She rose from the table. "I have a train to catch." Without further explanation, she pressed the napkin with her number on it into Reagan's hand. "If you ever want to get out of the city, call me," she said. Her voice flowed like honey. Reagan envied that voice. Her own always felt a little too large and loud for her slight frame. "You'd love Providence. It's lovely."

Reagan nodded dumbly, her words failing her again. Allison offered the befuddled girl a final smile in parting, gathered her purse and jacket, and exited out the front door of the Brooklyn restaurant, leaving Reagan behind.

Reagan looked down at the white napkin in her hand and the carefully scrawled numbers staring back at her. She crumpled the napkin and immediately contemplated throwing the number away. She'd been pleasantly shocked at how well behaved Allison had been during brunch, but if she never saw her high school tormenter again, it wouldn't be the end of the world. She instead could have this one morning, this one memory.

If they spent any more time together, her lasting memory of Allison certainly wouldn't be happy. It would just be a matter of time, she reasoned, before the real Allison Hoge showed her beautiful, yet bitchy, face.

She unclenched her hand and the paper napkin slowly uncoiled. The black inked numbers seemed to taunt her, jumping off the white, cotton napkin. Finally, going against her initial gut reaction, she carefully folded the napkin in half and put it inside of her jacket pocket.

+++++

When Reagan returned to her room, she was relieved to find that her roommate was out. As much as she loved her friend, Ashley had the particular habit of being nosy. And for once, she felt the need to not divulge every detail of her late morning meal. She knew it was just a matter of time before the Spanish Inquisition arrived, but for the moment, she was thankful for the opportunity to process that morning's events on her own. But not too much time; she had homework, after all.

Realizing if her roommate came home that she'd never get any schoolwork done, she grabbed her art history textbook and shoved it, along with some other books, into her backpack. She scribbled a quick note on a post-it for her roommate, letting her know where she'd gone, and headed to the library.

The holiday season was long over, but the New York winter showed no signs of relenting. Once back outside, Reagan flipped up the collar of her blue peacoat and tucked her head toward the sidewalk to shield herself from the brisk afternoon chill. The sun was out, but it was a deceptively sunny day.

She buried her hands deep into her pockets and lamented not having the foresight to have brought gloves with her. The university library was only a few blocks from her residence hall, but her fingers already felt like they were going to fall off. Her fingers brushed against the textured napkin tucked away in her jacket pocket. It took her a moment to remember what it was and whose number was written on it.

When Reagan had been thrust into the bustle of not just college life, but also living in the biggest city in the country, it had taken a while to adjust to the culture shock. And as she tried to navigate in her new surroundings, she had lost contact with practically everyone from high school. She wondered if it had been the same for Allison. Reagan mentally shook her head at the naivety of her high school self. She often wished Time Travel existed so she could travel back and talk to her sixteen-year-old self. It wasn't that City Life had turned her into a pessimist; she was just more realistic about things like life and love now.

She stopped walking when she suddenly found herself at the main entrance of the university library, having practically sleep-walked herself to the front steps. Showing her student ID, she entered the building and found herself a study table in one of the designated quiet areas.

She pulled her hands out of her pockets and the white napkin fluttered out as well. She frowned and bent to pick it up. She thought about throwing it away again. It was in her power; she'd never have to see and talk to Allison Hoge unless they miraculously bumped into each other again. Instead, she placed the napkin on the study table and smoothed out its edges. She had homework to focus on; she'd make her decision on the fate of Allison's phone number later.

+++++

"Is this seat taken?"

Reagan looked up from her art history textbook to see her roommate seated in the chair across from her. "What are you doing here?" she asked, pulling her ear buds out of her ears. "I didn't think you even knew where the library was?"

Ashley gave her roommate a sheepish grin and shrugged. "I had to ask directions."

Reagan smirked.

"I just wanted to be sure you were really here. Can't blame a girl for being concerned about her friend."

"I left a note back at the room," Reagan pointed out.

Ashley drummed her fingers on the tabletop and leaned backwards in her chair. "Yeah, but that Allison girl could have forged it."

Reagan arched an eyebrow. "And have done what exactly? Kidnap me?"

Ashley shrugged. "Maybe. Stranger things have happened."

"Well she didn't kidnap me," Reagan stated with some finality. "I'm fine."

Ashley grinned. "So how was it?"

Reagan couldn't help but roll her eyes – so much for finishing her homework that afternoon. "It was fine," she said, purposefully vague.

Ashley sat patiently, waiting for Reagan to elaborate. When it was clear her roommate wasn't going to accept her shortened answer, Reagan made a quiet, disgruntled noise, but continued. "Okay," she sighed, "so at first it was horrible." She rubbed at her face as she paused to remember how disastrous the morning had begun. "I was so nervous and angry and confused that I kind of yelled at her in the middle of the restaurant. And then I knocked my water over."

"Oh no," Ashley gasped sincerely.

"But then it got better; we left the diner and went to brunch in Brooklyn instead."

"Don't tell me you took her to that horrible vegan place you love?" Ashley looked horrified. "Wait, is this girl vegan, too? What's *wrong* with you Michigan people? Meat is delicious."

"Meat is murder," Reagan quickly countered and shook her head. "And no, Allison's not vegan. She was just being accommodating, I guess."

"So what else?" Ashley pressed. "Any other disasters?"

"Luckily no. But it was painfully awkward." Reagan worried her lip, remembering. "I didn't know what to say half the time and she wasn't helping either. We mostly just ate at the same table."

"Well, at least you gave it a shot," Ashley observed. "You should be proud of yourself for standing up to her."

Reagan hesitated. "She invited me to visit her at Brown."

Ashley's eyebrows furrowed together. "Well it couldn't have been a complete disaster then. Are you going to go?"

Reagan shook her head. "I don't think it's a very good idea."

"Why not?" Ashley pressed.

"At least here I was on my home turf," Reagan reasoned. She hadn't put much serious thought into the invitation until now. "Up in Providence I'd be trapped in her world, surrounded by snobby Ivy-League girls. It would probably be like high school all over again. Just with better clothes," she added.

Ashley looked thoughtful. "You're right. You probably shouldn't go," she said, nodding her head in agreement. "If you and this chick didn't get along in high school like you said you didn't, you're probably just tempting the Fates if you spend more time with her."

Reagan broke eye contact with her roommate in favor of doodling on a blank page in her notebook. She found it telling that Ashley's thoughts about spending more time with Allison had been her own initial reaction as well. But, she also hated being told what she could and couldn't do. "Maybe it wouldn't be so horrible," she said out loud, more for her own benefit than Ashley's. "And I've always wanted to see more of New England," she tried to reason. "I haven't really traveled much beyond the city."

Ashley leaned back further in her chair, nearly toppling it backwards. "Whatever you say, Prez. It's your funeral."

Reagan looked at the napkin. She looked at her cell phone innocuously sitting on the study table. She picked up her phone, its weight in her hand somehow grounding her.

"What are you doing?"

Reagan licked her lips and carefully pressed 10 separate buttons. "Probably making a big mistake."

+++++

Allison Hoge stepped onto the commuter train by herself. Her roommates and friends had left back for Rhode Island earlier that morning. Brunch with Reagan, regardless of the venue change, had caused her to miss meeting up with them. She actually preferred riding back to Brown by herself, however, rather than having to make pointless small talk for the duration of the trip with the girls with whom she'd lived. She saw them enough already. She'd only agreed to the New York trip because they'd harassed her so much about it. Running into Reagan Murphy was an unexpected consequence of that decision.

Allison took an empty seat by a window and carefully returned her ticket to her overnight bag. Her phone made a noise, indicating she'd received a text message. She dug in her bag briefly before producing the phone. She didn't recognize the number, but read the text anyway:

"Thank you again for brunch today."

The phone rattled again with a second incoming message.

"This is Reagan Murphy, by the way."

Allison smirked and immediately sent her reply: *"Did you think I had brunch with someone else this morning and therefore you needed to identify yourself?"*

A minute later, her phone chimed again.

"I didn't want to assume anything. You could have double booked."

Allison's response came easily: *"I might love pancakes, but one breakfast a morning is my limit."*

She fidgeted with her phone, waiting for Reagan to return the text with one of her own. Three years. It had been three years since high school. She typed out another text.

"What do you think about coming to Providence to see me?"

She frowned, eyebrows furrowed together.

"I suppose I could find a free weekend sometime."

"Well don't sound so excited about it." Allison scowled. Why did Reagan Murphy insist on being so difficult *all* the time? Apparently three years hadn't been enough to rid her of that habit.

"I'm sorry. I think I'm still in shock from the past two days."

Allison frowned deeper. She knew she'd made life difficult for Reagan in high school – impossible, even. Maybe nothing would ever be enough to make amends for her bullying. Maybe that was a bridge they'd never be able to cross.

"Don't make me beg."

As soon as she hit the send button, she immediately wished she could take it back. She wanted to jump into cyberspace, or whatever invisible space text messages traveled, and pluck the message from the ether.

"Do I have the right number?" came Reagan's response.

"What are you doing this weekend?" Allison knew she was being pushy, bossy; but that seemed to be the only kind of Allison to whom Reagan had ever responded. She didn't know how to be any other kind of Allison around her.

"I guess I'm coming to see you."

Allison read the message over a few times and suddenly felt a little queasy. She pushed it off as motion sickness; she'd never done well reading in a moving vehicle. She rested her head against the windowpane, soothed by the chill radiating from the glass. She closed her eyes and let herself be lulled by the perpetual rocking of the moving train.

Reagan Murphy was coming to Providence.

+++++

CHAPTER THREE

Reagan stared out the slightly tinted glass of her window seat as the New England coast rushed by outside. Beyond the confines of the Amtrak train it had started to lightly snow, giving the impression of driving through space. It reminded her of her father and driving through snowstorms at night in northern Michigan. She smiled at the memory. They'd pretend they were in a spaceship on their longer winter road trips and he would periodically flip on the high beams to make her squeal.

Her father had been her closest friend and confident all through middle school and high school. Ever since the summer before seventh grade, they'd been close. They were the only family they had anymore. Neither of her parents had any siblings, all of her grandparents had died when she was too young to remember them, and she herself was an only child.

Leaving her father behind in Michigan while she attended college in New York had been one of the hardest things she'd ever had to do. She had told him she would be fine attending a college closer to home, but when the acceptance letter to her top choice school had arrived, her dad had practically packed up her childhood bedroom for her.

"Do you mind if I steal your power?"

Reagan snapped out of her daydream and looked up to see a man standing in the aisle. He was tall and lanky in that East Coast hipster kind of way she'd become accustomed to, and his blond hair looked to be the product of a vigorous dye job. Her face revealed her confusion at the question, so the boy spoke again. "That seat. Is it taken?" he asked. "My laptop's almost dead and you have a plug-in."

"Oh!" Reagan exclaimed. "I'm sorry!" She collected her thoughts along with the oversized school bag currently occupying the seat next to her. The man waited patiently with a small smile curling the corners of his lips. "Sorry," she needlessly repeated as she pulled the bag onto her lap. "I guess I've been living in New York for too long, acting like I own the train or something."

The man sat down beside her in the sparsely populated train car. "You live in the city?" he politely conversed. "Where abouts?"

"Manhattan," Reagan responded. "I go to NYU."

"Wow. That's impressive," the man said with an approving nod. "I go to CUNY," he said with a shrug. "Nothing fancy."

"Don't sell yourself short," Reagan replied. "That's a really good school, too."

"Thanks for saying so. My parents think I'm a massive disappointment because I didn't get into NYU. I'm Christopher, by the way," he said, sticking out his hand.

"Reagan," she supplied with a winning smile. She shook Christopher's pale hand.

"Like the President?"

Reagan laughed. "Yeah. I think my parents were trying to be ironic or something; they're really not that conservative."

"So where are you heading to, if you don't mind me asking?" He held up his hands in mock surrender. "I promise I'm not a stalker."

Reagan laughed. "Would a stalker admit to being a stalker?"

Christopher smiled, his eyes crinkling at the corners. "You got me there."

"Providence, Rhode Island," Reagan supplied, only half-teasing about the stalker comment. But the train was sufficiently crowded and she had her whistle in the front pocket of her bag.

"Oh yeah?" Christopher's voice raised in excitement. "Me too. I'm visiting my grandma. It's her 90th birthday this weekend."

"That's got to be a line, right?" Reagan said, arching a skeptical eyebrow. "I bet you ride this train all day and tell girls how devoted you are to your grandmother."

Christopher laughed. "I don't know the guys you're used to, but in my experience being fond of your grandmother isn't good for a guy's rep."

Reagan hummed in agreement. The majority of boys she'd been hanging out with lately were her less-than-masculine art school classmates.

"My parents worked like all the time, so she basically raised me," Christopher explained. "Plus, she makes the best date bars you've ever had. She's awesome." He shook his head good-naturedly. "I'm sorry. I'm babbling, aren't I?"

Reagan nodded, but didn't comment on the boy's ramblings. She appreciated someone who wasn't afraid to talk and share intimate details with strangers. It was charming, in fact.

"What brings you to Rhode Island?" Christopher asked, turning the conversation to her. His floundering laptop seemed forgotten for the moment.

"I'm meeting up with…" Reagan paused. There was that word again. What *was* Allison to her? Yes, she was visiting her and even spending 4 hours on a train to get there, but that didn't mean they were *friends*. "…someone I knew in high school," she opted for instead.

Christopher's eyebrows furrowed. "That's awfully vague and mysterious," he noted. "Now I'm starting to suspect you're a Russian spy or something." He looked around in a comical, over-exaggerated manner. "Am I on an episode of *Alias* right now?"

Reagan found herself wanting to flirt with this boy, enjoying the unexpected attention. She batted her long eyelashes. "Well unlike you, maybe I don't reveal my whole life story in the first 5 minutes of meeting someone."

That of course, was a total lie, but this boy didn't need to know that. Actually, she was proud of how much she'd settled down since her freshman year at NYU. She'd quickly discovered that thrusting her hand in someone's face and launching into her "I'm Reagan Murphy, let's be best friends," spiel was just as unsuccessful in college as it had been in high school.

Christopher leaned a little closer and grinned a wide, mega-watt smile. "Then I guess I'll have to see you again if I want to learn more."

Reagan returned the smile, but didn't say anything else. If this boy liked a mysterious girl, she was only too happy to oblige.

+++++

Reagan chatted amicably with Christopher as they stepped off the train and onto the Providence train station platform. He helped her with her overnight bag when she briefly struggled going down the narrow stairs that led to the wooden platform below. Normally she liked to do things like that for herself, being a perfectly capable modern woman, but she wasn't too proud to dismiss an act of chivalry.

She thanked him for his help off the train and for the conversation, apologizing for keeping him from his homework. Three years removed from high school and she still felt like she had to apologize to people for talking to them. He brushed off what she insisted must have been an inconvenience and noted he still had all weekend and the train ride back to finish his college work. They said their goodbyes and shook hands again in parting with the promise that they'd talk soon and arrange another meet up back in New York.

Reagan watched Christopher walk away, his luggage trailing behind. The wheels made two tidy lines in the light layer of snow on the platform. She was shaken from the imagery when a familiar voice cut through the thin winter air.

"Friend of yours?"

Allison Hoge stood alone on the platform, her arms hugging her lithe form. Choosing to ignore Allison's icy tone, Reagan was more struck by how icy she *looked*.

"My goodness, Allison; you didn't have to wait outside for me!" she exclaimed in horror. "How long have you been waiting?"

"A while," Allison revealed, averted her gaze. "I didn't want you to get lost when you got off the train," she said miserably.

Reagan shook her head. "That's ridiculous," she chastised. "I live in *New York City*. How on earth would I get lost in Rhode Island?"

"Fine," Allison conceded. "I didn't want to miss you coming off the train and have you think I didn't show up."

Reagan clucked her tongue against the roof of her mouth. So much for feeling nervous around her former tormenter; now she was in total protector-mode. "You're taking me to your favorite coffee shop so you can properly warm up," she immediately ordered.

Allison appraised the smaller woman as she shouldered a comically oversized duffle bag. "When did you get so bossy,

27

Murphy?"

Reagan started walking toward the train station exit, not waiting for Allison. "Since you didn't have the good sense to wait inside the terminal for me," she shot back over her shoulder.

Allison moved at a brisk pace to catch up. "At least let me help you with your bag. That thing looks like it weighs more than you," she observed. "How many days did you pack for anyway? Are you moving in? I must have missed that memo."

Reagan snorted. "Very funny, Hoge. But less sarcasm and more walking."

Allison shook her head incredulously as she watched Reagan stomp away with purpose. Her awkward duffle bag managed to hit everyone in her path as she maneuvered through the dense commuter crowds like a true New Yorker.

As she watched Reagan put more distance between them, one thought popped into Allison's head: This might be a *very* long weekend.

+++++

"One café mocha, skim milk, with a sprinkle of chocolate dust."

Allison smiled and took the proffered, oversized ceramic mug. "Thanks, Jimmy."

After catching up with Reagan, who had stormed away without looking back, Allison had led her in the direction of her favorite coffee shop in downtown Providence. The downtown area, just a few blocks from the main campus, was quaint and picturesque in the way you'd imagine a New England town would be. Allison often found herself at this particular coffee place after discovering the university library too crowded to be conducive for studying. One of the drawbacks of going to an Ivy-League school where everyone was supremely competitive regarding academics was the difficulty in finding a decent study carrel in the library.

"Oh!" The man working behind the front counter lit up with excitement. "Marie just made a new batch of those white chocolate, macaroon muffins you like."

Reagan eyeballed Allison and her interaction with the barista. She looked amused as the man bent and disappeared momentarily behind the front counter. When he stood and reappeared, he held a muffin wrapped in wax paper. "On the house," he grinned.

Allison held up her unoccupied hand. "No, that's not necessary," she politely declined. "I don't need the extra calories today."

The lanky man snorted and pushed it closer. "I won't take no for an answer. Does your friend want one, too?"

Allison flicked her hazel eyes in Reagan's direction as if she'd forgotten she was still standing there during the exchange.

"I assume there are dairy products in your muffins?" Reagan spoke up, not content to be left out of the conversation. "As well as in the white chocolate?"

The grin fell from the man's face, and he nodded.

"Then I too will have to regrettably decline your kind offer," she said with a definitive nod.

The two women turned from the front countertop area, each with their own drinks. Reagan had opted for a cappuccino with soymilk. Allison, once again, had insisted on paying. And once again, Reagan had failed at turning down her hospitality.

"Is everyone in Providence so friendly?" Reagan asked in a hushed tone as they made their way to a small table near the front of the shop. The table offered a pleasant view of the postcard-like atmosphere just beyond the oversized windows. Even though the Christmas holiday had passed, the town still seemed decorated for the winter holiday.

"You've just gotten used to New York," Allison remarked, taking a seat at the table and setting down her drink. She took off her long winter jacket to reveal another three quarter-length cardigan that showed off her defined clavicle and skinny jeans that elongated her legs. "It's no different here than back home."

"For you, maybe," Reagan countered, settling down in the second chair. "Everyone's nice when you're gorgeous. Haven't you ever seen that episode of *30 Rock*?"

Allison waved a dismissive hand. "I just spend a lot of time here studying and doing homework," she noted. She cupped her oversized mug and blew across the top of her hot beverage. The heat felt comforting against her palms. Her bones ached from the cold, but she didn't want Reagan see her discomfort. She didn't know why she'd felt compelled to wait outside on the train platform. "They like me because I don't take up a lot of space, and I'm a decent tipper."

"Uh huh," Reagan said, unconvinced.

Allison shook her head and took a sip of her drink. "I don't know what it's going to take to convince you, Reagan, but I'm not that girl anymore. I'm not actively seeking out special attention."

Reagan, despite everything she'd seen so far from Allison, still felt skeptical – like all of these recent niceties was an elaborate ploy to get her defenses down and humiliate her. "What changed for you?" she felt compelled to ask.

"Just being in college, I suppose," Allison said with a delicate shrug. "Everyone at Brown is a little more talented than I could ever hope to be. A little smarter. A little richer. A little prettier."

"Well I find that last one hard to believe," Reagan interjected.

"Whatever," Allison scoffed. She was a little annoyed Reagan kept talking about her like that. She wanted to be more than just a pretty face. That was the whole point of reinventing herself in college. "Either way, it was humbling," she continued. "I wasn't at the top of the pyramid anymore. I wasn't even in the middle."

"So, what? You just gave up? That doesn't sound like you."

"I didn't *give up*," Allison denied with some heat. "I've got a 4.0 at an Ivy-League school. I hardly call that 'giving up.'"

Reagan shrank back. Allison's eyes flashed a hard look that reminded her too much of their high school days. She tried to keep the flashbacks at bay of clutching her books tight against her chest while walking down the high school corridor.

"My priorities changed," Allison said earnestly. The intensity and flicker of anger faded from her eyes. "Popularity, boyfriends, cheerleading…the same things that drove me in high school didn't seem so important once I got here."

Reagan took an experimental sip of her nearly forgotten beverage. It was still hot. "So what's important to you now?" she asked.

"Getting good grades," Allison noted with a shrug. "My writing." She hesitated and licked her bottom lip. "Making amends for the past."

Reagan looked up from the rim of her mug at the mention of the past. She was met with another intense gaze. "Is that what this is? Is that why you invited me this weekend?" she asked, feeling very small under Allison's unrelenting eye contact. "Am I part of your 12-step program to becoming a better person?"

Allison finally looked away and broke eye contact. "I don't have a checklist or anything," she mumbled.

She looked back when Reagan reached across the table to grab her hands. She stared down at where their hands connected. Hers, pale and unblemished, and Reagan's an attractive olive tone. She knew Reagan was saying something, but all she heard was white noise. She was too distracted by the feeling of Reagan rubbing her thumbs up and down her wrist bones to make out the actual words.

"Allison?"

She blinked once and looked up from their hands. "Hmmm?"

Reagan smiled softly. "Where did you just go?"

Allison shook her head and laughed, embarrassed. "Sorry. I totally zoned out on you, didn't I." She gently pulled her hands away, but not so quickly as to offend her. "What were you saying?"

"I was saying that even if this is part of some grand self-improvement scheme, I'm glad we reconnected."

Allison allowed herself a rare, genuine smile. "I am, too."

Reagan beamed. "Great!" she exclaimed. "So now that we've got *that* out of the way, where to next? I want to see all that Providence has to offer."

"I don't know what you're expecting," Allison admitted. "Providence isn't exactly New York, so I hope it's not too disappointing." She stood and bussed their table, setting both of their practically untouched beverages near the garbage cans.

Reagan stood as well. "My, how chivalrous," she remarked. She picked up her canvas bag from the floor and flung the strap over her shoulder.

Allison snorted. "Don't get used to it, Murphy. I fully expect to be waited on like this the next time I'm in New York."

Reagan clapped excitedly, causing Allison to laugh and roll her eyes at her antics. "You'd really want to hang out again?"

Allison smirked. "Sure. Why not? Besides, I've got those 12-steps to get through, remember?" she teased.

Reagan instinctively looped her arm through Allison's. The taller girl momentarily stiffened. She wasn't normally a touchy-feely person. Her family hardly hugged, only when it was necessary.

"Do I get to be your sponsor?" Reagan asked, leading them through the coffee shop door and out into the brisk Providence afternoon. "So whenever you're feeling like being a bitch you have to call me, and I'll talk you down."

"In that case, I'd be calling you *all* the time."

Reagan grinned. "I don't mind. I've got an excellent cellular plan. And there's always Skype. My dad and I talk on that all the time."

"God, you're a nerd," Allison chuckled. She tilted her head down as a particularly brutal gust of New England wind blew at them while they waited for the pedestrian signs at the intersection to change.

"Remind me why we didn't choose colleges down South?" Reagan asked. Her teeth practically chattered and she popped the collar of her jacket in a feeble attempt to keep the wind at bay. "We could be sipping Mai Tai's at the beach right now."

"Because serious artists study in New York City," Allison pointed out. "And you're a serious artist."

"And what's your excuse?" Reagan countered. "With all your blonde hair, you'd fit in perfectly in the South or on the West Coast."

Allison shrugged beneath her heavy coat. "I'm a frigid snob," she said simply. "And we snobs congregate in New England."

Reagan looked up at Allison, who was facing forward, looking ahead. She had always thought the girl walking beside her, their arms still linked in solidarity against the weather, had been the prettiest girl in their school. They'd been friends once, real friends, back in elementary and middle school. But the awkwardness of puberty had left Allison's elongating limbs much earlier than it had Reagan's.

While Reagan still played with Barbie's and Lego's in junior high, Allison had discovered make-up and heels. And in high school while Reagan hid behind her oil paints and photography, Allison had learned how to roll her eyes and hang prettily off the arm of the beefiest letterman jacket.

Long forgotten were the childhood days of lemonade stands and playing pirates in the tree fort in her backyard. Allison was popular. Reagan was not. And in high school, that was all that really mattered.

Allison stopped walking when she noticed the grim, far away look on Reagan's face. "Hey," she said gently. Reagan's eyes refocused on Allison's face. "Are you okay?" She grubbed her palms roughly up and down Reagan's jacket-covered arms as if coaxing the blood to better circulate in her limbs.

Reagan mentally shook herself. They were having a nice day; she didn't want to ruin it by dragging them through the muddied past. "Yeah, I'm fine," she said thickly. "Just low-blood sugar, I think."

Allison's features pinched in concern. "Let's move those legs faster then and get you back to my house. I'm not exactly sure what I have at home that's vegan, but I'm sure we can find something."

Reagan smiled and squeezed Allison's arm once in thanks. "And then I really do want to see your world," she insisted. "I want to see where this new Allison Hoge lives."

+++++

Reagan pulled off her hat and coat and looked around the front foyer, appraising the space that Allison called home. She was slightly surprised at what she saw. The rental home was immaculately cleaned, which wasn't a surprise. But the house was a little old, a little run down. The house felt...*historic*, she decided. It had a story to tell.

"I like your house," she said, handing Allison her jacket to hang up.

"It's a drafty shack, and it smells like mothballs," Allison retorted, "but at least I don't have to live in a dorm anymore."

Reagan frowned at the frank response. "I think it's charming," she protested.

Allison hung up Reagan's jacket on a hook in the foyer, took off her own coat, and did the same. "Let's see what we've got in the house you can eat. I'm sorry I didn't have time to go shopping before you got here," she sighed tiredly, walking toward the back of the house. "It's been a busy week."

"How many roommates do you have?" Reagan asked, following her down the long corridor. She didn't actually know if Allison had roommates, but it seemed odd that she would have this large rented space all to herself.

"Two other girls," Allison said, continuing down the hallway. "Meghan's room is over here," she said, pointing to a closed wooden door, "and Brice is at the back of the house. They go to Brown, too. Brice is a psychology major and Meghan is math."

Reagan wrinkled her nose. "Math? Gross."

"Yeah, I know," Allison said, nodding. "But she's surprisingly not weird or awkward. I think her dad is making her double major in economics and math so she can actually do something with her degree after graduation." She made a face. "Unlike me."

Reagan looked horrified. "I was so busy talking about myself when you visited New York, I didn't even think to ask about *your* major!"

"Don't worry about it," Allison dismissed. She started opening various cabinets, revealing boxes and packages of non-perishable food. "New York and NYU is much more glamorous than the life of an English literature major."

Reagan, not knowing what to do with herself now that she was truly in Allison's space, took a seat at the small kitchen table. "English Lit?" She crossed her legs and leaned forward with interest. "And what would you like to do with that?"

"Well, I'm not naïve enough to think I can make a living writing poems," Allison rolled her eyes.

"And why not?" Reagan sniffed. She wasn't sure why Allison continued to dismiss her life. First her house, now her major. Next she'd probably not make a big deal about being enrolled at an Ivy League College. She had changed since high school, that was certain, but Reagan didn't know how to interpret this more humble and understated version of her high school tormenter. "You're Allison Hoge, and you can do anything you put your mind to."

"Thanks for the pep talk," Allison smirked. "But I thought *I* was the former cheerleader?"

"You might have had the outfit, but I've always been your biggest fan." Reagan blushed as soon as the words tumbled out.

Allison blinked and shook her head. "You say the strangest things sometime."

Reagan ran her thumbnail over the kitchen table. "I know. You seem to bring out the awkward in me," she sighed.

A silence fell over the two and Reagan continued pretending to be interested in the finish on the wooden table. When she finally looked up, she discovered that Allison was staring at her with a particularly perplexed expression on her face.

"We'll have to work on that," Allison said. Her mouth twisted into a smile. "Salad for dinner sound okay?"

+++++

Reagan couldn't remember the title of the movie they were currently watching. She couldn't remember the names of the two protagonists either. All she could do was focus on keeping her eyes open. She was exhausted, but she didn't want Allison to think she wasn't having a good time.

After a thrown-together dinner of a simple salad and bread, neither girl had known what to do with the rest of the evening. Allison had reluctantly suggested they could go to a bar, but admitted that she wasn't much of a drinker. Reagan had insisted she didn't need to be entertained 24/7 and had, to the point of ridiculous, continued to apologize for being such a burden.

Finally, when all suggestions continued to float in the air unresolved, Allison had put a movie into the DVD player and plopped down on the couch. Reagan had sat down as well, putting what she hoped was an appropriate amount of space between them. She didn't want to invade Allison's personal bubble by sitting too close, but she didn't want her to think she didn't want to be there either by sitting too far away. Now that she was finally seated in a comfortable position and the radiator heat had kicked on, her exhaustion from traveling and the day's events was starting to settle in.

Allison's words wrapped around her head like a warm blanket. "Hey, sleepyhead."

Reagan's eyes fluttered open. "Hmm?" She nonchalantly wiped at her mouth with the back of her hand and was relieved to find she hadn't been drooling.

"Let's get you to bed before you pass out entirely on my couch," Allison coaxed. "You can sleep in my bed."

"Your bed?" Reagan echoed. "But where will you sleep?"

Allison stood up and brushed at the imaginary lint on her jeans. "I'll sleep out here on the couch."

"No, no," Reagan protested. She stood from the couch, now feeling more awake. "I don't want to put you out like that."

Allison sighed and ran her fingers through her hair. Why did she have to make everything so *hard*? "Reagan, I invited you," she pointed out. "You're my guest. I'll take the couch," she insisted. "It's actually pretty comfortable."

Reagan considered protesting again, but finally she bit her lower lip and nodded her consent.

Allison grabbed a few afghans from a nearby window seat and started to make up her bed on the couch. "Good night. If you need anything, I'll just be out here."

Reagan wordlessly nodded again and walked the few steps to Allison's bedroom, where she'd put her overnight bag earlier. She quietly closed the bedroom door and was greeted by the simple furnishings of Allison's room. In the center of the modest-sized room was a single bed, immaculately made. A few bookshelves populated the room, each struggling to contain the impressive amount of books on their shelves.

She felt like she'd been granted access to a holy place – the inner sanctum of an elite club. If anyone had told her just a few weeks ago that she'd soon be sleeping in Allison Hoge's bed, surrounded by her things and the scent of her light perfume, she would have bitterly laughed in their face and called them a liar.

+++++

CHAPTER FOUR

The morning after the initial awkwardness of arriving in Providence, Reagan woke up early. It wasn't unusual for her to wake up at an early hour, even on the weekends. She had her routines and her body obligingly stuck to them. She lay in Allison's bed for a few moments, just waking up and listening for any telltale sounds that people were up and moving around in the house. She had yet to meet Allison's roommates, but she was honestly a little nervous about it. What kind of people would Allison-version 2.0 be living with?

When she finally exited Allison's bedroom as quietly as possible so as to not wake up anyone in the house, she found Allison already awake, drinking coffee and sitting at the kitchen table with the morning newspaper. She wore black, rectangle-framed glasses, and her eyebrows were furrowed in concentration. The tip of her tongue was just barely visible, peaking out between two pale pink lips as she worked on the morning crossword puzzle. Reagan thought it unfair that anyone could still be so attractive in glasses and slightly disheveled from sleep.

"Morning."

Allison looked up and smiled warmly when she saw the brunette. "Morning," she returned the greeting. Her voice sounded deeper than usual. "Sleep okay?"

Reagan scratched at the back of her neck self-consciously and nodded. She had thought about changing out of her pajamas, but felt relieved that Allison appeared to still be in hers – a light blue Henley top and cotton pants with a drawstring. She wondered how she'd

37

gotten them since she'd taken over her bedroom. "How about you?" she asked. She still felt guilty that Allison had slept on the couch, but she didn't really know what protocol was for adult sleepovers.

"Good," Allison confirmed. Her eyes fell back down to her newspaper. "If you want coffee, there's some extra in the machine. Mugs are above the microwave."

Reagan padded over to the coffee maker and made herself a cup, black and strong. She cupped the ceramic mug in her hands and let it warm her. Allison's house was old, and therefore a little drafty. She was used to the muggy heat of her residence hall in the mornings, the result of so many women all taking hot showers at the same time. She sat down in the spare chair at the kitchen table and silently observed Allison for a moment as she continued to work on the crossword puzzle.

"What would you like to do today?" Allison asked without looking up. "I gotta warn you. Providence isn't that big, plus it's winter."

"Does Brown have an ice rink?"

Allison looked up at the unexpected question. "I think so," she said. Her fair eyebrows were still knit together. "I'm pretty sure we have a hockey team. Why?"

"It might be fun to go ice skating," Reagan said, drawing invisible patterns on the table with her fingers. "It seems like an appropriate winter activity," she added self-consciously. "I usually go skating with my dad on Christmas day, but we didn't get to go this year. Too many other things to squeeze in while I was home."

Allison seemed to let the idea marinate for a moment before responding. "I'll call the rink and see if that's something we could do today. I don't know if they let students skate there or if it's just for hockey."

"Could you ask if they have skate rentals, too?"

Allison nodded. "Good thinking. That would probably be important," she said with a quiet chuckle.

Now that a tentative plan had been made for the day, Reagan felt more at ease. If they had something concrete to do, there was less chance of her embarrassing herself or babbling endlessly and annoying Allison. "Do you have your own skates?"

Allison shook her head. "I've actually never gone skating before," she revealed.

"What?!"

"Geez, Murphy." Allison winced. "Trying to wake up my roommates?"

"Your parents never took you ice skating?" Reagan asked incredulously, dropping her voice to a hoarse whisper.

Allison's brow furrowed seriously. "No."

"I'm sorry."

"Don't apologize." Allison shook her head, looking frustrated. Reagan apologized too much. "It's not your fault."

"But we grew up in the middle of nowhere," Reagan pointed out. "What else was there to do in the winter months?"

Allison arched an eyebrow. "Under-aged drinking and premarital sex?"

"Skating, sledding, and making snow people?" Reagan countered.

"Snow people?" Allison echoed.

"Well I suppose they're better known as snow*men*, but it always seemed unfair to me that you could only build snowmen. What about snow*women*?" Reagan huffed indignantly. "They deserve a chance, too, you know."

Allison shook her head at Reagan's antics. Her energy was contagious. "Of *course* you'd get upset about that."

+++++

Reagan inhaled, enjoying the smell of the cold ice. She stepped out onto the sparsely populated ice rink and made a tentative stride. She hadn't been skating since two Christmases ago, but knew that after a little while she'd be back to her old form. Gaining confidence, she started to skate faster in a wide loop around the oval rink. She crossed her right foot over her left, making a sharp, crisp turn around the first corner. The sound of her sharp blades cutting into the ice was familiar and comforting, bringing her back to simpler days.

A loud crash pulled her out of her trance, and she looked in the direction of the noise to see Allison awkwardly opening the large gate to the rink. She stumbled out onto the ice surface and immediately grasped onto the sideboards surrounding the hockey rink to keep from falling.

"Devil shoes," she complained under her breath. "God never intended for people to fly or to ice skate."

"Well, for starters, you didn't tie your laces tight enough." Reagan pointed to Allison's unsteady feet and laughed. "That's why your ankles are wobbling around like that."

"And here I thought they'd rented me skates made out of Jello," Allison quipped and rolled her eyes.

Reagan cocked her head to one side, amused by Allison's lack of balance. The normally perfectly put-together girl looked anything but comfortable. "I still don't understand how you could have grown up in Michigan and never learned how to ice skate."

Allison scowled and her legs continued to wobble unsteadily. "It's Michigan, not the North Pole."

Reagan skated easily over to Allison and wrapped her arm around her waist. "C'mon," she cajoled, "I'll help you."

With a minimum amount of convincing, Allison released her tight clutch on the boards and allowed herself to be led back towards the zamboni entrance. Reagan momentarily released her hold to open up the sideboards.

Without the support, Allison immediately spilled onto the ice. "Hey!" she loudly complained, her back flat on the ice. "What was that for?"

"I'm sorry." Reagan held a mittened hand over her laughing mouth. "I didn't think you'd fall so easily." She reached down and pulled Allison off the slick surface and back onto her feet. The two wobbled unsteadily, both threatening to tumble, until Reagan planted her feet in the ice for better balance.

"Don't you dare let go again," Allison grunted through clenched teeth.

Reagan laughed. "I've got you," she reassured the shaky girl. She steered Allison back through the rink entrance and helped her step off the ice and onto the thick, black rubber flooring.

Allison wobbled over to a wooden bench and sat down. She breathed a sigh of relief to be on solid ground again.

Reagan stood in front of her and grabbed onto her skating partner's right ankle and elevated it so she could rest the skate blade between her knees. "This is how my dad used to tie my skates for me when I was little," she explained. She unlaced Allison's skate laces and retied the shoddy work. "You've got to get the laces really tight, especially around your ankles."

Allison grunted slightly when Reagan pulled the laces tighter. "Are you trying to cut off the circulation to my feet?"

"Do you want to flop around on the ice like a fish out of water, or do you want my help?" Reagan challenged. Without waiting for an answer, she grabbed Allison's other foot and retied the laces on that skate as well.

With both feet back on the ground, Allison flexed her toes, coaxing the blood back into her tiny appendages. "I don't think magic shoelaces will keep me from falling on my butt," she stated sourly.

Reagan laughed. "That's why you've got *me* to help you out," she reassured.

"Sure," Allison rolled her eyes. "Help me fall again, you mean."

"That was just once," Reagan protested with a soft laugh. "I won't let you fall again, I promise."

Allison sighed and pinched the bridge of her nose. "Why am I doing this again?"

"Because you don't want me to have to skate all by myself," Reagan lightly pouted. Her bottom lip made an appearance, signaling the end of Allison's protesting.

"Fine."

With the help of Reagan, the normally graceful girl stumbled back onto the ice. Once again, she clung to the hockey boards on the perimeter like an amateur swimmer staying afloat in a pool.

"Here," Reagan stated with a smile. "Do what I do."

Allison hesitantly allowed Reagan to wretch her grip from the sideboards. She held onto one of Allison's gloved hands and carefully pulled her towards the center of the rink.

"Hey," Allison remarked, allowing herself to pick up speed. "I think I'm starting to get the hang of this." Her legs felt more solid, but she was still unsure about letting herself go too fast.

"I knew you'd be a natural at this," Reagan noted with a crisp nod. "You're good at everything."

Allison gingerly turned on her skates, causing her to slow down. "Do you always put people up on such a high pedestal?"

Reagan wasn't quite sure what she was asking or what the right answer was, so she merely shrugged.

Allison started to skate towards Reagan, but her toe-pick caught on a divot in the ice and she started to fall. Her arms flailed comically at her sides as she tried to latch onto something to catch herself, but it only resulted in her plopping down hard on her backside.

Reagan tried to not laugh as she stared down at Allison. "Okay, so maybe you're not good at *everything*."

Allison groaned and rubbed at her tailbone. Falling on the ice felt like wiping out on concrete, only you got wet.

"Don't worry about it. It just proves that you're human after all." Reagan suddenly lost her balance and fell onto the ice surface, joining the other woman. She groaned unhappily. "I did that on purpose."

"Uh huh."

Reagan rolled onto her stomach and stared intently. "This is fun. Thank you for giving it a chance."

"It's really not a big deal. I told you, it's all part of the new Allison Hoge."

"I think I'm really starting to like this new Hoge," Reagan smiled back. "What do you want to do with the rest of the day?"

Reagan's words echoed in Allison's head. "What time's your train?"

Reagan's features scrunched together as she tried to remember. "Not until 6pm, I think. I could take a later train, but the 6 o'clock gets me back to New York at a respectable hour." It would have been more time and money efficient to stay Friday night through Sunday afternoon, instead of Saturday morning through Sunday evening, but she'd made the decision to make this initial visit as short as possible without offending Allison. She hadn't wanted to commit to spending two nights in Providence if it turned out to be a disaster.

"Right. Need to make sure you get your 8-hours of sleep," Allison snorted.

"My sleep schedule is very important to me." Reagan dug her toe-picks into the ice and pushed off, forcing her body to scoot across the ice, closer to where Allison still lay. She used her elbows to army-crawl until their bodies were parallel. Other skaters veered widely to avoid them.

"Are you a human zamboni now?" Allison cracked.

"No," Reagan pouted. "I just wanted to get closer to you."

"Oh." Allison sat up on the ice. She couldn't believe they'd been lounging on the ice surface for the past few minutes. "Are you hungry?"

Reagan sat up as well. She fluffed at her hair, knocking a few bits of shaved ice from the back. "Salad again?"

Allison frowned guiltily. "I'm sorry. I haven't been a very good hostess have I?"

Reagan stood up on shaky skates and wiped at her backside and coat where ice shavings had collected from the fall. "You've done an admirable job. I know accommodating someone with special diet needs isn't easy. My dad lived with me for 18 years and even he had problems with it."

Allison allowed Reagan to help her to her skated feet. They teetered once, threatening to spill back onto the ice, but Allison stuck her blades hard into the ice, determined not to fall again. "You don't have to be so nice to me, Reagan," she murmured. "I don't deserve it."

Reagan gave Allison a lopsided grin. "I know," she agreed. "But I also know you're working on it."

+++++

By the time they left the ice rink, the afternoon sun had sunk lower in the sky. Reagan squealed suddenly and ran off the sidewalk and onto the snowy campus green, which was currently covered in at least two feet of puffy snow. She stopped and flopped backwards onto the ground, giggling manically.

"What are you doing?" Allison asked, hugging herself as a brisk wind sliced through the New England afternoon. She glanced around, feeling anxious about the few pairs of eyes trained on them from fellow students. She really didn't care what they thought, but old habits were hard to break.

"I'm making a snow angel, obviously. Hop on in," Reagan crowed, "the snow's great!"

"I'm *not* going to do that," Allison stubbornly protested. "I'll get wet and cold. And I'm already sore from ice skating."

Reagan flapped her arms and legs back and forth in the powdered snow. "Don't make me make a snow angel all on my own, Allison," she pouted.

Allison rolled her eyes and sighed. "Fine," she conceded, far too easily for her liking. "What am I supposed to do?"

"You don't know how to make a snow angel?" Reagan asked,

suddenly stopping her flailing. "Seriously. Are you an alien?"

"Murphy, just tell me what to do," Allison snapped in an irritated tone.

"Just fall backwards," Reagan instructed as she went back to moving her arms and legs.

Allison warily eyeballed the frozen ground. "Won't it hurt?"

"The snow is soft," Reagan stated. "It'll break your fall. It's much better than falling on the ice."

Allison worried her bottom lip between her teeth and hesitated.

"Hurry up!" Reagan urged. "My butt is getting cold and wet. Just fall already!"

Allison sucked in a sharp breath. She hated not being in control, and she hated that Reagan Murphy was bossing her around. But more than anything, she didn't want to look like a stick-in-the-mud. That was the old Allison Hoge; that wasn't who she was anymore.

Taking one last fleeting glance behind her, she closed her eyes, tipped back on her heels, and let herself fall.

+++++

The sound of hospital sirens screaming in the background made Allison wince. The harsh fluorescent lights above hurt her eyes. EMTs rushed through the Emergency Room doors with someone laid out on a gurney. From where she sat, she couldn't make out the extent of the person's injuries. Doctors and nurses flooded to the scene yelling out codes from a secret language that she didn't recognize.

She felt a hand at her elbow. "At least you're not that guy," Reagan said in a quiet voice for only Allison to hear.

"But if I was, I'd actually get some attention," Allison scowled, equally quiet.

"Let me see it again," Reagan coaxed.

Allison pulled the makeshift compress away from the back of her neck. Reagan brushed Allison's long ponytail to the side. A jagged red line marred her porcelain skin. The bleeding had stopped, but the gash looked deep and would probably require stitches.

"I can't believe you hit a rock," Reagan murmured. Her fingertips were warm from being inside gloves, and Allison visibly shuddered at the tentative, gentle touch. Reagan bit her bottom lip. "I'm sorry.

Does it hurt?"

Allison released a shaky breath. "No," she said through gritted teeth. "It's okay. I've endured worse." Her eyes snapped shut when Reagan's fingers slid down the side of her neck.

"Have you ever had stitches before?"

Allison nodded, opening her eyes now that the wave of what she hoped was just nausea had passed. "Once. My cousin hit me in the head with a golf club when I was five." She was constantly getting bumped and bruised when she was young. Gracefulness had come late, despite the ballet and gymnastics and cheerleading.

Reagan's eyes bulged. "What?"

Allison shrugged. "It sounds worse than it actually was. I got cut, they stitched me up, good as new." She brushed her thin bangs away from her forehead. "That's what this scar is from."

Reagan inspected the tight white line, even whiter than Allison's already pale skin, just above her left eyebrow. Without asking permission, she ran her thumb along the slight indent. "So that's what's wrong with you."

Allison pulled away. "What's that supposed to mean?"

"I can blame your insanity on getting hit in the head when you were young," Reagan responded cheekily.

Allison turned the conversation back to Reagan. She knew she loved to talk about herself. In high school, it seemed to be her favorite topic. "Do you have any scars?"

"None that are visible," Reagan quipped. She smiled slyly.

Allison rolled her eyes. "You are an incredible dork."

"Oh, look," Reagan sing-songed. "I think a new scar is forming right now."

"Allison Hoge?" a nurse with a clipboard announced.

At her name, Allison stood up a little too quickly. Her knees wobbled when the blood rushed to her head.

Reagan shot to her feet and steadied her. "Are you okay?" she asked, her voice filled with concern.

"I'm fine," Allison insisted. She felt Reagan's hand at her waist. It felt warm. Had she always been this touchy? She couldn't remember.

"Do you want me to go in with you?" Reagan had started to stroke innocently near her hipbone. It was distracting.

Allison swallowed down an emotion she wasn't prepared to

identify. "No. I'll be fine."

+++++

The sky was a dark purple. Reagan looked up into the night sky and breathed out, watching her breath smoke in front of her face. Her lungs burned from the late winter chill, but she didn't mind. It was a familiar feeling, reassuring, and it reminded her of home.

The railroad platform creaked beneath Reagan's feet. There was something quant about the Providence train stop, like it had been cut out of a Norman Rockwell painting. Tall, spindly trees were painted with tiny white lights, leftover from the winter holiday. It was a far cry from the chaos of Grand Central Station to which she'd become accustomed. A light snow had begun to fall on their walk from the Emergency Room to the train station. The tiny snowflakes melted almost as soon as they landed, but over time it was sure to accumulate.

"You didn't need to walk me to the train station."

Allison shoved her hands deeper into the pockets of her wool jacket. "Well, after such an eventful weekend, it would feel a little anti-climatic to say our goodbyes at the Emergency Room." The doctors had quickly and efficiently stitched up her head wound, but they'd had to wait for so long in the waiting room that by the time they'd exited the doctor's office, it had been time for Reagan to catch her train back to New York.

"It would have served me right," Reagan said glumly.

Allison snagged Reagan's elbow, partially spinning her around. "Hey," she said softly. Reagan didn't think she'd ever heard her so soft-spoken. "It wasn't your fault, okay?" Allison's hazel eyes searched Reagan's face. "How were you to know my head would find the one rock for miles?"

Her words brought a small smile to Reagan's lips. "I guess we're lucky you have such a hard head."

Allison smirked. "Don't get cocky with me, Murphy," she teasingly warned. "It might not have been your fault, but I'm still gonna milk this for as long as I can. I had to get *stitches*, after all."

They stood in silence on the platform, both distracted by disparate thoughts. When Reagan's train arrived, Allison turned to face her weekend guest. "Thank you for today," she said in a quiet, yet genuine voice.

"Even though it ended with you in the hospital?" Reagan deflected. There was something about the look on Allison's face that made her nervous. But she looked so thoughtful, Reagan didn't want to chatter aimlessly.

Allison brushed away a few snowflakes that had settled on Reagan's cheek and eyelashes. She thought Reagan looked beautiful in this light. Before she realized what she was doing, Allison was leaning close and pressing her lips against Reagan's. The touch was light, her lips barely grazing Reagan's own. She slowly pulled back, face emotionless.

"What was...you just..." Reagan sputtered. She paused and inspected Allison's features before her nose crinkled. "Are you *sure* you don't have a concussion? Amnesia maybe?"

Allison smiled mildly. "Your train's here."

Reagan stared back blankly, the words not making any sense, but she jumped when the train's whistle blew its final boarding call. She spun on her heels and climbed aboard the train that would take her back to New York.

Once in the train, Reagan sat down, taking a window seat. Outside, through the frost-tinted windows she could just make out Allison's silhouette. The window was too distorted, however, to see her face clearly and her body language wasn't helping either. She was just *standing there*.

The train lurched forward and started on its way. Allison brought a hand up, her fingers motionless in her winter gloves, in a silent sign of parting.

Reagan raised her hand to the window, but her fingers never made it. Instead, they stopped and touched her lips, still tingling from the feeling of Allison Hoge's mouth.

+++++

Allison dead-bolted the front door behind her and released a shuddered breath she hadn't realized she'd been holding. She couldn't honestly remember how she'd made it back home. Her brain was loud and confused.

"Hey, Allison."

The voice coming from behind her made her jump. She spun around quickly to see one of her roommates, Meghan, eating noodles from a Chinese takeout box.

"Jesus, you scared me," Allison breathed.

Meghan frowned guiltily. "Sorry."

Allison threw her keys onto the small table in the front foyer that served as a catchall for keys and mail. "No, it's okay. I just didn't think anyone was home."

"Where were you all day?" Meghan asked, resting her chopsticks into the takeout container. "I texted a few times to see if you wanted to order Chinese with me."

"I was in the library. Down in the basement stacks." The lies easily flowed off her tongue. "I must not get reception down there."

"In the library on a weekend?" Meghan clucked her tongue disapprovingly. "Girl, we've gotta get you a social life."

Allison tensed and rapidly worked the muscles in the back of her jaw to avoid snapping at her roommate. "Midterms are coming up," she reminded her in a strained voice. "I don't want to fall behind."

"All right." Meghan shrugged and dropped the topic. "I'll be watching a movie in my room if you need me."

Allison released a long, tired sigh and let her shoulders slump when Meghan turned the corner to go back to her room. She took off her boots and methodically lined them up next to the other shoes near the front door. She walked past the kitchen and wrinkled her nose at the permeating scent of Chinese takeout coming from the room. Meghan must have ordered stinky tofu again. Both of her roommates hated cooking for themselves; it was a wonder they weren't 100 pounds heavier and perpetually poor from all the delivery food.

Allison walked past Meghan and then Brice's bedroom door. Brice's door, unlike Meghan's, was open and the room was dark. That her second roommate wasn't home didn't surprise her. Out of the three of them, Brice was the most social and was hardly home, especially on the weekends. Shortly after the three women had moved in together, Allison had given up trying to keep track of whomever Brice was currently dating. Her bedroom might as well have had a revolving door.

But Allison didn't live with the other girls because she was hoping to make best friends in college who'd be bridesmaids at her hypothetical wedding. They paid their rent and their share of the utility bills on time, and that's all she asked. College was temporary – 4 years of her life. She had no disillusions that she'd find, form, and nurture any lasting relationships during college, romantic or otherwise.

She made her way to the bathroom to wash her face, taking the time to go through her nightly ritual of removing her make-up and brushing her teeth. When her face was scrubbed clean, she stared at her pale reflection. She never wore too much make-up. She didn't consider herself high maintenance. Plus, her mother had always told her that only ugly girls needed make-up; and Allison Hoge was not an ugly girl.

As she continued to contemplate her reflection, a sharp sob bubbled up her throat and escaped past perfect teeth and parted lips. She grasped onto the edge of the bathroom vanity for stability, surprised by the intensity of the emotion.

With nothing else to occupy her mind, she finally allowed herself the one realization that she had shoved into a dark corner of her mind until she could no longer deny it.

She had kissed Reagan Murphy.

Safely tucked away in her bedroom and hidden by darkness, the tears started to freely fall.

+++++

CHAPTER FIVE

Allison walked two fingertips over the curve of an antique globe near her seat at her favorite coffee place in Providence. Unlike a carbon copy coffee chain, she preferred this shop for the randomness of its décor. And as an added bonus, no one ever bothered her to relinquish her table, even hours after she'd finished her coffee.

She loved the look of the antique globe – slightly yellowed by age – but it no longer served its purpose. It was obsolete. Her fingers traced over the country names carefully scrawled on the map. Czechoslovakia. Formosa. Countries and territories that no longer existed. Geography had always troubled her; it wasn't stable or fixed, but fluid and ever changing. That's why she loved words, particularly poetry, even if her father scoffed at it as a waste of time and his money. Language evolved, yes. But some themes were eternal. Love. Loss. Pain. Joy. Victory. Betrayal.

Her phone vibrated on the end table beside her. She picked it up and saw a message from Reagan: *"Aren't professors supposed to be liberal and progressive?"*

Allison typed her reply: *"Much to my father's chagrin."*

As much as Allison loathed the informality of text culture, she hated *talking* on the phone even more. Texting was a kind of paradox – intimate, but distant. You could launch yourself into the middle of a conversation without civilized formalities, but you never had to see how your words affected the text's recipient.

"Your father would love my Physical Anthropology professor."

"Why? What's up?" Allison responded. She put her phone back on the table and returned to her book. She'd learned that Reagan didn't just send texts – she wrote novels. She'd never be able to handle Twitter. It took her more than 140 characters to just say "hello."

A few minutes later, her phone rattled against the table's wooden top. She smirked knowingly when she saw the length of Reagan's message. She might as well have sent an email.

"It's like he's never heard of Jane Goodall before!" the first line steamed. Allison could practically hear Reagan's indignant huff. She scanned the rest of the message, which was a verbose rant about her anthropology professor, who apparently was anti-feminist and therefore now Reagan's arch-nemesis.

"When do I get to see you again?"

Allison stared down at the next text. She frowned. Reagan had a way of wording things that made her feel uncomfortable.

Since Reagan's visit to Providence, the two hadn't spoken much beyond a few random text messages. Reagan had first texted to let her know she'd made it back safely to New York and to thank her for her hospitality. She hadn't mentioned what had transpired on the train platform, and for that Allison was grateful.

"I've got to study for midterms," Allison wrote back. *"I can't get away."* It wasn't a complete lie. She *did* have midterms coming up, but they weren't until after Spring Break in a few weeks.

Reagan's response was immediate: *"Can we Skype later? I have a question for you, but I'd rather ask it face-to-face."*

Allison read and re-read the message before frowning. She couldn't imagine what Reagan had to ask her, or why it needed to be face-to-face, but a feeling of foreboding settled in her gut. Normally she would have said no. She would have run from the situation and never looked back. But this was Reagan, and she owed her this.

"Ok. When?"

+++++

"Is it coffee or a date?"

Reagan paused while applying her mascara long enough to glare at her roommate with the help of the room's full-length mirror. "Why are you so keen on labeling things?"

Ashley grinned from her location sprawled on top of her bed. "Because I like to know what's expected in certain situations."

Reagan finished her eye make-up and turned to give her roommate a skeptical look. "How would I even know the difference?"

Ashley tapped her fingers to her lips as though deeply considering the question. "Well, that all depends on if you're ordering coffee or if you're going for a more expensive latté or mocha or something."

"What does that have to do with anything?"

"It's all about the money, darling," Ashley said with an exaggerated drawl. "He's going to expect at least a goodnight kiss if you order a $5 drink and much more if dinner's involved." She gave her friend a peculiar look. "Don't you know anything about dating?"

"I know plenty," Reagan said stiffly. "Your made up rules are ridiculous, by the way."

Reagan thought about the coffee she'd ordered when she'd visited Allison at Brown. She was pretty sure it had cost more than $5. And Allison had kissed her goodnight. Maybe Ashley *did* know what she was talking about.

She probably wouldn't have agreed to see Christopher, the boy from the train, on such short notice if it hadn't been for Allison. He'd called her early that morning to see if she was free later. Typically she needed more advanced warning to mentally prepare, but Allison Hoge had kissed her. It had only been the lightest of kisses, lips innocently pressed against lips, but the memory was stuck in her mind.

She wasn't spending time with Christopher to re-affirm her heterosexuality, however. She just needed a distraction to help her get outside of her head. She couldn't imagine what excuse Allison had for the unexpected kiss, and she needed to stop obsessing about it until they talked later that week. Coffee with a new friend seemed like as good of a distraction as any.

The in-room phone rang, causing both women to jump.

"God, that's loud," Reagan complained. A bright grin crossed her features. "Kind of like you, Ash." They rarely used their dorm room phone except for ordering pizza or making on-campus calls. She would have given Christopher her cell number, but she was still concerned that he might be a crazy person. Her dad's warnings that New York City wasn't the Midwest still stuck with her, three-years removed from Michigan.

"Save your comedy for the third date, Prez," Ashley said, rolling her eyes. "You don't want to scare the boy off."

"It's not a *date*." Reagan stuck her tongue out and finally answered the annoyingly shrill phone. "Hello?"

"Hi. It's Christopher," came a muffled male voice. "I'm outside your building. I can't figure out how to get inside," he said. "Your dorm is locked up like Fort Knox. What are you guys keeping in there?"

"Just the innocence of about 200 co-eds," Reagan quipped.

His laugh was like a sharp bark. "I'm kind of afraid to ask to be buzzed up now."

"Give me three minutes and I'll be right down."

Ashley had returned to her Art History textbook by the time Reagan hung up the phone. "Have fun," her roommate said, not bothering to look up. Her voice sounded bored. "I won't wait up, so don't worry if coffee turns into more."

Reagan rolled her eyes as she grabbed a scarf and jacket from their wall peg. "I'll be back in a little while."

Ashley made a clucking noise and turned a crisp, textbook page. "You're such a disappointment to sexually-liberated, college women everywhere, Prez."

+++++

Not trusting her heels on the nine flights of stairs, Reagan took the elevator down. She felt soured by her conversation with Ashley. She loved her roommate, but she hated when she judged her Midwestern morals. It wasn't like she was a virgin, after all. She just didn't see the need to have sex with random strangers.

The elevator doors opened far too quickly, indicating she was at the ground level. She crossed the main lobby, and the heels of her stylish but reasonably priced boots clicked against the floor. She immediately spotted Christopher and his shock of peroxide blond hair just beyond the plate glass windows of the dormitory. He was appropriately bundled in an oversized winter jacket. He blew into his gloveless hands and stomped his feet to keep warm.

Despite her comparative lack of dating experience, Reagan didn't feel the nervous flutter of butterflies in the pit of her stomach. It was just coffee with a new friend, she reasoned with herself. If something more blossomed, she'd have plenty of time for nerves and anxiety later.

Christopher's gaunt, handsome face lit up when he spotted Reagan. She gave him a brief wave before pushing through the glass doors and was greeted by a stiff New York City winter wind upon exiting her residence hall.

"Hey you," he greeted, walking a few steps closer. "You look great."

"Hey," Reagan returned, her face immediately cold from the sub-freezing temperatures.

The two performed an awkward second meeting ritual on the sidewalk. Christopher leaned in for a hug, while Reagan stuck out her hand. Realizing her mistake, she kept her hand going forward until it curled around Christopher's tall, lean frame for a one-armed hug.

"*Oh no,*" she mentally panicked when Christopher gave her a perceptible squeeze. "*This is a date.*"

+++++

Christopher blew on his hands, white and raw from the winter weather. "What would you like?" he asked as he stared up at the beverage menu posted on the wall.

Since he wasn't very familiar with the Greenwich Village neighborhood, he'd let Reagan pick out a suitable coffee spot. They'd politely conversed on the short walk, making small talk about the stubborn winter weather and his grandmother's 90th birthday party.

Reagan hesitated with her drink order. She officially hated her roommate. Ashley's earlier words picked at her sanity. "Coffee."

Christopher turned his head to appraise her. "You sure that's all you want? I'm buying," he offered with a toothy grin. "I promise it won't break the bank if you want to order something else."

Reagan returned the reassuring smile with one of her own. "Don't let the rumors fool you; I'm really not a diva," she stated. "Coffee's perfect. Black, please."

Christopher turned back to the waiting barista. "I guess we're having two coffees."

+++++

It was late by the time Reagan returned to her dorm – late for a school-night by her standards, at least. After the initial awkwardness of the evening, she and Christopher had both settled down and seemed to shake off the first-date jitters. One cup of coffee had turned into two, and then they'd split a particularly decadent piece of vegan chocolate cake. Conversation had come easily and they'd talked and laughed for hours until the second-shift baristas had not-too subtly begun to put chairs on top of tables to close up for the night. After closing down the coffee bar, they'd walked back to Reagan's dorm, huddled together against the severe night chill, shoulders casually bumping.

As they'd come closer to her residence hall, Reagan's nerves had returned. Would Christopher be expecting a goodnight kiss? And more importantly, did she *want* to give him one? She'd had fun, yes – probably the most fun she'd had in the city in a while – but she wasn't convinced she could see more than friendship with the New York boy.

To her relief, but also equal chagrin, he hadn't tried to kiss her when they'd said goodnight. He simply went in for another hug, which this time Reagan was ready to receive and return. They'd verbally promised to hang out again soon, and Christopher had walked away, back in the direction of the subway to his own campus.

The lack of goodnight kiss threw her. She reflected on it as she took the elevator ride up to the ninth floor. Had it actually been a date? Or had she mucked up so badly Christopher had downgraded her to friend-status? Or was he just a good guy who liked to take things slow?

The elevator doors whished open, pulling her from her thoughts. As quietly as possible in case her roommate was already asleep, Reagan unlocked her door and let herself in.

"Oh my gosh," she gasped.

Seated in the center of their dorm room was Ashley. She had dragged an overstuffed chair from its corner and relocated it to the center of the room. The bedroom was bathed in darkness except for a corner lamp, which also had been repositioned so it illuminated Ashley, who sat cross-legged in the room's center.

"Quite a late night for you, Ms. Murphy," she drawled.

Reagan's hand still clutched at her chest – her heart had practically leapt from her body upon seeing her overly dramatic roommate perched in the middle of the room. "God, Ash. You about gave me a heart attack. How long have you been sitting there?"

Ashley uncrossed her legs. "Only like half an hour," she revealed. "But it was totally worth it," she grinned. "You should have seen your face."

Reagan turned on the main bedroom light and shrugged out of her winter coat and scarf. "You have too much free time," she complained. She hated pranks and Ashley was the queen of making her feel like a fool.

Ashley pulled her legs up to her chest and curled up on the displaced stuffed chair. "So did you put out?" she asked eagerly.

"No, I did not 'put out,'" Reagan said, making a face.

The excited look fell from her roommate's features. "Well then why were you gone for so long?"

Reagan began to change into her pajamas and get ready for bed. "It's called having a conversation," she quipped. "You should try it sometime."

"Boring," Ashley sang. She stretched out her long, dancer legs. "There are so many more interesting things you could be doing with your mouth."

"I can't believe you sometimes," Reagan groaned. "You're going to move the furniture back, right?" She treaded over to her bed, intent on going to sleep. Normally her nighttime regime was more extensive, but she needed to get to sleep right away. She had a physical anthropology lecture to suffer through in the morning.

Ashley threw her legs over the arm of the easy chair. "I don't know," she said, looking around. "I kind of like the *feng shui*."

"Turn off the light," Reagan grunted. She felt soured by Ashley's cavalier attitude about casual sex, and she hated the feeling of being judged for not sharing it. "I'm going to sleep."

Ashley made a frustrated noise. "Why do I agree to room with you, year after year? I could be partying it up in Manhattan with a *fun* roommate."

Reagan puffed up her pillow and got comfortable, pulling her duvet tight around her. "Uh huh. And flunking out of school. I make sure you get to class and actually do some homework."

Ashley sighed. "I know. I know. You're liked my personal Jiminy Cricket."

"And you're my personal *Penthouse* magazine," Reagan remarked.

"Hey, speaking of which," Ashley said, her voice perking up, "you never told me how tonight went with that guy."

Reagan snorted. "That's because you were too busy trying to scare me."

"Oh, there was no *try*. I'm just sorry I didn't have a camera set up. That little footage could have been worth money. But enough about that. How was your date?"

Reagan was too tired to reiterate it wasn't a date. Plus, she was pretty sure it had been one, and she didn't want to admit that Ashley had been right. She stared up at the ceiling. "It was fine."

"Just fine?" Ashley pressed for more details. "You were gone for hours."

"It was fun," Reagan admitted. "Christopher is fun."

"But is he boyfriend material?" Ashley questioned. "Or at least boinking material?"

Reagan rubbed at her face. Even after sharing a room for three years, she still found her roommate too graphic for her sensibilities. "We only just had coffee," she said pragmatically. "It's a little too soon for me to decide on that."

"Then you're doing it wrong," Ashley noted. "You're either attracted to him or you're not. It's not rocket science, Prez."

"If he calls," Reagan said slowly, letting the idea swim around in her brain, "I'd go out with him again."

"It's the 21st century. You could call *him*."

"You make it sound so easy," Reagan sighed. She pulled the covers up around her head and tried not to think about how few hours she had until she had to be awake again.

"If it's meant to be, Prez. It is."

+++++

"How did your exam go today?" Allison propped her pillows up and settled herself more comfortably against her bed's wooden headboard.

"It was fine," came Reagan's voice over her laptop's speakers. "The professor gave us a study guide with the essay questions beforehand, so I was naturally overly-prepared."

"Wow. That would never happen at Brown. What kind of Monopoly education are you getting over there, Murphy?" Allison teased.

After dragging her feet for a few days, Allison had finally caved and had agreed to a Skype session with Reagan. She'd never used the technology before, but Reagan had assured her that even an Ivy-League student could figure it out. Allison noticed that Reagan was awfully stuck on the phrase "Ivy League," and seemed to use it in conversation with her whenever possible.

Reagan frowned. "Are we ever going to talk about what happened at the train station?"

Allison stiffened. She cleared her throat delicately. "You mean when you got on your train?"

"Don't play dumb," Reagan huffed. "You're a very smart girl, Allison Hoge. You go to an Ivy-League School."

Allison shook her head. There was that phrase again. "It wasn't a big deal. I kissed you, yes." The words felt strange in her mouth.

"But why?" Reagan pressed. The question had been pulling at the edges of her sanity ever since she'd left Providence. She was, by habit, an impatient person, and she felt she'd already shown an amazing amount of willpower for delaying this conversation this long. She wasn't going to let Allison hide any longer.

"Is that the question you wanted to ask me?" Allison sighed, looking visibly frustrated. She pushed her hair away from her eyes. She really needed to get it cut. "The one you had to ask me face-to-face?"

"Yes. I thought I'd get a more honest answer this way."

Allison sat silent. She'd already admitted to kissing Reagan. What more could she possibly want from her?

"Do you kiss all of your friends goodbye?" Reagan demanded when Allison's continued silence became too much. "I mean, I didn't mind it; I'm a very affectionate person," she quickly added. "I'm just curious."

She couldn't recall ever having seen Allison kiss her high school girl friends. But that didn't mean this wasn't all part of the new

Allison 2.0. She didn't want to read too much into the action, but it was so far removed from the Allison she had known during their high school days, she had to ask.

Allison touched the side of her laptop, tempted to slam the lid shut so she wouldn't have to face Reagan. It would be all-too-easy to sever ties from her forever. Reagan's incessant need to know the meaning behind every action and every conversation was as exhausting as ever. "It's really not a big deal, Murphy," she grumbled. "Let's just chalk it up to my recent head injury and move on."

Reagan was far from satisfied with that answer, but experience told her she wasn't going to get a straightforward response like this. She'd just have to bug her about it at a later time until Allison finally broke down and opened up to her. "Are you going home for Spring Break?" she asked, changing the subject to something safer.

"Yes. Unfortunately," Allison confirmed. Her features pinched together with the topic change. "You?"

"Mmhm." Reagan's features brightened hopefully. "Maybe we could hang out?"

"Sure. If I'm not busy."

Allison's roommates were traveling someplace closer to the Equator for Spring Break. She'd been invited along, and her parents would have paid for the trip now that she could legally drink, but the whole co-ed Spring Break phenomena wasn't her scene. So instead of flocking to sandy beaches, wet t-shirt contests, and all-day booze cruises, she was returning to her hometown for a few days. She would have stayed in Providence and enjoyed the rare quiet of a completely empty house with no roommates disturbing her, but she hadn't seen her family in a few months and felt obligated to visit, especially since she had no plans on returning to Michigan for summer break.

Reagan raised an eyebrow. "Big plans when you're home?"

"No. Not really. I just don't want you to get disappointed if we can't hook up over break." Allison grimaced at her word choice. *Hook up?* God, she was supposed to be articulate. Why did her mouth continue to betray her?

Reagan seemed undisturbed by Allison's choice of words. "Well, you have my number. Call me if you have some free time and want to grab lunch or something."

Allison nodded tersely. "We'll see."

+++++

CHAPTER SIX

Allison tilted her face into the early afternoon sun. She closed her eyes to enjoy the warmth caress her skin. Northern Michigan didn't often experience such mild weather so early in the year, so she was determined to enjoy the novelty.

Her flight had arrived the evening prior, but she was already eager to return to school. It wasn't that she didn't get along with her parents, but their expectations of her could be stifling. When she'd first arrived on the Brown campus three years ago, she'd felt like she was able to breathe for the first time.

Her mom had made Allison's favorite dinner and the meal had started out pleasantly enough with each person taking turns talking about their day – a routine they'd started when Allison and her sister, Lucy, were young. But when her father had redirected the conversation to her college major and limited career options, it was as if a dark cloud had come to hover over their house.

As soon as she'd cleaned her plate and was excused from the table, Allison had raced upstairs to call Reagan. They didn't share the same academic schedule, but their Spring Breaks overlapped for a few days. They'd talked on the phone the rest of the evening, commiserating about the difficulties of being under their respective parents' watch again and had made plans to see each other the next day.

She opened her eyes at the sound of a familiar voice calling her name.

She squinted into the sun and raised a hand up to shield her eyes from the bright glare. Reagan beamed down at her, her smile nearly as radiant as the sun. They hadn't seen each other in person since that night on the Providence train platform, but they'd texted and talked on Skype a few times. It had been just enough distance to let Allison forget that they'd kissed. Well, almost.

Allison stood to be polite, but Reagan went in for the hug. Arms immediately wrapped around her, and for perhaps the first time in her life, Allison didn't freeze up. "You smell good," she said without thinking as she pulled back from the friendly hug.

"Do I?" Reagan's face scrunched. "Well, I *did* shower today," she remarked.

Allison released an uneasy breath and returned to her seat. "That must be it. I know showering is a rarity for you." She let the playful taunting displace the uncomfortable twisting in her gut.

Reagan pulled off her oversized sunglasses and carefully set them on the table. The patio furniture was normally still stored away until warmer weather descended on their hometown, but the unseasonably warm temperatures had prompted the sandwich shop's owners to dust off the outdoor seating earlier. "I'm glad I found you."

Allison smirked. "I wasn't hiding, Murphy. I told you where I'd be at exactly this time."

Reagan raked her fingers through her loose hair and released a shaky, high-pitched laugh. "I know that; I'm just nervous, and it's making me behave awkwardly."

"What are you nervous about?"

"Being here with you."

Allison shifted in her plastic chair and leaned forward. "Explain."

Stalling, Reagan played with a small hole in the plastic tablecloth. She continued to fiddle with the rip until Allison set her hand on top of hers, stopping the nervous movement. Reagan's gaze remained stuck on the tabletop.

"It's different seeing you in New York or in Rhode Island. I can handle that. But being back here..." she trailed off. "I'm sorry," she said shaking her head. "I'm being ridiculous."

"You're not ridiculous. You're remembering all the horrible things I did to you in high school," Allison finished for her. "And you're remembering that I'm a bully who doesn't deserve another chance." She realized she hadn't removed her hand from its place on top of

Reagan's, and that she'd started rubbing small circles with her thumb. She immediately stopped and dropped her hand onto her lap.

"Yeah."

Allison had worried this might happen. Being back in their hometown brought with it a flood of memories for her, too. It was part of the reason she'd escaped to the East Coast in the first place and rarely returned.

"But you're wrong about the second chance thing," Reagan said. "Everyone deserves that."

Allison shook her head. "You're too forgiving."

"Oh, I never said you were forgiven," Reagan said with a sly smile. "I'm still going to make you work for that."

"How about I start off by buying you lunch?" Allison offered.

"Are *you* going to buy lunch or do I have to send your dad another Edible Arrangement?"

Allison laughed and brushed the hair out of her eyes. She felt better now that the conversation had taken a lighter tone. "If it'll get me closer to redemption, I'll actually pay. No Rodger Hoge credit card today."

"Well in that case," Reagan smiled, "I will accept."

+++++

Reagan pushed her fork around on her nearly empty plate. Vegan options were scarce in their small hometown, and she felt unsatisfied by the iceberg lettuce "salad" she'd ordered. Her palate had gotten spoiled after living in New York for over three years, but she couldn't deny that spending more time with Allison made the lackluster salad less offensive. "So it's weird being back here, right?"

Allison finished the final bite of her sandwich and vigorously nodded. "I don't know what it's like for you," she said when she finished chewing, "but I can't handle being at my parents' house. I've gotten too accustomed to living on my own, in my own space, with my own rules. Being back here makes me feel like a child."

Reagan hummed in agreement. "I know. Don't get me wrong, I love my dad, but -"

"Hold that thought," Allison cut in as she abruptly stood up. "I just stuck my hand in something sticky, and I'm quietly freaking out over here." She wiggled the fingers on her right hand and grimaced.

Reagan chuckled. "Ok. Do you want to sit inside instead? I could move our stuff to a new table."

"No, this is nice out here," Allison insisted. "I miss being by the lake. I just need to rinse my hand off, and I'll be right back." She spun on her heels and tromped across the wooden patio inside to the sandwich shop's single bathroom.

After washing the mysterious goo off her hands, Allison checked her reflection in the bathroom mirror. She pulled her lip-gloss out of the front pocket of her jeans and re-applied a coat. She pursed her lips, but stopped when she realized she was primping as if getting ready for a date.

After a rocky start, lunch had gone surprisingly well. She still worried that Reagan might bring up that unfortunate kiss though. She hoped Reagan could forget it happened and they could continue rebuilding their friendship. If Reagan insisted on talking about it, however, she knew she'd be forced to divorce herself from the situation. But she really wanted that second chance with Reagan.

She stared hard at her reflection. Large hazel eyes stared back at her beneath a curtain of blonde hair. She really needed to get it cut. Maybe she'd hunt down her old hair stylist and see if she could squeeze her in before the end of Spring Break.

Taking one last look at herself in the mirror, she left the bathroom. When she swung the bathroom door open, she nearly ran into someone standing just outside of restroom. She blindly mumbled an apology.

"Allison? Allison Hoge?"

Long arms were suddenly surrounding her torso and squeezing her hard. Only when the hug ended and she could pry herself away did she recognize her hugging assailant.

"Carly?"

The lanky girl waved her arms around. "Beth! Vanessa!" she called out. "Look who's here!"

Two other women appeared at Carly's side and Allison soon found herself in the middle of a high school reunion sandwich. She would have covered her ears to muffle the ear-piercing shrieks, but her arms were pinned to her sides. She shut her eyes and waited for it to be over.

When the squealing died down, she tentatively opened her eyes. Carly, Beth, and Vanessa, her three closest friends in high school stood in front of her, shoulder to shoulder, like an impenetrable wall.

"What are you doing back in town? It's been, like, forever!" Carly exclaimed.

Allison nodded. "I know. I haven't been back that often," she acknowledged with a small frown. "I've just been too busy to make the trip." She was guilty of not staying in touch, despite the promises scrawled on the inside cover of yearbooks. But giving up her high school friends had been just one casualty in the quest to re-invent herself.

Carly and Beth were fraternal twins. Rumor was they shared a brain, but that Beth got to use it more often. High school was unkind, even to the most popular kids. Their family had moved to town at the beginning of high school and lived in the house next door to Allison's family. The three had become fast friends. Carly and Allison had been on the cheerleading squad together. Beth, more solemn and serious, wasn't the cheerleading type. She'd been just as popular, however, with her girl-next-door good looks and warm demeanor.

"It must be like a high school reunion or something," Beth spoke up. "Did you guys see who's here, too?"

"No. Who?" Carly chirped curiously.

"Reagan Murphy."

"Oh my God." Vanessa nearly shrieked at the name. "Where? I *have* to see this."

Unlike the twin sisters, Vanessa was less charming. If every high school had a token Mean Girl, she was it. Allison briefly entertained the thought that perhaps she and Vanessa had shared that title. It had made for an uneasy tension during school with each vying for the top of the pyramid, both figuratively and literally as cheerleaders. They'd been friends, but only because the alternative was much worse.

"She's out on the patio," Beth noted, nodding in that direction.

Vanessa peered out at the girl sitting by herself on the back patio area. "Good old Reagan Murphy, sitting with all her friends," she chuckled. "Hey, remember when you took her clothes from her gym locker and she had to wear sweaty gym stuff all day long? God, Allie. You were the Queen of Mean," she giggled approvingly.

"Do you have any plans for today?" Beth asked, turning to her high school friend. "A lot of the old gang is home on break, so we're having a bonfire at the beach."

"Yeah, I heard Chad is back from college, too. Maybe you guys could reconnect," Vanessa laughed conspiratorially.

Allison felt three pairs of eyes on her, waiting. She hazarded a glance once more in the direction of Reagan, still sitting outside. In her absence, she had pulled her oversized sunglasses back on and was gazing out at the harbor, unaware of the conversation happening inside at her expense.

"I'm free," she heard her voice say.

"Great!" Vanessa chirped excitedly. "I want to catch up and hear all about the rich Brown men you've been tormenting." She linked her arm with Allison's and pulled her outside with Beth and Carly following behind.

Allison crawled into the back of Beth's SUV, leaving her own vehicle behind in the parking lot. She figured she could pick it up in the morning or later that night. As she buckled her seatbelt in the backseat, her stomach lurched. She knew she had to do something about the girl she'd left behind.

She grabbed her cell phone out of her bag and quickly typed off a text message: *"My mom called while I was in the bathroom, and I needed to leave. I'm so sorry."*

The reply was instantaneous: *"Is everything all right?"*

Allison frowned. Why did Reagan have to be so nice all the time when she was such a rotten person?

"Everything's fine," her fingers replied. *"If I don't see you again before you head back to school, have a nice break."*

Reagan's polite response flashed on her screen: *"You, too."*

Allison sighed. She'd successfully maneuvered out of an uncomfortable situation, but that didn't make her feel any less guilty. She started to type another text when her phone vibrated again with a third message: *"By the way, say hi to Carly, Beth, and Vanessa for me."*

Allison's eyes went wide and she threw her phone back into her purse so she didn't have to look at it anymore. She felt sick. Nauseous. How could Reagan have caught her in the lie so easily?

While her old high school friends chattered excitedly in the background, Allison stared out the back window at the town she used to call home. The familiar scenery blurred before her.

Way to go, Hoge, she bitterly thought. *So much for growing and maturing.*

+++++

Spring Break had ended and Allison was back at Brown. She'd temporarily gone off the grid, not responding to emails, voice mails, or text messages in order to buckle down for that semester's round of midterms. Once she'd emerged from the tests and papers that kept her busy mid-semester and finally got back to technology, she was sure she'd be the recipient of at least a dozen messages from Reagan. She was terrified, however, to discover that Reagan hadn't once tried to contact her – not even a single text message with the words "I hate you."

There was no other word that better represented her feelings about the situation – *terrified.* Something must be wrong. Reagan must have died. There seemed no other logical explanation for her to have not reached out to at least pontificate why Allison Hoge was a horrible person who had not changed since high school.

She couldn't deny that her ego hurt just a little that Reagan hadn't tried to contact her after the Michigan trip. She knew it was a remnant of her high school persona, and she tried to mentally choke back those indignant feelings. Being angry with Reagan for having a backbone wasn't going to rectify the situation.

In the absence of any messages from Reagan, Allison decided to send one of her own: *"Are you going to pretend like I don't exist?"*

If Reagan wanted to cut her out of her life, she knew she deserved it. She'd all but done the same to her, ditching like that at their hometown sandwich shop. It might have even been crueler than if she'd stood her up altogether.

She chewed on her thumbnail, a nervous habit she couldn't shake, and stared at her phone, willing it to *do something.* When it was clear Reagan wasn't going to respond to her text, she called her phone number instead. The phone rang until it went to her voicemail. Reagan's recorded, perky, professional voice told her she wasn't around, but to leave a message and she'd be happy to respond as soon as possible.

Allison seriously doubted if left to her own devices that Reagan would call her back. She called the number again and glanced at the time displayed on her cell phone. It was late in the afternoon, but maybe Reagan was still in class. She hung up and immediately redialed the number. The phone continued to ring and she contemplated leaving a voice mail.

Across her bedroom, her laptop started to jangle. She hopped up from her bed and crossed the room to the desk where she kept her computer. Her Skype program, which she had only ever used with Reagan, opened and Reagan's screen name appeared on the screen. She sat down at her desk chair, tucked her long hair behind her ears, and hit the Accept button.

When Reagan's scowling face filled her laptop screen, Allison didn't give her the opportunity to start the conversation. "I'm sorry, Reagan."

"For calling my phone repeatedly and interrupting my homework time?"

"No. You know for what," Allison frowned.

"If you wanted to apologize, you could have just left me a voice mail like a sane person," Reagan said, her tone exhibiting her annoyance. "Or you could have written me an email."

"And if you wanted to ignore me forever, why are you web-chatting me?" Allison countered.

"I never said I wanted to ignore you forever."

Allison sighed. "You didn't call me after Spring Break."

"Neither did you," Reagan pointed out. "And *I'm* not the one who messed up."

"Do you have to be so dramatic all the time?" Allison felt increasingly agitated by Reagan's newfound backbone. She knew she was in the wrong and that Reagan was going to make things difficult for her. But beyond apologizing repeatedly, she didn't know what else she could do to make things right. "Why didn't you just pick up the phone when I called?"

"Self-preservation. In my experience, you have a harder time being mean if you can see my face," Reagan snapped. "When I'm out of sight and you can't see how much your actions hurt me is generally when you're at your worst." Her voice started to shake on the last few words.

Allison's determination to be angry immediately crumbled at the show of emotion. "Reagan, I'm really sorry. What I did to you was uncalled for and incredibly cruel."

Reagan released a long, tired sigh and she ran her fingers through her hair. She looked away at something off-screen. "Is it really *that* embarrassing to be seen in public with me?"

"No," Allison insisted. "Of course not."

"You just can't be seen with me in our hometown."

Allison hung her head. She'd been so busy once she'd gotten back to campus that she hadn't let herself dwell on what she'd actually done to Reagan. But now as she sat here with Reagan refusing to look at her and her voice coming through her laptop speakers, the full weight of her cruelty sank in. She was disappointed in herself. Even High-School-Allison was disappointed by her actions. "I know I'm a coward," she choked out. "And I'm sorry."

"This isn't going to work." Reagan continued looking away, and it drove Allison crazy. Reagan always maintained perfect eye contact.

"What isn't?"

"A friendship." Reagan turned back to the computer screen. Her eyes flashed with anger. "I'm not going to let you make me feel like it's high school all over again."

"Please, Reagan. I'm *trying*." Allison couldn't deny the desperation in her voice. "I overestimated myself. I thought I was ready to be a better person – a *different* person than who I used to be. But Carly and Beth and Vanessa blindsided me. I wasn't ready for that kind of confrontation."

Reagan looked curiously at the woman pictured on her computer screen. She hardly resembled the confident, self assured bully of years ago. "You know, you were horrible to a lot of people in high school. Why is *my* friendship so important to you?"

Allison twisted the silver band she wore on her right ring finger and looked uncharacteristically fidgety. "I've asked myself that same question." She spoke so softly that Reagan had to lean forward to hear her. "And I don't know. But it is."

Reagan bit her lower lip. She wanted this friendship. She'd wanted it every day of their entire high school career. But not if it was going to hurt like this. "I'm sorry," she said thickly. "I just can't do it anymore."

"One more chance. Please, Rea."

The use of the familiar nickname both tugged at Reagan's heart and made her equally furious. She couldn't tell if Allison had purposely used it to manipulate her feelings or if it was a throwback from their middle-school friendship.

"Let me visit again," Allison pressed. "This weekend. I want to be a better person."

Despite her misgivings, Reagan felt her resolve faltering. "Maybe."

"Really?" Allison's eyes brightened, and she looked hopeful.

Reagan continued to frown. "I'm serious. You make me feel insignificant one more time, Allison, and I'm done."

Allison's face immediately grew somber. "I understand."

"Are you serious about wanting to visit this weekend?"

"If you're free," Allison said with an eager nod. "I don't want it to be an inconvenience."

In truth, Reagan had no plans. Most weekends, in fact, she had no plans. But Allison didn't need to know that. She looked down at her nails, not trusting herself to continue making eye contact. "I guess I could rearrange my schedule."

+++++

CHAPTER SEVEN

Reagan stood on her tiptoes and craned her neck to see above the crowds milling around Grand Central Station. The extra inches did her no good. She was still too short to see over the other heads. Her stomach felt uneasy. She knew she should have insisted on a more specific meeting place. But Allison had told her not to worry. She'd insisted they'd find each other outside of the busy terminal and that she'd text if delayed.

Reagan glanced at the time on her phone. 7:17pm. The electronic signs around the station all indicated that Allison's train had arrived 15 minutes ago, yet she was nowhere in sight.

The last time they'd seen each other, not counting their disembodied faces over Skype, Allison had ditched her to hang out with her high school friends. Reagan felt justified in worrying that she'd been abandoned again. She also knew that she only had to dial Allison's number and she'd be able to track her down. But Reagan Murphy was stubborn, and she wasn't going to call first when Allison could just as easily do the same.

She was still unsure about agreeing to see Allison that weekend. She wasn't convinced they could get past their high school differences. *"One more chance,"* she told herself. *"I'll give her one more chance to prove she's changed."* She felt a little better now that she'd set some personal perimeters. Now all she had to do was find Allison in this sea of people.

"Hey, Murphy."

Reagan spun on her heels at the sound of the familiar voice. "You made it!"

Despite having just crossed the borders of several states, Allison looked fresh-faced and glowing. The sun was getting ready to set and the red-orange rays played against her pale hair and equally pale features. Reagan, with her naturally darker skin tone, need only stand in direct sunlight for a few hours before turning a full shade tanner. She wondered if Allison spent any time outside or if she was too busy with school to do so. She hated the thought that she might be caged inside a library, her bedroom, or even a coffee shop while the world outside continued on without her.

"Yes. I somehow managed to board the right train and get off at the right stop," Allison deadpanned with a quick roll of her eyes. "Go me."

Reagan shook her head. "I just meant you found me. I was worried we wouldn't be able to find each other without a designated meeting location."

"I guess it's a good thing you wore that orange trench coat."

Reagan looked down at her jacket. "Huh. I didn't notice I did that."

"I can't even imagine what your closet must look like if that color orange didn't make an impression," Allison chuckled, not unkindly. "Did you kill a family of clowns and steal their wardrobe?"

Reagan momentarily bristled. Comments about her clothes reminded her too much of high school. But then Allison was hugging her, and she couldn't remember why she was angry anymore. Reagan closed her eyes and let herself enjoy the moment. *Allison* had initiated the hug. Allison Hoge was hugging *her*.

+++++

"And this," Reagan announced, turning the key in her lock, "is my dorm room."

She stepped to the side and let Allison go in first. Allison was momentarily taken aback when she saw another girl in the room. "You should really knock when the door is locked, Prez," the girl said. "You never know what you might walk in on."

Reagan made a face. "And that's my roommate, Ashley."

"Hey," Ashley said in greeting. She returned her attention back to her laptop screen.

"Ash, this is my friend Allison. The one from Michigan who goes to Brown."

Ashley rolled her eyes and finally pulled herself up to a seated position. "As if there's any other Allison's who I might get her confused with. You only told me about a hundred times this week that she was coming to stay."

Allison's extensive etiquette training kicked in. "Ashley, it's nice to meet you. Reagan's told me a lot about you."

"And it's great to final meet the Great and Powerful Allison Hoge. Reagan does nothing but talk about you."

Allison quirked an eyebrow at Reagan who was busy looking everywhere except at her friend and her roommate.

Allison turned back to Ashley. "Thank you for letting me intrude on your space this weekend," she said graciously.

Ashley held up her hands. "No need to thank me."

"Allison is constantly thanking people," Reagan chirped. "It's kind of her thing."

Allison made a face. "There's nothing wrong with having manners," she defended herself.

"Well, Reagan's had to suffer through enough of my old high school friends visiting," Ashley noted. "I'm just happy she finally brought one of her Michigan people here. I was starting to think I embarrassed her."

Allison arched an eyebrow. "I'm the first person to visit you?"

"I've had people visit. They just haven't spent the night," Reagan grumbled. "I'm not a *complete* leper."

Allison laughed lightly and bumped her hip against Reagan's. "I'm just teasing. Maybe I like the idea that I'm the only one who's gotten to stay in your room."

Reagan raised an eyebrow. "Why?"

Allison shrugged. "I don't like to share," she said simply.

Ashley watched the two women's bantering with interest. She hadn't been exaggerating – Reagan *did* talk non-stop about Allison, and she was curious to see more. "Oh, before I forget, Prez, that boy keeps calling the room phone. Give him your cell number or I'm demanding a roommate change. I have a heart attack every time that damn phone rings."

Allison set her bag down on the floor. "*Boy*? Are you dating someone, Murphy? You keeping secrets from me?"

"It's nothing." Reagan waved a dismissive hand. "Just this guy I met who goes to CUNY. We've gone out a few times, but it's nothing serious. Actually," she said, looking thoughtful, "we met on the train when I came to visit you the first time."

"Oh. Well that's convenient." Allison's lips pressed together. "I expect an invite to your wedding since I'm the one responsible."

"Do you guys have big plans for tonight?" Ashley asked, interrupting the banter.

Allison looked to Reagan for confirmation. Reagan shrugged. They hadn't really discussed what they might do over the weekend, and she hadn't had the time to make elaborate plans during the week. Allison was surprised Reagan didn't have an agenda, typed and laminated, for the weekend. She tried to not be offended though; she hadn't even taken the time to stock her refrigerator with vegan-friendly food when Reagan had visited.

"Not really," Reagan said.

"You should come to the party down at the Delta house," Ashley said. "The place is a total dive, 'cause you know, *frat house*, but they always have a nice spread. All the booze you could ask for. I could get you two on the list."

"Is that something you'd be into?" Allison asked Reagan.

She shrugged. "Maybe."

"It's your city, Murphy. I'm just visiting."

"But you're the one visiting," Reagan pointed out. "We should do what *you* want to do."

"You mean like go ice skating and end up in the Emergency Room?" Allison teased.

Reagan stomped her foot a little and huffed. "You said that wasn't my fault."

Ashley watched the two go back and forth like an animated ping-pong match. "*Today*, ladies," she taunted. "I've gotta call a guy to get you on the list in time. They hate reprinting that crap. Saving the Earth one piece of paper at a time or something equally lame."

"Yes," Allison supplied for them. "We'd love to come. Thank you, Ashley, for the invitation."

The other girl waved it off and grabbed her phone grumbling something about Midwesterners being too polite.

"Are you sure?" Reagan asked uncertainly. She lowered her voice while her roommate was on the phone. "We could find something else to do."

Allison smiled placidly. "I'm not a total snob. I do know how to hang out with the unwashed masses."

"Are you sure? We could find something else to do tonight. It is the greatest city in the world."

"I'm sure. Let's go to this party." Allison nudged her. "It might actually be fun."

Reagan looked a little bashful. "I know it's not a big deal to you, but it's not like I went to the popular parties in high school. My 16-year-old self would be really psyched to be going to a college frat party."

Allison smiled fondly at the sheepish girl. "Then for the sake of 16-year-old-Reagan, let's go."

+++++

The air was thick and humid, slightly perfumed with the stench of cigarettes, cologne, and body odor. Couples danced in the front dining room area. It looked more like dry humping to Allison's critical eye. Although the music was upbeat and the bass rattled the front windows, couples danced to their own tempo. Clusters of girls danced in tight circles while co-ed men hung back on the perimeter, bobbing their heads to the beat, not quite drunk enough to actually dance.

Away from the designated dance floor, Reagan and Allison stood in the kitchen of the local fraternity house. The room was crowded, particularly around the keg, but where they had congregated was relatively open. Upon arriving and ditching their jackets on the bed of an open second-floor bedroom where Ashley insisted they'd be safe, Reagan's roommate had immediately pulled them to the kitchen. Boys with red plastic cups in their hands cheered her on as she shot-gunned a beer with gusto.

Reagan felt a light touch at her elbow. "Is she always like this?" Allison murmured in her ear.

"She works hard and plays hard, too." Reagan felt the need to defend her long-time roommate.

Allison knew she could have a very critical and judgmental personality, especially when she felt threatened and uncomfortable. She couldn't pinpoint what was bringing out this side of her, but she brushed it off as being at a fraternity party in an unfamiliar city. She herself rarely went to these kinds of activities at Brown. It was too much like her high school experience and she kept telling herself that wasn't who she was anymore.

"Do you go drinking with her often?" Allison leaned in to make sure Reagan could hear her.

Reagan shook her head. She wrapped her arms around her torso, hugging herself and looking uneasy. "I've been to a few parties with her, but I'm usually doing homework on the weekends, not binge drinking."

"You guys are falling behind," Ashley hollered over the loud music. She grabbed a bottle of unrecognizable alcohol and began setting up shots on the kitchen island. She handed one of the tiny plastic cups to Reagan and one to Allison and chugged down one for herself.

Allison looked down at her shot glass's contents and grimaced. *Why are there gold flecks in my drink?* she silently lamented. She quickly downed her shot, not wanting to appear inexperienced in front of either Ashley or Reagan. She sputtered slightly, half choking on the seemingly toxic alcoholic concoction.

Ashley handed Reagan a second shot, this time of something clear. "Bottoms up, Prez!" she hooted.

Allison put her hand on Reagan's wrist, stopping her as she brought the tiny cup to her lips. "Are you sure that's a good idea?" she cautioned.

Reagan smiled. "I've got this," she said. "This isn't my first rodeo." She promptly slammed down the drink. She coughed just a little as the burning liquid hit the back of her throat. Her blue eyes were bright and wide.

Ashley cheered on her roommate and grabbed a vodka bottle off the counter. "Now the party's started!" She gave Allison a triumphant smile.

Allison narrowed her eyes in return. She couldn't understand Ashley's angle. Was she *trying* to make Reagan sick? Were they *competing* for Reagan's attention? Was she actually *threatened* by this girl and her close relationship with Reagan?

Reagan slammed back a third shot before Allison could stop her. She didn't want to act Mom-ish, but she also had no intention of babysitting a drunk Reagan Murphy the rest of the night. "Do you want to dance?"

Reagan flashed a dimpled smile and nodded. She grabbed Allison's hand to lead her toward the front of the house. They worked their way towards the dining room, weaving through the tightly packed mass of bodies. Finally satisfied with a small pocket of space, Reagan turned around. Allison suddenly found herself invading Reagan's personal bubble. Or maybe it was the other way around.

Reagan reached out and toyed with the jade pendant at the end of Allison's necklace, ignoring the way she tensed at her touch. She trailed her finger down the length of the Allison's neck, stopping just above her clavicle. "I meant to tell you earlier I really like your necklace," she said, her enchanting mouth curling into a lazy smile.

Allison touched her fingers to the pendant. "Oh, uh, thanks," she said. It suddenly felt very warm in the room. The music was no longer the house beats that had been blaring when they'd originally arrived – it was slower, more primal. "It was a present from my mom."

"So are you actually going to dance with me?" Reagan teased. "Or are you waiting on a lesson in how to move your body?"

Allison's eyes narrowed slightly. It sounded like a challenge; she never backed down from a challenge. She grabbed onto Reagan's hips and pulled her close. Reagan's eyes widened in surprise, but she quickly recovered by spinning around and pressing her backside against Allison's front. The dance had unexpectedly become a game of chicken – how far could they push before one of them buckled.

Not one to be outdone, Allison pulled Reagan close and splayed her hands across her hipbones. She began to sway her hips to the beat, encouraging Reagan to do the same. She attributed her desire to keep up with Reagan's advances as her being naturally competitive. She was her father's daughter. She was a Hoge. And they always did things 100%.

Reagan closed her eyes and allowed herself to get lost in the moment. She leaned her head back, resting it on Allison's shoulder. She could feel the pulsing of the bass vibrating against her body, the energy from the frenetic dancers that surrounded them, and the intoxicating sensation of Allison's breath hot against her neck. Her skin felt hot. She couldn't tell if it was from Allison's proximity or if the alcohol was starting to catch up with her. She didn't know why she'd felt compelled to take so many shots in rapid succession. She wasn't much of a drinker, but being at a fraternity party with Allison made her nervous. She didn't feel so anxious anymore.

Reagan raked her short, manicured nails down the sides of Allison's denim thighs. The hands at her hips tightened, holding her impossibly closer. Her top had ridden up slightly and she felt the delicious burn of Allison's heated skin against that exposed patch. She spun around again so they faced each another. Her thigh found its way between Allison's and began a slow, sensual grind. She was mildly surprised that Allison had not pulled away, embarrassed to be seen with her so intimately in public, so she continued to dance, a small, lazy smile of contentment on her face.

Despite only having had one shot herself, Allison found herself powerless to the movements of Reagan's body. She felt like she was suffocating from the hypnotizing beat engulfing her senses and the raw promise of sexuality evident in Reagan's expressive eyes. She swallowed down the urge to run, but she knew she needed to at least step back.

"I have to pee," she yelled into Reagan's ear, making sure she could be heard over the house party's music.

Reagan nodded, eyes looking unfocused. "Okay. I'll be right here."

Allison hesitated, not confident about leaving Reagan on her own, but she needed some space to clear her head. She wandered back towards the kitchen area where she remembered seeing a bathroom. The line was surprisingly short, and within a few minutes she was safely locked away in the small bathroom.

She stared at her reflection in the dingy mirror. Her face looked flushed, her hair slightly array, her make-up a little smudged. She turned on the faucet and ran her hand beneath the cool water before clamping her now damp hand near the base of her neck. The water instantly cooled her pulsing skin, but not necessarily the pulsing need between her thighs. She turned the faucet off and gripped the edges of the porcelain pedestal. She needed to regain control.

Allison exited the bathroom once she felt sufficiently stable. She focused next on reclaiming her spot beside Reagan and enjoying the rest of the night. She turned sharply when she felt a hand graze over her ass. "Excuse me?" she snarled at a dumbstruck co-ed who wore the letters of the fraternity house they were in.

The male student held up his hands in surrender. "Sorry," he grinned. His feet moved back and forth along with the music. "I got bumped into. I really didn't mean to grab your ass."

Allison's hardened features momentarily softened and she prepared to retract her viciousness.

The boy leaned in. His breath smelled like mint and cheap beer. "Although if I *did* grab it on purpose, could you blame me?" He beamed, flashing two rows of even, white teeth. Some girls might find the anonymous boy charming and laugh it off. But Allison wasn't "some girls."

She leaned in, and the college boy's smile widened, encouraged by the attractive woman's proximity. "Touch me again and you'll lose body parts," she stated coolly in his ear. She pulled back and arched an eyebrow in challenge.

The smile fell from his face. He nodded, his eyes shifting in his head as though afraid to make eye contact again, and he promptly left the dance floor in search of another dance partner or a beer.

Allison audibly sighed and rolled her eyes. She'd always believed that boys would mature during college, but if the few fraternity parties she'd attended were any indication, boys tended to devolve in college.

She returned her attention to the dance floor. It was more crowded now than when she and Reagan had first started dancing. She stood on her tiptoes to see over the taller heads of other co-eds in search of her friend. When she finally spotted her, a frown tugged at the corners of her mouth. Off in a corner of the room, Reagan was dancing with a significantly taller boy who appeared to have his hands cupping her ass.

Allison immediately felt her mood shift and darken. Unthinking, she stormed across the party, practically shoving people out of her way to get to where Reagan danced. When she reached her, she yanked on her wrist, pulling her away from the tall frat boy. "Finding friends?" she asked tensely.

"Oh, I ran into…" Reagan blinked a few times, looking confused. "…this guy. I think his name is Matt. We have Stats together."

"I think we should go," Allison said, hazel-eyes flashing. "That alcohol's going straight to your brain. And maybe other parts," she growled, looking lower.

Reagan's lower lip stuck out. "But we just got here," she pouted. "And I'm having fun."

"Fine!" Allison hissed, not wanting to make a scene. "Drink yourself sick. I'm sure any one of these fine gentlemen you were dry humping will hold your hair while you puke."

"Hey." Reagan touched Allison's wrist, but she flinched and pulled away. She was feeling remarkably sober despite the amount of alcohol she'd had in a short time-span. "Where is this coming from?"

Allison ignored her and stomped across the house.

Reagan followed behind until she reached the second-floor bedroom where they'd stashed their coats. Allison grabbed her jacket off the bed and pulled it on, roughly shoving her arms through the fitted sleeves. "I'm sorry if my idea of fun isn't watching you do keg stands and getting groped by meatheads," she sniffed.

"I wasn't doing keg stands, Allison, and no one has been groping me," Reagan snapped off in a retort. "Give me some credit; I'm more responsible than that."

"Well, whatever," Allison scoffed. "I'm going back to the dorms." She slung the strap of her purse over her shoulder.

"I'll come with," Reagan said, despite the confusion and anger she currently felt.

"No. You should stay. You're clearly having a good time."

Reagan hesitated. Allison's face was unreadable and her tone civil and clipped. She couldn't understand what had happened. They had just been dancing and having a good time – or so she had thought.

"You shouldn't walk back by yourself," Reagan tried again. "It's late and this is New York City, not Rhode Island."

"I am perfectly capable of taking care of myself," Allison said coolly.

Reagan shook her head and reached for her jacket. She wasn't going to let Allison stop her. "I'm sure you can handle walking back to the dorms, but I'd never forgive myself on the off-chance that something *did* happen."

Allison rolled her eyes. "Whatever," she huffed. "Just hurry up before I change my mind."

Reagan hated this attitude. It reminded her of the Allison Hoge she had known in high school and resembled nothing of the girl whom she had gotten to know over the past few months. She wanted to point this out, but knew that standing in the bedroom of some stranger was not the place to have such a conversation.

The two women traipsed down the staircase to the front door. Reagan stopped at the bottom of the stairwell. She suddenly remembered that they were about to leave someone behind. She touched her hand to Allison's elbow, causing her to pause her hasty exit. "I should tell Ashley we're leaving so she doesn't worry."

Allison frowned hard. "Aren't you worried about *her* walking home by herself?

"No," Reagan said with a dismissive wave. "She'll be fine. Let me just find her. I'll be two minutes. Don't leave."

Without waiting for Allison's response, Reagan spun on her heels and maneuvered her way back through the crowds and into the pulsing center of the party.

Allison stood awkwardly by the front door. She contemplated leaving, but something made her stand in place, as though cemented to the floor.

+++++

Reagan found Ashley, still holding court in the fraternity house kitchen. "Allison and I are gonna head back," she told her roommate. "Are you okay on your own?"

"Leaving so soon?" Ashley pouted.

Reagan nodded. "Yeah, uh, Allison's not feeling that well." The lie was easier than the truth; plus, she didn't know the truth. She couldn't figure out what had happened to make Allison snap.

Ashley quirked an eyebrow. "Everything okay?"

"Yeah," Reagan said. "We're just gonna get back to the room."

The answer seemed to satisfy her roommate. "Okay, be safe."

Reagan hesitated. Her teeth tugged at her lower lip. "What do you think of Allison, by the way?"

Ashley shrugged. "She's nice."

"That's it? She's 'nice'?"

Ashley chuckled. "Chill out, girl. I just met her like two seconds ago. I don't know her like you do. Speaking of which, are you *sure* you two hated each other in high school?"

"I'm positive. I've got the therapy sessions to prove it. Why?"

Ashley shrugged. "You just seem pretty chummy for two people who only very recently stopped torturing each other."

"We have history. It's complicated."

Ashley gave her roommate an unconvinced look.

"Are you suggesting she has ulterior motives?"

"Maybe I've watched that movie *Carrie* too many times," Ashley started, "but in my experience, people don't change. At least not that much."

"Allison did," Reagan said stiffly. She wasn't altogether sure of that, but she desperately wanted to believe that people could change – even Allison.

"Just watch out for that bucket of pig's blood, okay? You're my friend and I don't want to see you get hurt."

"Allison won't hurt me. It's…I think things are different now."

Ashley nodded slowly. "If you insist, Prez. Just be careful, okay?"

"*You* be careful," Reagan countered. "You've had a lot to drink tonight."

"Sure thing, *Mom*," Ashley sighed as she accepted Reagan's brief parting hug. "I'll behave."

Reagan's smile grew when she saw Allison still standing by the door. She had expected her to grow impatient and leave, forcing her to run after her along the streets of New York. But seeing Allison still there caused a strange, warm sensation to flush over her body.

"Did you find her?" Allison asked, although her face and tone showed nothing but disinterest.

The warm sensation immediately cooled. "Yeah," Reagan confirmed. "We can go now."

+++++

The walk back to Reagan's residence hall was quiet. The city bustled around them on a busy Friday night, but Reagan and Allison ignored each other.

When they reached the front entrance of the dormitory, Allison stopped. She pushed out a deep breath from her lungs. "Maybe I should just go back to Providence," she said.

Reagan's eyes grew wide. "Tonight? It's after midnight," she pointed out. "I don't even think there's trains leaving the city anymore."

Allison looked away. "It's...I'm not feeling very well."

Not buying Allison's excuse, Reagan gathered her courage. "Can we talk about your total Dr. Jekyll and Mr. Hyde act from the party now?"

Allison's features were stoical. "I don't know what you mean," she said with equal passivity.

"Don't give me that. We were having such a good time, or so I thought," Reagan said, exasperated. "What happened to trigger High-School-Allison? I thought we were through with her."

"I don't know," Allison said in a quiet voice. The sidewalk was suddenly very interesting and her gaze remained downcast.

Reagan continued to stare at the uncomfortable girl before her. Something Ashley had said at the party poked at her brain – *Are you sure you two hated each other in high school?*

She repeated her original answer: "It's complicated," she whispered.

Allison looked back up, not having heard Reagan clearly. "What'd you say?"

"Don't move," Reagan husked. She took a step forward.

"Huh?" Allison's eyes widened in alarm as she followed the trajectory of Reagan's mouth. She watched her momentarily hesitate. Reagan bit down on her lower lip before pressing her mouth fully against Allison's own.

Allison's eyes remained open for a second before she felt Reagan press harder against her. Her eyes fluttered shut and she released an involuntary groan. She was startled by how soft and pliable Reagan's mouth was. Although she'd often found herself staring at her thick, dimpled lips (although she'd always told herself that it wasn't unusual for one girl to admire another pretty girl), she'd never imagined a kiss could feel so tender. It was a far cry from the chapped lips and rough stubble of a man's kiss.

She felt something gnaw at the pit of her stomach. At first she thought it was dread, but when Reagan's teeth softly nipped at her bottom lip, she realized what the feeling truly was – *desire*. With their lips moving freely against each other's, Allison threw caution to the wind, shut her eyes, and threw herself eagerly into the embrace.

Pulling away from Reagan's mouth, she scraped the tips of her top canines across her neck, inhaling her scent and relishing the feel of her soft skin, vulnerable against her mouth. She licked the side of Reagan's neck, tasting the thin sheen of sweat that had accumulated there, and nearly swooned when she felt Reagan shudder beneath her touch. The movement made her remember herself, and she abruptly pulled away.

"I'm so sorry," she gasped. She touched her fingertips to her burning mouth. "I don't know why I did that."

Reagan's heart hammered in her chest and she desperately tried to regain control of her breathing. "It's okay. Technically I kissed you first."

"But I didn't have to go all vampire on you."

Reagan stared carefully at Allison, sensing her unease. "Am I the first girl you've ever kissed?"

Allison's eyes darted around nervously. Who knew how many people had seen them kiss? "Can we talk about this inside?" she asked in a quiet, desperate voice.

Reagan nodded solemnly. "Of course."

+++++

They rode up the elevator in silence. When Reagan pulled out her keys to open the door, she felt self-conscious. She couldn't understand from where the feeling originated, but she was pretty sure it had something to do with the fact that she had just kissed Allison in front of her residence hall. And Allison had more than returned the kiss.

Reagan pushed into her room and instinctively shrugged out of her spring jacket to hang it up near the front door. Allison silently entered the room behind her and closed the door.

Reagan cleared her throat and dislodged the lump that had taken residency there during the elevator ride. "So, uh, we should probably talk about this."

"I'm suddenly very tired," Allison announced in a voice much louder than was needed. She averted her gaze and she too removed her jacket. She made a beeline for her suitcase, grabbed clothes to sleep in, and before Reagan could stop her, was out the door again, no doubt in the direction of the community bathroom.

Reagan sat down heavily on the edge of her bed and sighed. She rested her head in her hands and tried to not let her thoughts overwhelm her. She only looked up again when she heard the door open.

Allison re-entered the room and Reagan allowed herself an indulgent appraisal. She'd always known that Allison was beautiful in that Anglo-Saxon perfection kind of way. There was nothing exotic-looking about her to make her stand out in a crowd, but she certainly wasn't someone who didn't draw second, and even third, glances from admirers. But this Allison Hoge, the one standing in her dormitory bedroom in her pajamas, was a revelation.

Allison had thrown her hair up in a high, loose ponytail and had changed into cotton shorts and a tank top. In her hands were the clothes she'd worn that night. Reagan took a moment to admire the strong, lean thighs that tapered into well-formed calves. Allison's sleeping shorts were cut high on her upper thigh, revealing enviable toned muscles that flexed when she walked. Her breasts sat high on her chest despite not wearing a bra. That warm, familiar feeling returned when Reagan noted the undeniable outline of two erect nipples poking through the cotton material. When she realized Allison was staring back, she quickly averted her gaze.

"I should sleep on the floor."

Reagan looked back up. "What? Why?"

"I just thought with what happened…" Allison trailed off, unwilling to finish her train of thought.

Reagan stood. "Has anything changed between us? Are we not friends anymore?"

"No. Nothing's changed, I guess." Allison felt annoyed at how cavalier and comfortable Reagan appeared with this situation when she could hardly make eye contact.

Reagan blinked once. "And are you going to molest me in the middle of the night?"

"Of course not," Allison snapped. She blushed at the thought.

"I might not mind if you did."

Allison's eyes widened. She almost looked *afraid*. "Oh, uh, I don't…I don't know if I'm, uh," she stammered.

"I'm just teasing. Sorry. You know I say stupid stuff when I'm nervous." Reagan worried her bottom lip.

"So you're okay with us sleeping together?" As soon as the words spilled out, Allison pressed her lips together. She was mildly horrified she'd phrased her question like that. Her mouth was betraying her tonight in all kinds of new and unexpected ways. "I mean, not like *that*," she quickly tried to clarify. "I just mean in the same bed."

"I knew what you meant," Reagan smiled. "I'm going to get ready for bed. Don't, uh, don't leave, okay?"

Allison looked down at her sleeping attire. "Where would I go?"

"I don't know. Just. Don't go," Reagan said. She grabbed her sleeping things and rushed out of the room as if she really worried Allison would bolt if left alone for too long.

When Reagan returned, the room was plunged in darkness. She used the light spilling in from the hallway to orient herself before shutting the door and committing the room to darkness again. Her eyes weren't yet adjusted to the dim lighting, but it was her room, so she had little problem finding her way to the bed.

When her knees brushed against the fabric of her down comforter, she experimentally patted the bed to avoid sitting on top of Allison. Things had been awkward enough between them that night without her unintentionally crawling on top of her. She lifted the corner of the blanket and slid between the sheets; but since it was only a twin mattress, she quickly found Allison's body.

"Sorry," she mumbled when her shoulder knocked into an unidentified body part.

Allison held her body rigid until she felt Reagan relax beside her. "It's okay," she reflexively whispered back.

It wasn't really okay, though. It was the kind of response you give when someone runs into you or walks into the bathroom stall you're occupying. You say it because it's the polite thing to say, not because it's actually fine. The truth was Allison felt completely rattled, and even the simplest, unintentional touch made her want to lean in for more.

The silence eventually became too much for Reagan – a girl who never dealt well with unresolved tension. "Are we really not going to talk about this?"

"There's nothing to talk about," Allison said to the black space above her head.

Reagan sighed dramatically. "Allison," she sighed. "We can't just...It's not healthy to..."

"*Please*, Reagan," Allison cut her off. The desperate plea was obvious in her tone. "I-I can't do this," she breathed. "Not right now at least."

Reagan was silent, but only momentarily. "In the morning then?"

Allison bit her lower lip and hesitated before giving her response. "In the morning," she reluctantly agreed.

+++++

CHAPTER EIGHT

Allison woke up to the muffled sound of doors slamming and the high-pitched chatter of excited co-eds. It took her a moment to remember where she was. New York City. In Reagan Murphy's bed.

The woman in question was currently curled on her side with an arm and leg thrown over Allison's midsection and hipbone. Her bangs were slightly matted to her forehead, the sheets thrown off, and her tank top had crept up during the night to reveal a patch of lightly bronzed skin. Her eyes were lightly lidded and her mouth slightly agape. Allison could hear the sound of light breathing and she watched the gentle rise and fall of her chest with each deep breath.

She couldn't remember if she'd ever woken up to find herself being so thoroughly cuddled. She'd serial dated in high school, but never had sleepovers with the boys she'd been in relationships with. Early in college she'd experimented with her new independence from her parents and conservative community, but none of those scattered one-night-stands had amounted to anything significant – just a series of Walk of Shames across the campus green. Her flirtation with sexual fluidity had never extended to the university sorority houses, however. Waking up with another girl draped over her was new territory. The question was, how did she feel about this new set of events?

Before she could really contemplate that unsettling question, she felt Reagan begin to stir. First, the arm across her torso tightened. Small, feminine fingers curled around her bicep. Next, a small nose nuzzled its way into the crook of her neck. Finally, a low, sleepy hum of approval rattled in her ears.

Allison quietly sighed. She allowed herself this one moment to enjoy Reagan's closeness and early morning intimacy. The arm draped over her suddenly flew up in the air, however, and Reagan abruptly sat up like a marionette whose strings had been jerked.

From her reclined position, Allison looked quizzically at Reagan. "Are you okay?"

"Yeah, um, sorry about that," Reagan mumbled, looking away. Her voice was thick with sleep. "I'm not used to sleepovers."

"It's okay." This time, Allison found herself actually meaning the words. And that was a realization too disturbing on which to dwell.

"Morning," Reagan greeted. She wiped at her mouth with the back of her hand, self-conscious that she might have been drooling in her sleep. She hazarded a glance at Allison's tank top and felt a mild reprieve from her embarrassment when she saw no visible evidence that she'd drooled on Allison during the night.

"Good morning," Allison returned. She made no effort to get up.

Reagan, still embarrassed to have woken up only to discover she'd been using Allison as a pillow, scooted over in bed to afford her more room. It wasn't much though, considering the size of the mattress.

"Did your roommate come home last night?" Allison asked. "I didn't hear her come in."

Reagan craned her head to peak in the direction of Ashley's bed. It was empty and the blankets disheveled, but that didn't mean she'd slept there the previous night. She hardly ever made her bed. Reagan tried to remember if she'd heard Ashley come in, but failed. She was an infamous heavy sleeper; Ashley always teased her that she could die in the middle of the night and Reagan would sleep right thought it.

For the second time of the early day, Reagan was in panic mode. She jumped out of bed and began digging through her purse for her phone. She was more than disappointed in herself. Ashley had insisted she'd be fine on her own and Reagan had stupidly left her at the party to fend for herself. She'd been so anxious to get back to Allison before she could run away, she'd overlooked her roommate's safety.

As she watched Reagan frantically search for her phone, Allison frowned, missing the heat of Reagan's body. When she realized why she was frowning, she frowned even deeper. This was getting out of control.

Reagan held her phone up triumphantly. "She's okay!" she announced, breaking Allison from her troubling thoughts. She stood to her full height. "She texted me last night that she was going to stay at our friend Denise's dorm room." Her features revealed her relief as she continued to read the message out loud. "So we could have some time alone."

Allison bolted upright. "What does she mean, 'have some time alone?'"

Reagan looked up from her telephone screen. "Uh, I imagine she means so you and I could spend some time by ourselves."

Allison's hands went to the top sheet and she bunched the material in her clenched fists. "Why would she think we need time by ourselves?" she asked in a strained voice.

Reagan stared at the girl in her bed. If possible, Allison's porcelain skin looked ever paler than usual. Her hazel eyes shifted erratically. "Allie?" Reagan asked concerned. "Are you feeling okay? You look a little…not like you."

Allison's eyes snapped into focus and she leveled an intense glare on Reagan. "Why would your roommate say those things about us?" she demanded. "What did you tell her?"

Reagan held up her hands in retreat. "Whoa. Slow down. I didn't say anything to her."

"Then why would she say that?" Allison seethed.

Allison was like a grenade, about to implode and Reagan feared the shrapnel of her rage. She'd been on the receiving end of that temper during high school and it never ended well. "Don't get mad at me, okay? But I don't see what the big deal is."

"Big deal?" Allison practically shrieked. "Big deal? This could *ruin* me!"

"Ruin you?" Reagan naively echoed. "What are you talking about?"

Allison launched herself out of bed and immediately began throwing her things into her open suitcase.

"Wait," Reagan said, stunned and dumbfounded by the morning's events. "What are you doing?"

"What does it look like I'm doing?" Allison growled. "I'm packing my bag. I'm going home." She yanked the zipper shut and stood up stiffly. "And when I get back to Providence, I think it's best if we don't talk for a while."

Reagan grabbed the handle of Allison's wheeled suitcase and yanked it out of her hand. The suitcase noisily fell over.

"Don't touch me, Murphy," Allison rasped. The sudden use of her last name felt like an open-palm slap to the face. "I need some time and space to get my head on straight."

Reagan's mouth twisted. "Is that word choice deliberate?"

Allison quickly replayed her previous statement in her head. When she realized what she'd said, she gave Reagan a sour look. "Is this funny to you?"

Reagan instantly grew serious. "Of course it's not," she declared. "But I also don't think this is something time away from each other is going to resolve." She gave Allison a peculiar look. "What are you trying to accomplish by doing this?"

Allison's face scrunched up, and for a moment, Reagan thought she might cry. "Being around you is too confusing right now."

"Confusing how?" Reagan demanded.

"Why do you always need me to explain myself?" Allison stated with heat. The longer Reagan refused to drop the subject, the more her frustration grew.

"Because I don't want to lose you again!" Reagan said with equal ferociousness.

Allison stood still. Reagan's volume surprised her.

"High school was hell," Reagan announced, seemingly out of nowhere.

"I know it was," Allison fumed, angry to be back on this topic. "I was purposely cruel. I thought we were past all that."

"You were a bully, yes," Reagan agreed, "but that wasn't the worst part. High school was torture because we used to be best friends and then suddenly we weren't. I had to see you in the hallways everyday knowing what I'd lost," she noted with a frown. "We'd been inseparable all our lives, and I couldn't figure out why you didn't like me anymore, and my mother had just ..." Reagan's eyes filled with tears and she choked back a sob. "And my mother had just..." she tried again. She clamped her mouth shut and her shoulders slumped forward.

"Reagan." Allison frowned.

Reagan's shoulders began to shake as she tried to control her emotions.

Allison felt sick. She knew she'd been unnecessarily mean to Reagan in high school. If other students were preoccupied tormenting Reagan with her, they would be too busy to recognize how insecure she felt all the time. Popularity was fickle and fleeting and she'd worked hard, no matter the cost, to stay at the top of the food chain. But until this moment, with her first friend shaking with anguish in front of her, she'd never fully realized the depth of her cruelty. She had been mean, but even worse, she'd denied her friendship at the one moment Reagan had needed it the most.

Ignoring her brain's pleas to just stay away, Allison threw her arms around Reagan's rocking form and pulled her tight.

With Allison's long limbs solidly around her frame, Reagan finally let herself fall apart. The sobs came harder now, and without Allison's silent stability, she knew she would shatter. Reagan buried her face into Allison's neck. Tears fell freely against her skin.

When she felt the dampness, Allison gripped Reagan tighter. "Reagan," she hushed again. "It's okay. Just let it out."

Reagan turned her face into Allison and her warm breath fell hot against her throat. Allison stiffened, her own breath catching. She felt perversely turned on.

"What time is your train?" Reagan sniffled, wiping at her eyes. Her tears had dried on her face, making her skin feel salty and tight.

Allison glanced at the digital clock near Reagan's bed. "In about an hour."

Reagan's features immediately crumpled. "Okay," she choked out.

"I'll take a later train," Allison said. Her resolve was almost depleted. If she stayed, she'd regret it. But if she left on the next train with Reagan still so visibly broken, she'd hate herself.

"You don't have to do that," Reagan sniffled, shaking her head. "I'll be fine."

"I'll take a later train," Allison repeated, this time more forcefully.

Reagan sucked in a shallow breath and nodded. "Okay."

+++++

The sheep's meadow at Central Park was surprisingly vacant that afternoon. Everyone in the park seemed to be coupled up, lost in each other. A few individuals did yoga on foam mats, undisturbed by the sounds of children playing and squealing in the distance from a nearby playground.

Allison bit into her chicken Caesar pita. On their way to the park, they'd stopped at a corner grocery store and had picked up a few items for a makeshift picnic. She tilted her face up to feel the sun warm against her skin.

"More grapes?"

She opened her eyes and squinted into the bright sunlight until she could make out Reagan holding a small plastic container filled with red seedless grapes. Allison smiled her thanks and plucked a few grapes from the translucent contained before popping them into her mouth. "It's a nice day, huh?" she observed around the sweet, bursting fruit.

"Mmhm," Reagan agreed. She set the container down on the blanket they were sitting on and began to pick at a frayed corner.

"Hey, are you okay?"

Reagan wordlessly nodded, but didn't look up. She continued to fiddle with the blanket's worn edge. She finally looked up when she felt Allison's hand, warm on top of hers, stopping her from destroying the blanket.

"You're awfully quiet," Allison observed. "What's going on inside that head of yours?" She ran her thumb across the top of Reagan's hand.

Reagan looked down to where their hands touched. "I guess I'm just a little embarrassed about my outburst earlier."

"You? Embarrassed? I didn't think that emotion was in your repertoire," Allison lightly teased.

Reagan pulled her hand out from under Allison's touch. It should have felt comforting, but instead it made her skin crawl. "You've become quite tactile," she observed.

"Tactile?"

"Touchy."

"I know what the word means, Reagan," Allison scoffed. "I got a 32 on my Verbal ACTs." She frowned hard. "But if it bothers you, I won't touch you anymore."

"No, that's not it," Reagan said, grabbing onto both of Allison's hands as if proving her point. "I'm sorry. I just was making an observation, that's all."

"Do you come here often?" Allison asked, changing the subject.

Reagan nodded and let go of Allison's hands. "I miss open spaces," she admitted. "It can feel awfully claustrophobic, especially in Manhattan." She looked off into the distance and her eyes seemed to focus on a faraway spot.

"Do you think you'll stay here after college?" Allison flexed her toes, enjoying the sensation of tall, soft grass against her skin.

Reagan's gaze refocused on the girl next to her. "Maybe. It would make sense. But there are things I miss from home."

"Like what?"

"I miss the horizon. I miss Michigan sunsets."

Allison smirked. "Now *you* sound like the writer."

Reagan sat up straighter. "Are you ever going to let me read something you've written?"

"Probably not."

"Well that's not fair."

"Are you going to let me see one of your paintings?" Allison countered.

A suddenly bashful smile reached Reagan's lips. "Probably not."

Allison turned to look directly at Reagan. "Why not?"

Reagan shrugged. She picked at a long blade of grass. It ripped away from the earth and she rolled the single blade between her fingers. "It's personal."

"And you don't think my writing is personal?" Allison countered.

"I don't know. You've never let me read anything," Reagan said cheekily.

"Maybe some day."

Reagan bit down on her lower lip. "I really wish you were coming home this summer."

Allison shook her head. "There's no reason for me to go back. There's nothing for me there."

"*I'd* be there," Reagan pointed out.

"I know." Allison frowned guiltily. "I'm sorry. I just…can't. I'm fine visiting my family over short holiday breaks, but not for an entire summer."

"Your mom is nice," Reagan noted. "Or at least I remember she was when we were younger."

"She is," Allison confirmed with a tense nod. "I just can't handle my dad. It gets to be overwhelming if I'm home for too long. He and I are too alike, but at the same time not at all similar."

"You could stay at my house if your dad gets under your skin?" Reagan offered.

Allison shook her head. "I wouldn't want to put you and your dad out like that."

"Stop being so damn polite all the time," Reagan complained. "Just...think about it, okay?"

Allison chewed on her lower lip. "Okay."

Reagan stood up and brushed at her backside. Allison looked up after her. "Leaving me?"

"No. I just thought you'd like to see more of Central Park."

Allison looked around. "There's more than this?"

"You're kidding, right?"

Allison chuckled and shook her head. "Of course I am."

Across the vast green openness of Central Park, Allison spotted a couple holding hands and feeding breadcrumbs to the ducks. She had to do a double take, but on her second perusal, she realized it was two women.

It wasn't the first openly gay couple she'd ever seen – her college town was pretty liberal – far more than the town and household in which she'd grown up. As she observed the two women who were obviously together, she couldn't identify the emotion she was currently experiencing. Discomfort? No. She didn't think of herself as bigoted. Envy? She quickly dismissed the idea. That was ludicrous.

Reagan noticed that Allison appeared distracted. She followed the trajectory of her stare and it landed on the women holding hands. "They make a cute couple," she observed with some hesitation. "It's nice seeing people being so open and comfortable. It's one of the things I love about living in a big city."

"Uh huh."

Reagan's phone buzzed in her purse. She cursed under her breath and dug around before producing the phone. She glanced once at Allison guiltily.

"It's okay. Answer it," Allison allowed.

Reagan hit the answer button. "Hey, Chris. What's up?" she

chirped. She took a few steps away from Allison to take the call.

Allison frowned watching Reagan chat amicably to the disembodied voice. Reagan's eyes crinkled at the corners and she laughed at something the caller said. She found herself stepping closer as if to overhear the topic of their conversation.

"Tonight? Yeah, I could probably do that." Reagan flicked her eyes in the direction of Allison who appeared to be creeping closer. "I have a friend visiting from out of town, but she's heading home soon."

Allison quirked an eyebrow. Apparently her presence was no longer needed.

Reagan's forehead scrunched when she felt a hand at her hip. She looked down to Allison's hand and then up to her face. Allison's eyes had taken on that unmistakable intensity. Reagan wondered if she even realized when she did that or if it was something she could queue on command.

"I'll, uh, I'll have to get back to you about tonight, Chris," she said. "Something might have come up." Without waiting for a response, she hung up. "What is it?" she asked. Her chest seized watching Allison flick her tongue to the cleft in her lower lip. "Is-is something wrong?"

Allison's response was low. "Yes," she rasped. "Everything." The hand at Reagan's hip tightened. Allison brought the other hand to the side of Reagan's face. "I don't know what I'm doing," she said, her dark hazel eyes boring into Reagan.

Reagan closed her eyes when the thumb at her cheekbone stroked down the length of her face. She breathed in shuddered breaths through her nose. "Is this because of Christopher?" she asked without opening her eyes. Fingertips traced the outline of her mouth.

Allison swallowed and clenched and unclenched the back hinge of her jaw. "Who?" she asked thickly.

Reagan opened her eyes and was greeted once again by that intense hazel stare. "Chris," she repeated. "That boy I met on the train to Rhode Island." She no longer felt Allison's fingertips on her face. She frowned, knowing she had ruined the moment. But she also knew they couldn't keep this up without some kind of confrontation occurring.

"Oh. Him." Allison pressed her lips together.

"Yes. *Him.*" Reagan bit back a laugh. "So you're not denying that his call upset you?"

Allison's fair eyebrows scrunched together. "He interrupted our...uh." She struggled to find an appropriate word. "...*day* together."

"What is this, Allie? I dance with some guy at the party last night and you get angry with me, I talk to Chris," she said, waving her phone, "and you start acting weird. Are you jealous?"

"Jealous?" Allison echoed the word as if she didn't know its meaning. "Of what?"

Reagan licked her lips. "I don't know. You tell me. Am I misinterpreting this? Am I reading too much into your mood swings?"

"I know I behaved poorly last night," Allison said, dropping her gaze.

"You did," Reagan acknowledged. "But when you saw me dancing with that guy, what did you *feel?*"

Allison blinked a few times and looked startled by the question. "I don't...I'm not..." she sputtered.

Reagan surprised even herself by seizing Allison's waist. "How about *this?*" she husked, tightening her grip. "What do you feel when I do this?"

"Reagan." The growled name sounded like a warning. Allison hooked her fingers through the front belt-loop of Reagan's jeans and pulled her even closer. Reagan gasped into Allison's open mouth when the material of her pants rubbed against her sex. Allison slowly traced the length of Reagan's full, lower lip with the tip of her tongue, pulling a quiet groan from her.

Reagan pulled away, panting. "You can't just do that...you don't get to..."

"Why not?"

Reagan cocked her head to one side and appraised Allison. She once again looked uncharacteristically uncomfortable. Seeing her frazzled was strangely reassuring, and Reagan felt bold enough to venture onto a potentially dangerous topic. "If you want to date me, why don't you just ask?"

Even though Reagan's tone was mild and unassuming, the question itself felt like a scathing accusation. "Because I'm not gay," Allison balked. "Are you?"

"I've never given much though to it," Reagan pragmatically admitted. "It's not like I seriously dated anyone in high school, and I hardly have in college. I suppose I'm open-minded though. I've always thought I'd fall in love with a *person*, not a gender."

"Well, whatever," Allison said so hastily it wasn't clear if she'd even listened to Reagan's response. "Even if I felt that way, *which I don't*," she was quick to add, "I totally abandoned you in high school. Just thinking about it makes me sick. You couldn't possibly ever forgive me."

Reagan looked mildly amused. "So you think I just go around kissing every pretty girl I hate?"

Allison tried to ignore the hammering in her heart caused by Reagan calling her "pretty." She received compliments about her appearance all the time, but something about hearing it from Reagan made her pulse race.

"I don't know," she scowled. She put on a sour front to keep herself from feeling anything else. "Maybe you get some sort of perverse pleasure out of it. I can't pretend to know what goes on inside that strange brain of yours."

Reagan snorted and shook her head. Allison was clearly in a mood, and there was no talking to her about anything of substance when she got this way. "What do you want to do before you have to leave?"

The anger drained from Allison's features and the scowl on her face smoothed out. "Would it be okay if we stay in the park?" she asked in a far more measured tone than before. "It's so nice out," she observed, "I'm kind of having fun just hanging out in the sun with you."

Reagan smiled warmly. "Me too. I just didn't want you to get bored."

"You don't have to entertain me constantly," Allison chastised. "I'm not your family visiting from out of town or something."

"Then what *are* you?"

"I'm your friend," Allison immediately replied. "Aren't I?"

Reagan's lips pressed together. "Right. Friends."

+++++

Reagan threw herself on her bed.

"What's wrong with you, Drama Queen?" Ashley said, not looking up from her laptop screen.

"We kissed again," Reagan mumbled into her pillow. She sat up and rubbed at her face, annoyed by the day's activities. Allison had recently left on an evening train back to Providence. They'd hugged at the train station, but hadn't re-enacted their Central Park antics. It was all starting to get very confusing.

Ashley closed her laptop. "This is getting to be quite a habit with you two."

Reagan hadn't originally told her roommate about their first kiss at the train station since she had passed it off as a one-time fluke. She'd eventually and hesitatingly told her later though. It wasn't that she wanted Ashley to know her business – she was nosy enough on her own – but Reagan had been so confused, she needed to decompress and verbally work out her and Allison's situation.

"It's not normal, you know that, right?"

"*What's* not normal?" Reagan snapped off. "Are you implying that two girls showing affection for each other isn't *normal*?" she spat out with emotion. "Do you think there's something *wrong* with being gay?"

"Whoa." Ashley held up her hands. "Simmer down, Prez," she said in what she hoped was a calming tone. The look on her roommate's face was one she hadn't seen before – rage. "I wasn't saying anything about that. I've got nothing against gay people," she noted. "I was just saying that it's not *normal* that two girls who insist they're 'just friends' keep making out."

"Oh." The anger on Reagan's face immediately slipped away. "Sorry," she said sheepishly, "I didn't mean to snap at you. I thought you were being an asshole."

"It's okay, Prez. I *am* an asshole," Ashley said matter-of-factly. "I just wasn't being an asshole *this* time." She cocked her head. "That's quite the temper, by the way. I think Allison's starting to rub off on you. I was almost afraid of you."

Reagan threw a pillow in her roommate's direction. "I hate you."

"Don't lie." Ashley caught the pillow in mid-air. "You're going to miss me all summer. Whatever will you do without me?"

"I'm sure I'll manage," Reagan noted before sticking out her tongue. "Can you believe we're finishing up our Junior year?" she remarked wistfully. "It feels like yesterday we were both fresh-faced

First Years moving to the big city."

"And now look at you," Ashley remarked. "You're a raging homo."

"You know I hate labels,"Reagan scowled.

"You're so gay for that girl, Prez," Ashley countered with a playful smirk. "I don't know why you don't just ask her out."

"Because Allison Hoge is the most infuriating person I've ever met," Reagan announced with conviction. "I could never go out with her."

"And yet your mouth keeps accidentally bumping into hers," Ashley said pragmatically.

Reagan made a frustrated noise. "I don't know what our deal is." She absently punched the top of her mattress. "And whenever I try to bring it up, she completely closes off."

"Well, you'll have all summer to figure it out, right?"

Reagan shook her head. "She's staying in Rhode Island," she pouted. A sudden look of panic passed over her features. "What if I come back to school in the Fall, and she's forgotten all about me?"

"It's not the end of the world, Prez. You can still talk to her on the phone, write emails, write letters, talk on Skype," Ashley ticked off on her fingers, "or send carrier pigeons."

"I know, I know," Reagan huffed. "But it's not the same as really spending time together."

Allison wiggled her eyebrows suggestively. "I guess you'll just have to sext her and give her something she'll *really* remember."

Reagan lamented having thrown her pillow at her roommate; she was out of ammunition. "Remind me never to ask you for relationship advice," she deadpanned.

+++++

PART 2: SENIOR YEAR

CHAPTER NINE

The Amtrak train had barely rolled to a complete stop before Reagan was flying down the stairs and onto the wooden platform. She hurled herself towards the familiar blonde standing by herself, arms open and laughing.

She and Allison had kept in contact over summer break, texting, calling, and the occasional Skype session, but both had been busy, Allison with a job at a local bookstore and Reagan with an unpaid internship at an art gallery in their hometown. It had been a casual connection, but now, seeing Allison again, a flood of emotions that had remained dormant for months bubbled to the surface.

Allison laughed at Reagan's enthusiasm. Her hazel-green eyes shone brightly in the early afternoon sunshine.

"I missed you so much," Reagan mumbled into Allison's neck.

Allison didn't respond, but she squeezed Reagan tighter.

Reagan pulled back and inspected Allison's face. Her grin got bigger. "You cut your hair," she said breathlessly.

Allison tugged at the shaggy ends. She'd finally prioritized getting a serious haircut. She'd found a stylist in Providence who'd chopped off at least four inches. She was still getting used to the shorter length having always had enough hair to at least put it up in a ponytail. "I thought it was time for a change." Her eyebrows pinched together and she looked concerned. "Do you not like it?" she worried out loud.

"I *love* it," Reagan gushed. She took another step backwards so she could fully appraise her. "You look sexier than ever, if that's even possible."

Allison's eyes shifted uneasily in her skull and she cleared her throat. "Uh, thanks. Let me help you with your bag."

Reagan sighed and watched Allison stiffly stalk away with her suitcase rolling behind her. "Here we go again."

+++++

Reagan tapped her fingers against the countertop of the Providence coffee shop and hummed a wordless tune as she waited for the barista to finish making their drinks. She glanced once in the direction of Allison who sat nearby at a table for two. Reagan smiled at her and reveled in the smile that Allison gave back. Even though they hadn't seen each other all summer, it felt as though no time had passed.

"Vegan hot chocolate and a dark roast with skim milk." The man behind the counter set the drinks down and nudged them towards Reagan.

"Thank you," Reagan said, putting her extra change in the tip jar. She grabbed the drinks and turned. "Oh, I'm sorry," she sputtered as she nearly ran into two girls about her age. She'd been daydreaming and hadn't realized anyone was standing right behind her.

"Watch where you're going," one of the girls snapped. "This jacket's worth more than your entire wardrobe."

"God, this coffee shop is such a dump," the girl standing beside her snorted. "They'll let *anyone* in."

"We should stick to campus," the first girl noted, already dismissing Reagan's presence. "Townies make me uncomfortable."

Reagan rolled her eyes, but a tiny seed of discomfort and insecurity still remained. Being dismissed felt like high school all over again. Her muscles twitched, getting ready to take flight and escape the situation, but she took a deep breath, clamped her hands tighter around the two beverages, and walked over to the table where Allison sat.

"I hope this table by the window is okay," Allison said when Reagan set the drinks down. "I know you love to people watch."

Reagan nodded stiffly.

Allison's nose scrunched up. She recognized that look on Reagan's face. She'd seen it enough in high school when she'd been harassing her; Reagan's discomfort was palpable. "Hey," she soothed. "What's wrong?"

Reagan took a deep breath and rolled her shoulders. She could handle this. She wasn't going to let an anxiety attack ruin their day. "I'm okay," she breathed. "Some assholes in line said something to me."

"What did they say?"

Reagan shook her head. "It's not important."

Allison frowned. "Yes it is. Who said something to you, Reagan?"

Reagan nodded in the direction of a particularly boisterous group that sat at a collection of tables near the front entrance. The mixed crowd all wore at least one item of clothing that labeled them as Brown students. They appeared oblivious to the silent death stares the coffee shop's other patrons shot in their direction.

Reagan watched as Allison stood up; her body tensed and her hazel eyes locked on the group. Reagan knew in an instant what was going to happen – Allison Hoge was going to bitch-slap someone.

When Allison took her first step towards the group, she only paused when a hand grabbed her wrist.

"What are you going to do?" Reagan worried.

"That group over there isn't just anybody," Allison said heatedly. "The ring leader is Brice, my bitch of a roommate."

Reagan's eyes widened. "Don't, Allie," she pled. "Just let it go. I don't want to make your roommate situation uncomfortable."

"I'm not going to do anything uncalled for," Allison said with forced calmness. "I'm just standing up for my friend."

Reagan dropped her hold on Allison's wrist, dumbstruck. "You just said the f-word."

Allison made a pained look. "And that right there is why I need to do this." Not waiting for Reagan's reply, she strode toward the overly loud group.

Their chattering mildly subsided when she approached. A few of the boys present gave her appreciative smiles. Allison deflected them all with an icy glare.

"Allie!" A slender redhead hopped up from her seat when she saw Allison.

Reagan watched the events unfold from across the coffee shop.

The redhead looked familiar, but she couldn't quite place her face. She suddenly recognized her as one of the girls Allison had been with the night they'd run into each other on Broadway so many months ago. Brice. She finally had a face to go with the name.

She inched a little closer, hoping to catch a scrap of their conversation. She felt guilty for not trying harder to stop Allison, but not guilty enough. She'd never been in this position before, getting a front row view of Allison on the attack. It was terrifying – like watching a snake slowly wrap around a small mammal to squeeze the life from it just before finishing it off with a deadly strike. Reagan shook her head. She really needed to stop watching National Geographic late at night.

Reagan strained her ears, but without being obvious, she couldn't hear what Allison was saying to Brice and the rest of the group. But the redhead looked properly wounded and the formerly noisy group was now standing up and sulking out the front door.

When Allison returned, looking calm and restrained, Reagan threw her arms around her and hugged her tight in thanks. Allison stiffened at first at the contact. Public affection always made her uncomfortable, regardless of its source. But she reasoned that she'd earned this hug for finally doing the right thing. And Reagan smelled like warm honey. The observation made Allison pull back awkwardly. "You're welcome."

Reagan held her hand and swung it back and forth. "It still wasn't necessary, but thank you." The excitement and pride fell from her face suddenly. "Oh no!" she exclaimed, sounding horrified. "Where are we going to sleep tonight?"

"Huh? At my house; where else?"

"Won't that be awkward with Brice being there?"

Allison waved a dismissive hand. "She's hardly around on the weekends; I'm sure she'll be bunking with her Flavor-Of-The-Week. Besides, if she starts anything again, I'll just put her in her place with my super bitch powers."

Reagan tugged on her lower lip with her teeth. "I knew I shouldn't have let you tell her off. Now it's going to be horribly uncomfortable all weekend. Oh God," she moaned dramatically. She clutched at her stomach. "I might give myself an ulcer. I can already feel the acid eating away at the tender stomach lining."

Allison's eyebrows lifted to her hairline. "Are you being serious right now?"

Reagan nodded glumly. "I hate confrontations," she whimpered. "They make me physically ill."

Allison whistled lowly. "Wow, Murphy. You've got issues."

Reagan turned her bright blue eyes to her friend. "This is serious, Allison. Please," she pled. "Can we figure something else out for tonight? Even if we were locked in your bedroom the whole time, I'd still be on edge."

The thought of being locked in her bedroom with Reagan for the entire day and night made Allison's stomach feel funny. Maybe she was getting an ulcer, too. "I suppose we could always stay at a hotel."

The words tumbled out of her mouth before she could stop them. As soon as she realized what she'd suggested, her stomach felt uncomfortable all over again.

Reagan's eyes immediately widened in excitement. "Could we really do that?"

Allison pretended to look interested in her cuticles. "Yeah, I guess. There's some reasonably priced places near campus."

"We could order room service and lounge around in bed all day and be lazy together!" Reagan clapped excitedly. "Oh, this is going to be amazing!"

Allison smiled, but it felt more like a grimace. "Yeah...amazing."

+++++

"We need a room," Reagan loudly announced.

Allison anxiously looked around. Realizing what she was doing, she silently berated herself. No one who knew her would be in the hotel lobby. Besides, there was nothing suspect about two girls checking into a hotel room in the middle of the afternoon, she reasoned to herself.

The front desk receptionist flashed a warm smile. The name engraved on her nametag read Darcy. "Name on the reservation?"

The eager smile fell from Reagan's lips. "Oh, we don't have one. This was kind of last minute."

"I'm afraid we're totally booked this weekend," the hotel

employee apologized. "There's an academic conference being held at Brown this weekend. Let me just see if we've had any cancelations, however." Her fingers flew over the keyboard and she inspected the computer monitor in front of her. "Oh, you're in luck. We've got one king suite available."

Reagan looked anxious. "Suite? That sounds pricey."

"We'll find something else," Allison spoke up, talking for the first time since they'd arrived.

"It's a pretty big conference," Darcy warned. "This may be your only option in town."

Reagan gave Allison a sad look. "I guess we don't have to stay at a hotel tonight."

Seeing how crestfallen this revelation had made Reagan, Allison immediately fished out the credit card her father paid for. She didn't know how she was going to explain the charge on her monthly statement, but she'd figure something out. "We're paying with a VISA card," she said crisply to the hotel staffer.

Reagan's blue eyes were round. "Allison," she whispered as the woman behind the front desk started typing up their room request, "I can't let you pay for that."

Allison drummed her fingers on the granite counter and waited for the woman to run her card. "I'm not paying for it," she said, not looking at Reagan. "My dad is."

Allison heard the quiet gasp. "Are you sure he'll be okay with that?"

Allison finally turned her head to face Reagan. "It's totally fine," she insisted with a bright smile. "He pays for stuff like this for me all the time," she lied.

Reagan still looked unconvinced. But Allison was so confident and so unwilling to bend; she had little choice but to believe her. Reagan shouldered Allison's backpack. After the coffee shop confrontation, they'd briefly stopped at Allison's house so she could grab things for an overnight bag. "A little more hustle, Hoge," she playfully ordered. She punched the elevator button and spun to grin broadly at her friend who lagged a few steps behind. "This is going to be the best night ever!" she cheered.

"*Or the longest,*" Allison silently bemoaned.

+++++

"Holy cow," Reagan admired. She ran her fingertips along the edge of the massive in-room whirlpool. "This is like something out of *Pretty Woman.*"

"So since I paid for the room, does that make me Richard Gere?" Allison clamped her lips together. "I don't know why I just said that; how horribly inappropriate."

"Only if I was a prostitute," Reagan sing-songed. She tossed her bag on the floor and jumped on the bed – a single king bed. Its presence seemed to mock Allison from its location in the center of the room.

Allison dropped her backpack on the ground. "There's only one bed," she said flatly.

Reagan hopped up and down on the mattress. "What were you expecting?" she said, her voice hitching from jumping up and down. "It's a king suite. Ergo, a king-sized bed."

Allison stared at the bed and gave herself a silent pep talk. She could to this. Everything would be fine. They'd spent the night together in a far smaller bed before. She released a shaky breath. Surviving one night in a hotel room with Reagan would be no big deal.

"You interested in breaking in that hot tub?" Reagan asked. She stopped jumping and plopped down in the center of the mattress. "It seems like a waste of your dad's money not to."

"I didn't pack a bathing suit. Did you?"

"No. I didn't anticipate going swimming in Providence."

"Then what are you proposing we wear in the hot tub?"

"Bra and underwear aren't that different from a bikini," Reagan pointed out with a shrug. "Besides, we're both girls. It's not like you have anything I haven't seen before."

"I wondered how long it would be before you tried to get me out of my clothes." Allison's lips snapped shut. "Sorry." She made a face. "Again. Something about this hotel room is making me say all kinds of inappropriate things."

"You know, you don't have to keep your walls up around me. You don't have to be Miss Manners all the time."

"I'm trying, I really am." Allison rubbed at her face in frustration. "But old habits die hard."

"Maybe you need a cocktail," Reagan suggested, her face serious. "Loosen you up a bit."

Allison bit the tip of her tongue before another sexually suggestive comment stumbled out. Apparently the combination of a king-sized bed and an in-room hot tub turned her into a high school boy.

Before Allison could suggest another idea, Reagan had rushed to side of the whirlpool tub and turned on the faucets. She grabbed small bottles of shower gel and dumped their contents into the tub. Large, sudsy mounds of bubbles began to swell up.

"Wait! What are you doing?" Allison exclaimed when she saw Reagan reach for the bottom hem of her sweater.

"Well I'm not going to get in there with clothes on, Allison."

"You're going in there *naked*?" Allison stumbled on the final world.

Reagan pulled off her sweater. The camisole she wore beneath it came off as well. Allison swallowed hard. Reagan's toned upper torso and flat stomach were on full display. She wore a dark purple bra that contrasted attractively with her olive hued skin. The tops of her breasts swelled over the demi cut of the flimsy undergarment.

Even without seeing Allison's panicked, but appreciative stare, Reagan knew she looked good. She kept her small frame limber with a balance of cardio and yoga.

Reagan's fingers hesitated at the top button of her jeans and Allison bit back a groan. She coughed to mask the unwanted noise. She remained near the edge of the bed, looking like she wanted to run away.

"Are you coming?" Reagan asked.

Not yet.

Allison yanked off her top and just as quickly stripped off her shoes, socks, and jeans. She went to the opposite side of the oversized tub and slid in, burying herself in the pile of fluffy soapsuds. Reagan's grin returned, mistaking Allison's speed for enthusiasm. She popped the button on her tight-fighting jeans and slid them down shapely hips and thighs.

Even though Allison was already in the tub, Reagan stuck her hand in the water to test its temperature. Satisfied, she turned off the faucets and climbed into the tub as well. "Ooooh," she cooed as she was nearly swallowed by a mountain of soap. "It's like a pool!"

"Stay in the shallow end, Shortie," Allison scowled. "I don't do mouth-to-mouth." She slouched down in the water so her entire body was submerged. The tip of her chin skimmed the crest of the water. She didn't like anyone seeing her with so few clothes on. She felt self-conscious about her figure, and Reagan's soft, feminine curves and naturally darker skin tone made her feel boyish, pasty, and altogether unattractive.

Reagan wiggled around in the whirlpool in search of a comfortable position. The water displaced with her movement and lapped at the inner edges of the tub. "I love baths. Don't you?"

Allison sat up a bit straighter so she could respond without getting soap in her mouth. "I guess so," she said noncommittally. "But I usually prefer taking baths by myself."

Reagan skated her palms over the water's surface and watched the tiny ripples. "Ever since watching *Pretty Woman*, I've wanted to take a bath with someone. It seemed so terribly romantic."

"Soaking in someone else's dirty water? Yeah," Allison deadpanned. "Real romantic."

"Allison," Reagan scolded. "That movie is one of the greatest romantic comedies ever made."

Allison rolled her eyes. "It's about hookers and Johns and everyone is shitty to Julia Roberts' character."

"It's a classic love story," Reagan countered.

"It's misogynist. Not everyone needs to be saved."

"This was a bad idea," Reagan sighed. "We should get out."

"Are you getting cold? You could drain the water a little and add more hot water?" Allison suggested.

Reagan shook her head. "I'm just going to hop in the shower and rinse this soap off. You're not having fun." She started to stand up, but stopped when Allison's hand grabbed her knee under the water.

"I'm sorry I'm being so grouchy," Allison apologized. She let go of Reagan's knee. She felt embarrassed that she'd grabbed her like that. "It's just that I'm not comfortable with my body. I'm sorry I was taking it out on you."

Reagan stared in disbelief. "Allison, you're like the prettiest girl I know."

Allison slouched down further in the tub. "You must not know many people, Murphy."

Reagan pressed her lips together. "Let me see you."

Allison nearly slipped. "Huh?"

"Stand up," Reagan ordered. "I want to see this grotesque body."

"Well, when you put it that way," Allison scowled.

"I mean it, Allison. Stand up and let me see for myself."

Allison opened her mouth to once again offer her protest, but Reagan had her arms folded across her chest and resolve clearly etched across her face.

"I can't believe I'm doing this," she grumbled. She grabbed onto the edge of the massive tub for stability and stood up. She winced as the water level immediately lowered. It did nothing to help her already shaky body-esteem. Soap clung to her skin in bunches and her wet bra and underwear clung uncomfortably to her skin. She shivered uncomfortably and rubbed her hands along her bare arms, trying to keep warm.

"I don't see it," Reagan said.

"Don't see what?" Allison asked, teeth practically chattering.

"The ugly parts." The water moved around Allison's knees as Reagan shifted closer. "All I see is a beautiful woman."

Allison reflexively scoffed. "You're not looking close enough."

"I can see just fine." Reagan bobbed even closer. "I see flawless, smooth skin. I see long, slender dancer's legs. I see a perfectly proportionate backside, thin muscled thighs that connect to delicious hipbones. I see a flat stomach with just the slightest hint of abdominal muscles, the perfect combination of femininity and strength." She paused and looked up at Allison, unsure of her reaction.

Allison licked her lips. "What else do you see?"

Reagan swallowed and worked the muscles in her neck. "I see your arms, long and graceful like a ballerina. I see a defined clavicle, sharp enough to slice through flesh. I see...I see your breasts." She audibly sucked in a sharp breath. "Perfect in size and shape. I see a beautiful woman who I know doesn't see the same thing as I do when she looks at herself in the mirror. I see a strong, accomplished woman who's her own worst critic because she can't see how amazing she is."

"You really see all that?" Allison's voice sounded meek and small.

Reagan looked up at her from beneath thick eyelashes. Her fingertips just barely brushed against the back of Allison's knee. "It doesn't take a microscope to see your beauty, Allison."

Allison cleared her throat. She wasn't quite sure what to say. So she did what felt natural. She was polite. "Thank you, Reagan."

Reagan pushed backwards in the tub and floated back to her original seat. The abrupt movement broke Allison out of her quiet trance. "You can have the shower first if you want," Reagan offered.

Allison plunged back down into the tub. "No, you can go ahead. I think I'll float around a little longer."

"Ok." Reagan stood up and rearranged her bra top and underwear so they better covered her body. Allison tried not to ogle her ass too explicitly as she climbed out of the tub.

"I saw that, Hoge."

"Saw what?" Allison asked, eyes wide.

Reagan stopped just outside the bathroom door. "You appreciating my beauty, too," she said with a sly smirk.

The door to the bathroom closed with Reagan inside. Allison fell back into the tub and dunked herself under the water.

+++++

CHAPTER TEN

Allison turned on the shower as high as the pressure would go and stepped inside the tub. She pulled the curtain back in place and released a long, satisfied sigh as the rush of water pelted against her skin. She loved showers. It was where she did her best thinking - if she had Writer's Block or needed to mentally work through a particularly challenging text, she took a shower, even if she'd already showered just a few hours prior.

She grabbed the tiny bottle of the hotel-provided shampoo-conditioner combination and worked the soap through her hair. She hated the all-in-one product, but in her haste to pack an overnight bag, she'd forgotten her own shampoo and conditioner. Reagan had hurried her along, urging her to be as brief as possible, certain that Brice would return home while they were still there. In addition to Reagan's desperate pleas to hurry, her brain had also been preoccupied with the knowledge that she'd be spending the night with Reagan at a hotel.

If they'd stayed at her house like she'd originally intended they would have spent just as much time together, but something about a hotel room made the weekend feel more like an illicit affair than a friendly sleep-over. As soon as they'd arrived she'd felt on edge. She was sure Reagan noticed how awkward she was behaving, but she was just ignoring it or silently over-analyzing Allison's behavior.

Allison had thought time apart from each other over the summer months would change things - at least temper her growing feelings - but as soon as Reagan had hugged her after flying out of the train,

113

dormant emotions seemed to come out of hibernation. She couldn't count how many sleepless summer nights she'd mentally replayed their last New York weekend together, just trying to make sense of it all. They'd kissed. Twice. Reagan had initiated the first and she the second, but both times she had been the one to expand their activities to Reagan's neck. She flushed with a combination of embarrassment and arousal at the memory.

She couldn't help herself though; Reagan always smelled so good. She couldn't pinpoint what it was though. She grabbed Reagan's shampoo bottle and popped open the top to discover its scent - lavender. It was pleasant, but it wasn't the same scent that made Allison's knees buckle. Maybe it was her perfume. She'd have to rummage through Reagan's toiletries later. It had to be her perfume. It was far less complicated than the alternative explanation – that Reagan's pheromones turned her on.

Allison grabbed a tiny bar of soap and worked up a lather. When her soapy hands passed over her naked breasts, she wobbled unsteadily. All of this thinking about Reagan was doing nothing to help the perpetual ache between her thighs. It didn't help that she could hardly remember the last time she'd had sex. Something had to give. She was going to pop. Her hands went back to her breasts and she cupped their modest weight in her palms. She didn't often masturbate. It was a lasting remnant of her strict Christian upbringing that had scared her into believing it made you blind or you'd grow hair on the back of your hands. Even the word itself felt cold and clinical.

She bit her bottom lip as she continued standing in the shower, hot water beating down on her. She didn't trust herself to go back out there and sleep next to Reagan. Not unless she took care of herself first. Leaving her breasts, she slid her hands down to her smooth abdomen. She could feel her hipbones slice into her palms as her hands traveled further south. What word had Reagan used to describe her hipbones? *Delicious.* Yes. If she had had any doubts before, Reagan's speech only confirmed that she was attracted to her. Her fingers curled along the inside of a lightly muscled thigh, and the tops of her fingers just slightly brushed against shaved, smooth skin.

Her stomach clenched when her fingertips brushed along the

outside of her clit. Her eyes fluttered shut and she tried to imagine how Reagan would touch her. Would her fingers feel light and delicate? Would she take her time to torment and tease? Or would she be wild and ravenous, consuming and burning hot like liquid fire?

Allison's hand had become Reagan's hand. She knew she should feel embarrassed or guilty or *something* about using Reagan as mental candy, but it seemed to be working. Like, really working. Her skin felt flushed, more so than just the effects of the steamy shower. Why couldn't it be Reagan's fingers now stroking along her sensitive clit? Why couldn't it be Reagan's hand now parting her pussy lips?

Allison bit her bottom lip to stifle the moan that stumbled up her throat when she pressed hard against her clit. She rubbed the sensitive nub around and around in tiny clockwise circles and a sharp wave of pleasure stabbed her insides. Her fingers drifted further and she could feel her arousal accumulating, a wetness different and distinct from the water that continued to fall from the showerhead. She subtly widened her stance and used her free hand to steady herself with the help of the shower wall. A quiet whimper escaped when she increased the pressure and dipped between her folds.

With hooded eyes she peered through the translucent shower curtain over to the door and focused on the doorknob. *"Shit,"* she silently lamented. She couldn't remember if she'd locked the bathroom door. Reagan could walk in at any moment and catch her touching herself. The thought momentarily sent her into a panic, and her wandering hands stopped wandering. But the more she let that thought and that image swim in her already lust-ridden head, the more turned on she became: *"Uhn, she could walk in on me."*

The scene that now formed in her head resembled the beginning of a cheesy porno - not that she had ever watched one before. *"Need some help with that, Allison?"* Reagan would smile innocently as she peeked around the slightly opened bathroom door. *"Need an extra hand?"*

Allison knew her thighs would quickly clamp together and her face would burn a million shades of red, embarrassed to have been caught. She'd try to cover her body as best as she could. But her body would be begging for Reagan to jump into the shower, clothes and all. Her body would demand that Reagan use her knee to part her thighs, just like she'd done on the dance floor at the frat party.

She would uselessly protest, vainly insisting that that wasn't what she wanted. But Reagan would take control, take the lead, and take her. The shower curtain would be thrown back, water spilling onto the bathroom floor, but she wouldn't care. With the weight of her knee behind her hand, Reagan would penetrate her with her fingers until Allison's eyeballs rolled back into her head.

As Allison slid her own digits inside her wet sex, she imaged they were Reagan's persistent fingers, filling her. Her body would finally surrender itself to Reagan and the tension that had been building between them. She bit down on her lower lip as the tightness in her stomach spread lower.

But she knew that her brain wouldn't allow it. Her brain and her body would be screaming different demands. After all, Allison Hoge didn't do those kinds of things.

+++++

Allison emerged from the bathroom in a billow of steam. She'd dried her hair just enough so it wouldn't drip all over her sleeping shirt, but it still fell in damp tendrils that framed her heart-shaped face. Her skin was free of make-up and the heat from the shower had flushed her skin, red cheeks and a slight blush that crawled down her pale neck.

"How do you do that?"

Allison stopped and raised a perfectly manicured eyebrow. "Do what?" She sat down on the bed, but maintained a respectable distance from Reagan. Although she'd scrubbed her skin thoroughly, she still worried that she might be able to smell the sex on her.

"How are you always so put-together?"

Allison's steady gaze faltered momentarily as her eyes dipped to the duvet. "Years and years of practice."

"You make it look so flawless though," Reagan complained.

Allison paused and wet her lips. "Have you ever considered that maybe I'm envious of *you*?"

"Me? That's ridiculous. I'm a mess."

"I know you are." Allison smiled softly. "And that's what I envy. You're *allowed* to be a mess."

"I'm not sure if that's a compliment," Reagan countered with a scoff. "And why aren't you allowed to be a mess?"

The smile on Allison's face dropped and she sighed. She picked at the mattress top. "What would people have said if I showed up to school looking like I'd just rolled out of bed? What would our teachers have said if I didn't have my homework completely done? How badly would I have disappointed my parents if I wasn't living up to my potential?"

"It was high school," Reagan said, shaking her head. "No one's supposed to have it all figured out."

"Tell that to my 16-year-old-self," Allison said stiffly. "She must have missed the memo."

"Well, I guess we have a new goal for tonight," Reagan remarked.

Allison didn't look amused. "And what's that?"

Reagan grinned mischievously. "To give your 16-year-old-self a second chance."

"I don't know if I like the sound of that."

"Just trust me. Are you hungry?"

"I guess so."

Reagan grabbed a black folder off the bedside table and flipped through the binder until she found the local dining options. "What are you hungry for?" she asked as she scanned the pages.

"Whatever. I'm not picky." Allison grinned broadly. "Or vegan."

Reagan looked up and stuck out her tongue. "It's not that hard to find vegan options," she defended.

"Maybe not in New York, but Providence is hardly the culinary capital of the world."

"How about pizza?" Reagan proposed.

"What does a vegan pizza look like? Flat bread and tomato sauce?"

"You should be a comic," Reagan muttered. "If I pay, will you call?"

Allison shook her head. "Why stop now? Let's just have my dad pay for it."

"Are you sure?"

"Might as well."

"What do you want to do while we wait?"

"I don't know." Allison had a few ideas. They mostly involved Reagan being naked, so she kept those thoughts to herself. "Watch TV, I guess."

"Wait." Reagan bounced up from the bed. "I have a better idea." She grabbed the in-room phone and pressed the button for the front desk.

+++++

"C1."

"Miss."

The vegan pizza arrived 20-minutes later. Allison had been right – tomato sauce and pizza bread – but she didn't make a point of complaining about it; not when Reagan looked so pleased that she was eating vegan food with her. "Pizza and board games, huh? Is this what 16-year-olds do on the weekend?"

The board game selection at the hotel's front desk had been meager. The Monopoly game had no hotels or houses, the Game of Life was missing its cars, and who knew how many vowels were absent from Scrabble. In the end they'd settled on Battleship. There looked to be enough red and white pegs to play and only one of the submarines was missing.

"It's what *I* did on the weekends," Reagan defended. "I know it's probably not as fun for you as getting drunk and being felt up by boys."

Allison raised an amused eyebrow. "Is that really what you think I did in high school?"

"Well, maybe not you, but I'm sure some of your other friends, like Vanessa."

"Vanessa's a bitch," Allison bit off. "I don't think we were actually friends – more like frienemies waiting for the other person to make a mistake."

"But Allison Hoge doesn't make mistakes," Reagan teased.

"Which is why I never fell from the top of the food chain," Allison noted with a crisp nod.

"Were you really friends with any of them?" Reagan tried carefully. She didn't know if this was a safe topic to talk about. She was half-afraid digging up these memories would cause Allison to snap or revert to her former self.

Allison picked at the cheese-less pizza. "We hung out all the time, but I don't think I was ever really close to them. Carly and Beth were probably the closest thing I had to a best friend because they lived next door, but it's not like I ever shared my secrets with them."

Reagan smirked. "Allison Hoge doesn't make mistakes, but she has secrets?"

A strange, almost hostile, look passed over Allison's features. "We weren't friends then, Reagan. You didn't know what I was going through."

"You're right," Reagan nodded, trying hard not to feel defensive. "We weren't friends. To me you were just the scary blonde who tormented me for no good reason."

"At the time I'm sure I had good reasons that made sense to my borderline personality."

Reagan sighed. "I hate that I can't tell if you're joking about that."

"It's in the past," Allison said, the irritation palpable. "Let's not ruin the weekend by digging up skeletons."

Reagan looked sufficiently wounded. "Okay."

"I'm sorry." Allison reached for Reagan's hand. "I'm just not comfortable talking about those years. Especially not with you." She stroked her thumb across the top of Reagan's hand, feeling the fine bones beneath the pad of her thumb. "You may have forgiven me, but I can't forgive myself for my behavior. I had things I was working through, sure, but so did you—with your mom..." She trailed off, still uncomfortable with that story. "But you never used that as an excuse to be cruel."

Reagan's eyes became unfocused. "No, but I did use it as an excuse to keep everyone but my dad at a distance," she countered.

Allison chewed on her lower lip contemplatively. "Do you want to talk about it? About her?"

Reagan swallowed hard. "Not really."

"This isn't the slumber party you expected, huh?" Allison softly chuckled and shook her head.

"I'm having fun," Reagan protested. "Aren't you?"

Allison squeezed Reagan's hand. "Best day of my life."

"Don't tease me."

"I'm not!" Allison's voice pitched. *Oh, how I'd love to tease you. Damn it. Where did that come from?* "I'm having a lot of fun," she insisted, her tone returning to its usual raspy husk.

"I missed you this summer." Reagan dropped her eyes away from Allison's intense gaze. She could feel her cheeks burning from the admission. "I know we talked, but it's not the same."

"I missed you, too," Allison responded in an equally quiet tone. She wanted to lean across the expanse of the bed and kiss the girl.

She grabbed a handful of sheets instead. "It's still your turn, Rea."

"Oh, right." Reagan's eyes re-focused on her playing board. "A2."

Allison pulled out a white peg. "Miss." Battleship was safe. Battleship was mindless. And it gave her hands something to do. *But they could be doing Reagan.*

"How have I not hit *anything?*" Reagan complained.

Allison shrugged. "I'm stealthy. B4."

"Hit." Reagan made a frustrated noise. "Damn it. You sunk my cruiser. C6."

"Miss." The smile on Allison's face grew with each incorrect guess.

"Do you even have any ships on your board?" Reagan whined. She was naturally competitive and hated losing, even at a meaningless game of Battleship.

Allison covered a laugh by clearing her throat. She looked particularly pleased by something. "I'm looking at all five ships right now."

"I don't believe you." Reagan grabbed Allison's board. Red and white pegs scattered across the mattress top.

"Hey!" Allison protested.

"I can't believe you!" Reagan exclaimed. "I didn't think it was possible, but you found a way to cheat at Battleship."

"How is that cheating? All of my ships are on the board."

"But you stacked them on *top* of each other!"

Allison sat back with a smug look on her face. "Show me the rule that says that's cheating."

"I would," Reagan huffed, "but the rule booklet is missing."

"It's not cheating if there's no rule book."

"But…" Reagan couldn't come up with a clever retort. Instead, she folded her arms across her chest and pouted.

Why is she so adorable when she pouts? Allison mused to herself. "We should go to sleep."

"But the game…"

Allison shook her head. "Is over." She picked up a red peg and tossed it back onto the duvet. "There's pieces all over, Rea."

Reagan wrinkled her nose. "Fine. It's a tie."

"A tie?" Allison scoffed. "You didn't even get *close* to hitting my boats. I clearly won."

"If the game isn't completed, then it ends in a tie."

Allison stood up and walked toward the head of the bed to pull back the covers. She ran her palm over the top sheet and pieces of the game fell onto the floor. "And where's the rule that says that, Murphy?"

Reagan slid under the covers on the right side of the bed and fluffed up her pillows. "In the absence of a rule book," she said, wiggling and getting comfortable, "I make up my own."

Allison laughed and shook her head. She climbed into bed and tried to not focus on the fact that she was *climbing into bed* with Reagan. She let out a shaky breath. Maybe masturbating in the shower hadn't been such a good idea. Instead of calming her, it had only awoken her libido – like her body had forgotten what an orgasm was and now craved more. She rolled onto her side and turned off the bedside lamp closest to her. The room was swallowed by darkness.

Allison rolled onto her back and stared up at the ceiling. Even though they were in a king-sized bed, she swore she could still feel the heat of Reagan's body beside her. She was like a tiny radiator. *It would be so easy*, she thought, *just to roll over and kiss her.* She sighed. No, she was wrong. There was nothing *easy* about that at all.

"Ow!"

"What's wrong?" Allison tried to make out Reagan's body in the dark.

"Nothing. But I think I finally found your battleship."

121

CHAPTER ELEVEN

The next morning, Allison sat in one of the stuffed chairs of their hotel room, looking out the window with her journal and pen in hand. Even though she rarely left her house without the leather-bound book, she hadn't been able to put pen to paper since visiting Reagan in New York. Every time that summer she had picked up the journal, she had put it away. She was too afraid that the ink might betray her confidences.

Her Muse itched at the base of her brain, urging her to take advantage of all the emotions and thoughts that currently troubled her. And a part of her hoped that if she could just write them down, maybe they would go away. If she spilled the contents of her brain into her journal, maybe she could control them.

But the last time she'd written something about this…No. She couldn't write about this. She'd just push this down. Shove it down deep so she could focus on something else. Anything else. Writing it down only made it more real.

The shower turned off in the next room and after a few minutes, Reagan emerged from the bathroom. The white fluffy towel wrapped tightly around her torso made her olive skin-tone seem even more exotic than usual. In a city like New York, she fit right in. But in a small town in Northern Michigan, it had only served as another reminder of how she didn't quite belong.

"It's so nice not having to shower with other people," Reagan beamed.

Allison snapped her journal shut. "You make it too easy,

Murphy."

Reagan self-consciously pulled her towel tighter around her figure. "Too easy for what?"

"For me to make pervert comments."

The paranoia fell from Reagan's face. "Or maybe your head is just permanently stuck in the gutter, Hoge," she countered.

Allison shook her head. "I never used to be like this."

Reagan grinned. "Maybe I just bring it out of you."

Allison stood suddenly.

"What are you…"

Allison brought her hands up to rest on Reagan's toweled hips. The material was damp and scratched her palms. "I'm tired of this, Reagan. I'm tired of us tiptoeing around."

Reagan's mouth twitched. "Tiptoeing around what?"

"I'm not very good with words." Allison visibly swallowed. "You'd think as a writer, I'd be better at expressing emotions. But if I don't have a pen in my hand, I get tongue tied." *And I'd rather get my tongue tangled with you.* "Oh, fuck it."

Allison grabbed a hold of Reagan's shoulders and pushed her back onto the mattress. The movement was gentle, but aggressive at the same time. As Allison fell onto the mattress with Reagan beneath her, she was acutely aware that while she was fully clothed, Reagan wore only a loosely bound towel. She had only to reach between their bodies and Reagan would be naked. Allison groaned against Reagan's open mouth as thoughts of Reagan naked and pressing against her slammed against her consciousness. She bit down on Reagan's lower lip, pulling a moan from her.

When Reagan felt Allison's fingers toy with the bottom hem of her towel and brush against her naked upper thigh, she knew they needed to stop before things went too far. "Wait," she panted, sucking in mouthfuls of air. The combination of Allison's teeth now raking across her neck and her light, fluttering touch on her thigh was making her head spin. "You have to stop."

Allison looked up, annoyed. "Why?"

"Because," Reagan said, sitting up and pulling her loosening towel tighter around her, "we have to talk."

Allison released a disgruntled sigh. "What about?" She knew the answer, and she knew Reagan was right. She just didn't want to have that conversation. Avoiding talking about whatever was between them was the reason she'd kissed her in the first place. She realized now, however, it had only hastened that discussion.

"About why you were kissing me."

"I didn't hear any complaints," Allison shot back defensively.

Reagan grimaced. She knew she'd have to proceed with caution. "That's because I liked it."

The hurt expression softened on Allison's face. "Really?"

Reagan scooted a little closer. She touched her fingers to the side of Allison's face and rubbed the pad of her thumb along her cheekbone. Allison's eyes fluttered shut and Reagan could hear her quiet sigh.

"I'm sorry if me stopping you hurt your feelings."

Allison opened her eyes, and Reagan let her hand fall back into her lap. "I'm sorry I threw myself at you and made you feel uncomfortable."

"You didn't –."

"Rea," Allison interrupted, "I kind of did."

Reagan smiled. She was unsure how to proceed now, but rather than the uncertainty and the quiet that had fallen over them making her anxious, she felt comfortable with the silence. She still had questions she needed answers to though.

"Can we talk about this?" she tried again.

Allison blew out a deep breath, ruffling the hair that framed her face. "I suppose that would be the mature thing to do."

"I should put on some clothes," Reagan said, standing up from the bed.

"Yeah, that probably would be a good idea."

Allison watched Reagan pad over to her suitcase. She picked out a few things and then let her towel fall. Allison quickly averted her eyes to afford her some privacy, but not before getting an eye-full of Reagan's naked silhouette. She tried not making any uncool noises. Now that she'd begun admitting to herself that she might actually be attracted to Reagan, her mind was taking her to inappropriate, but wholly pleasant, places.

Reagan came back to the bed, fully dressed and smiling. Allison wasn't sure if she knew what the sight of her naked body did to her and was purposely teasing her, or if she was oblivious to it all.

"So," Reagan started. She crossed one leg over the other and rested her hands on her kneecap. "When did you realize you were attracted to me?"

"Reagan, you don't just ask people that."

Reagan shrugged. "Why not? I think it's a perfectly reasonable question."

"Would you ask a boy that?"

"I might. Especially if I had known him for as long as we have and he had never shown any interest in me before."

Reagan had the strangest gift for making the insane sound rational. "Well I could ask you the same question," Allison deflected.

Reagan tapped her fingertips against her bottom lip and looked deep in thought. "You've always been beautiful, Allison. Even when I was terrified of you in high school I could appreciate that."

Allison leaned forward and licked her lips. "But just in a subjective way, right? You never fantasized about kissing me in high school."

"Well first, I'd argue that you're objectively beautiful. And second, we're not talking about me," she deflected. "Why did you kiss me at the train station last year?"

Allison leaned back to her original position. *That* again. She realized it was a justified question, however. That was when everything had started to change for her. "When you came to visit me for the first time, I didn't know what to expect. I didn't know if we were going to have fun, or if we were going to devolve into our high school selves and fight the whole time." She took a breath before continuing. "But I honestly had a lot of fun - minus the part where I cracked my skull open on a rock - and I wanted to thank you for that."

Reagan's eyes hadn't left Allison's face the entire time. "You could have sent a fruit basket or, I don't know, said 'Thank You.'"

Allison's lips pressed together to form a straight line. "I thought you looked really pretty, okay Murphy?"

Reagan's long eyelashes fluttered. "Really?"

Allison sighed and rubbed at her face. "It was the whole atmosphere. There were twinkle lights, and it had just started to snow, and the snowflakes were getting caught in your hair and on your ridiculously long eyelashes, and it was all so overwhelming."

"Why did you kiss me in Central Park?"

Allison made a pained expression. "Are we really going to do this? Do you want a play-by-play of every time I've kissed you?"

Reagan sat up a little straighter. "I think it could be beneficial for us both."

"I felt jealous. Territorial." She was tired of the lies and the deflecting. She just needed to be honest with Reagan so she could be honest with herself. "That guy had just called you, and I felt like you were going to bail on me to hang out with him."

"You don't have to worry about Chris. He's just a friend."

Allison's lip curled. "Well how was I supposed to know that? And what would I be worried about in the first place?"

Reagan ignored the questions and asked another one of her own. "What about just now? Why did you kiss me?"

Allison leaned forward and cupped the side of Reagan's face. "Can you blame me? Have you seen how good you look in a towel?"

Reagan pulled away and turned her face. A cascade of brunette hair concealed her face. "I'm sorry."

Allison's eyes flickered with intensity and her nostrils slightly flared. "It's fine." Her mouth formed the words, but her face and tense body language suggested it was anything but fine.

"I like kissing you, Allison." Allison waited for the other shoe to drop. "I'm just not sure what that means."

Allison stiffened. "I'm not asking you to be my girlfriend, Murphy."

"Right. Because you're not gay," Reagan routinely echoed.

"I don't believe in long-distance relationships. Not at our age."

Reagan bit her lip. Allison hadn't reacted to her comment about her sexuality like she'd expected she would. She hadn't confirmed that she wasn't gay, but she also hadn't disagreed with the statement.

Reagan's phone rang on the bedside table, interrupting the moment.

"You can get that." Allison looked tired, like she wanted to slide under the hotel duvet and never come out.

"No. Whoever it is can wait."

With an exasperated sigh, Allison grabbed Reagan's phone. She didn't recognize the area code and no name was associated with the number. She answered the call. "Hello? Reagan Murphy's phone."

A confused male voice came across the line. "Uh...is Reagan there?"

"Hold on." Allison shoved the phone in Reagan's face. "Take it." Reagan shook her head, but Allison made an impatient sound. "*Today*, Murphy."

Reagan sighed and took the phone. "Hello?"

"Hey, Reagan. It's Chris. I'm sorry I haven't called lately. I've been swamped with school and my part-time job."

Reagan made a face. *When it rains, it pours.* "It's okay. I know how that is."

"I was calling to see if you wanted to hang out soon—maybe dinner and a movie?"

Reagan chewed on her bottom lip. She couldn't tell if Allison could overhear the content of their conversation. Her face was maddeningly unreadable.

"I'm sorry, Chris. I'm seeing someone new. Well, they're not really new—but it's a new relationship." The words just seemed to leap out of her mouth. "And it wouldn't be fair to either of you if we continued hanging out."

"Oh, uh. Are you sure?"

Reagan nodded once, even though she knew he wouldn't see it. "I'm positive."

When Reagan hung up with Chris, she was afraid to look at Allison. But she felt good. She didn't feel the normal guilt that came with rejecting someone—although she didn't have much experience with that. But more importantly, she didn't feel that anxiety that comes with knowing you've put all your eggs in one basket. Allison was her basket, and she thought she was ready to give her eggs to her. She wrinkled her nose; she'd have to rethink using that analogy though.

"So you're seeing someone new?"

Reagan cleared her throat. She fiddled with her phone, still unable or unwilling to look in Allison's direction. "That's to be determined."

"So you just lied to that guy?"

Reagan looked up from her phone. Allison was staring hard at her. Instead of looking away as she was wont to do, she stared back with equal intensity. "I don't know. Did I?"

+++++

Reagan climbed the bleachers, clutching her bag of unbuttered popcorn. "I have to warn you," she said, looking back briefly, "I know nothing about sports."

Allison followed behind, one step at a time. "Don't worry. I'll teach you everything you need to know." She was thankful for the warm weather. It was the perfect day to watch a college football game and without the need for heavy jackets, it gave her the opportunity to admire Reagan's tight backside as she ascended the metal bleachers.

Reagan scooted down the aisle until she found a space that afforded them a clear view of the football field, even though she didn't know what she was supposed to be looking at. She wasn't kidding – she knew nothing about the rules of the game. But with Allison, she was happy to try new things. *Like making out.* She tried censoring her thoughts about all the other new things Allison seemed eager to do with her. *To* her.

After hanging up with Chris that morning, they'd talked a little more about their situation. Yes, they were attracted to each other. Yes, making out was a lot of fun. Yes, the idea of Reagan dating someone else drove Allison mad with jealousy. But beyond these few, brave admissions, they'd come up with no real conclusions. She knew that verbally admitting these things was a big step for them both, but she wasn't sure where that put them now.

When Allison had suggested they spend the afternoon watching Brown's football team, Reagan had been tempted to ask if it was a date. She'd kept that question to herself though, knowing it would only lead to another confrontation.

She desperately needed to talk to her roommate. Ashley was good at these things. She'd know if it was a date. She'd have to sneak off to the bathroom later to call her.

"Popcorn?" Reagan tilted the small paper bag in Allison's direction.

"No thanks."

Reagan shook the bag's contents. "I don't have cooties."

"If I thought you had cooties, I wouldn't have shoved my tongue down your throat this morning."

Reagan violently coughed, drawing stares of concern from the people seated around her. "I can't believe you said that," she wheezed. She wiped at her eyes, which had watered up from choking on a nearly fatal popcorn kernel.

Allison looked smug, but didn't say another word.

+++++

"I need your help." Reagan stood outside the field house and the public bathrooms at the football stadium. She cupped her hand around the base of her phone.

"Did you fall down a well?" came her roommate's response. "I keep telling you to watch where you're walking."

"Allison and I stayed at a hotel last night."

"Oh no," Ashley bemoaned. "She's turning you into a Call Girl. I knew that girl was no good. Don't let her pimp you out, Prez. Just remember – you say who, you say when, you say how much."

"Why can't you ever be serious just once?" Reagan stomped her foot.

"Because I've seen the alternative, and it's not a happy life."

"If I go back to the hotel with her tonight," Reagan worried out loud, "I think we might have sex."

"Is that something you want? Is she pressuring you? Do you need me to come pick you up? God," Ashley complained, "I feel like an overprotective mom."

"I don't know what I want. I'm worried if we do this thing, if we sleep together, it's going to ruin everything we've been working to build together. I could see myself being more than friends with her, but I don't know where her head is at. What if she's just using me for my body?" God, she never thought she'd *ever* be asking that question. Especially not about Allison Hoge.

"These are all good questions," Ashley acknowledged, "but you should be asking Allison, not me."

Reagan ran a hand roughly through her bangs. "I know," she grunted. "Thanks for listening to me vent, Ash."

"No problem. Your life keeps me young."

Allison smiled when she saw Reagan maneuver back up the bleachers and reclaim her seat. "Hey you," she greeted. "I was starting to worry you fell in."

"Or ran away with my high school friends?"

Allison's face darkened. That thought had never crossed her

mind, but she was sure Reagan probably thought about that memory every day. She cleared her throat. She didn't want them to fight. She wanted to continue having a light, easy day. She needed it after the heaviness of their conversation that morning. "I'm sorry, Rea," she apologized, looking properly shamed.

Reagan tersely shook herself. "No. *I'm* sorry. I don't know why I said that."

"It's okay. I deserve it." Allison's shoulders slumped and she tried to get back into the game. She secretly loved football. Besides the popularity, it was one of the biggest things she missed about not being a cheerleader anymore.

She looked away from the playing field when she felt Reagan tug her hand into her lap. Reagan's face revealed her anxiety. "Is this okay?"

Allison looked down to Reagan's lap where their fingers were currently intertwined. She licked her lips and nodded. *It was more than okay.*

"Fall break is coming up."

"Mhmm." Reagan remained focused on the playing field. She was worried that if she looked away, she'd lose track of what was going on. Or worse, that she'd get lost in Allison's hazel stare.

"Are you going home?"

"I wasn't planning on it," Reagan said. "I usually save my dad's money and go back for Thanksgiving. It's my favorite holiday." She scrunched up her nose when a Brown player took a particularly vicious hit. She didn't understand why anyone would voluntarily play football.

"Even if it's an annual turkey genocide?"

Allison's words were enough to pull Reagan from the carnage down on the field. "One vegan pizza and now you're protesting the ritual slaughter of innocent animals?" She quirked an eyebrow. "Am I converting you?"

In more ways than one. "Hardly." Allison rolled her eyes. "I'm just surprised, that's all."

"Thanksgiving's about more than food, you know. But I do have to admit to a particular weakness for cranberry sauce."

"I'll have to keep that in mind."

Something about Allison's tone and the way her hazel eyes seemed to darken even under the early afternoon sun made Reagan's stomach twist. "Are we going back to the hotel after this?"

"I hadn't really thought about it." *Lies.* It was all Allison could think about.

+++++

Brown lost the game, but if prompted, Allison wouldn't have been able to recall the final score. For most of the second half, her mind was preoccupied instead with the feeling of Reagan's hand enclosed around her own. The simple gesture and the heat of Reagan's thigh were the only things she could focus on. She wasn't uncomfortable openly holding hands in the stands. She didn't really care what the people at Brown thought of her – after the current semester came to a close she was only there for another semester until graduation.

Every time she thought she was getting immune to the handhold, Reagan would shift on the bleachers and their enjoined hands would touch a new part of her lap or thigh. At one point Reagan had absently stroked her thumb against Allison's palm, and she thought she might combust right there in the stands.

The worst part was, Reagan had no idea what this was doing to her. Unless she had abruptly cupped her hard between her thighs, she would have had no way of knowing that even the simplicity of holding hands was making Allison melt. She couldn't imagine how she'd respond if they ever did more than hold hands or kiss.

Back from the game and with stomachs full of pasta and breadsticks, Reagan and Allison continued to hold hands as they lay in bed next to each other, watching late night television. They'd untangled themselves just long enough to have dinner at a corner Italian restaurant, but as soon as the check had been paid for, their hands had found each other once again. Far from threatening and uncomfortable, holding hands felt safe, like this kind of affection was permissible.

"What time is your train tomorrow?"

"It's one of the earlier one," Reagan said, her tone apologetic. "I have a paper to finish before classes on Monday, so I have to get back earlier."

Allison's face scrunched. "You didn't have to come this weekend if you had work to do, Rea. We could have rescheduled for another weekend."

Reagan stuck out her bottom lip. "But I wanted to see you this weekend. I missed you. We hardly talked all summer."

"I know. And I'm sorry about that," Allison sighed. "Things were busy, but I should have made more of an effort to stay in touch."

"No." Reagan shook her head. "I'm just as much to blame. I let that internship consume me."

Allison turned on her side, but continued holding hands with Reagan. She was surprised their hands hadn't gotten overly sweaty yet. "Did you like it? Working at the gallery?"

Reagan nodded. "I like creating my own art, but it surprised me how much I enjoyed helping curate special exhibits and plan events."

Allison rested her weight on her elbow. "Sounds like you've got it all figured out." She was acutely aware that even though her senior year had just started, graduation would soon be upon her. She didn't know what she was going to do after college, and that feeling of uncertainly wasn't something she enjoyed.

"Hardly." Reagan sighed. "There's so many things I want to do. I can't settle on just one."

"But at least you've got multiple prospects. If I want to do anything with my English degree I can be a journalist or a professor."

"A professor?" Reagan cooed. "I bet you would be great at that."

"How do you figure?"

"Well, you already have the serious professor glasses. I saw you in them last winter. Very fetching," Reagan giggled.

"That's all you've got? I already own the glasses?" Allison laughed.

"Well, you're also super intimidating; students would pay attention to avoid your wrath. *And* you look fantastic in skirts. I've figured it all out for you." Reagan looked particularly pleased with herself. "You're destined to be an English professor. "

"Your logic baffles me, Murphy."

Reagan traced along the fine lines of Allison's wrist. "How does one become a professor?"

"Lots and lots of school." Allison licked her dry lips. She tried to stay focused on their conversation even though Reagan was doing her best to distract her. "Probably like another six or seven years."

"Holy cow. Seven? I had no idea. No wonder all of my

professors are so ancient."

Allison nodded. "I've sent in some applications to grad schools for their PhD programs in English, but I'm still not sure that's what I want to do next year. It's a pretty big commitment."

"Where have you applied to?" Reagan hadn't given much thought to what Allison might do after graduation. Her intended career path had her settled in New York City for life, but this was the first time she was realizing that Allison's future profession might send her someplace else.

"Kind of all over."

"Do you have a number one choice?"

"Stanford," Allison said without any hesitation. "They have a really strong program, and ever since I was a little girl I've wanted to go there. I think it's a hangover from my *Saved by the Bell* fan-girl days. Jessie Spano, the smartest girl at Bayside High, was obsessed with Stanford."

"Jessie Spano," Reagan echoed with a laugh. "Didn't that actress become a stripper?"

"No." Allison shook her head. "I think she just played one."

"Same thing." Reagan looked pensive. "Stanford. That's in California, right?" She let go of Allison's hand.

Allison could practically see the gears churning in Reagan's head. "Columbia or NYU might not be so bad either," she added.

"We should go to sleep."

Allison took Reagan's hand again, but she could tell the other girl wasn't reciprocating. "Reagan, did I do something wrong?"

"No."

"Then what's wrong?" Allison pressed.

Reagan shook her head and looked more than a little melancholy. "Don't worry about it. Just a little dose of reality."

Allison wanted to say more, but her words failed her. Instead, she rolled onto her side and turned out the light.

+++++

CHAPTER TWELVE

"This place is like frozen in time," Allison looked around the familiar sandwich spot with its walls covered in kitschy memorabilia.

Reagan nodded. "I think the wait staff has been the same since we were 12. My dad used to take me here after church every Sunday."

Allison looked up from her coffee cup and smiled politely at a girl who walked by and sat at a nearby table. She looked vaguely familiar – they'd probably gone to high school together, but back then Allison hadn't bothered to learn the names and faces of her graduating class unless it was advantageous to her status at the top of the social pyramid. "Should I know her?" she quietly asked while lifting her coffee cup to her lips. "I think we went to school together."

Reagan swiveled her head and blatantly stared. When she caught the attention of the girl in question, she waved with purpose. "Oh yeah! That's Traci McGowen. She looks great!"

Allison smiled cordially over her coffee mug, but it didn't reach the rest of her face. "And that name should mean something to me because…"

Reagan swung back around in her seat. "Because we went to school with her since preschool?"

The smile fell from Allison's lips.

"Really? You don't remember her? Her dad works at the hospital, and her mom is the head librarian at the public library."

Allison focused on the coffee mug cupped in her hands. "I really was self-absorbed in high school, wasn't I?" It wasn't much of a question – just a defeated statement.

Reagan reached across the table for two and laced her fingers with Allison's free hand. "You're getting better," she stated, careful with her eye contact. "And that's what's important."

Allison tightened the grip. "I'm glad our breaks overlapped." Her thumb reflexively ran along the top of Reagan's hand. "And I'm glad you changed your mind about coming." She was making it her personal mission to make sure this Fall Break didn't end up like the previous Spring Break.

They hadn't seen each other since Reagan's last visit to Providence. The semester had gotten busy, papers and midterms looming, and that had made it impossible to take a weekend to visit each other. They'd kept in contact though, emails and late night phone calls, but this was the first time they'd been face-to-face since Allison's confession weeks ago in their Providence hotel room.

She didn't quite know where they stood. Were they dating? Were they just friends? Were they something else altogether? Every time she tried to have that conversation with Reagan, she felt more confused than ever. Neither of them had explicitly asked if they were dating. They continued to skate around the topic despite numerous attempts to come to some kind of agreement.

"I am, too," Reagan returned. She hadn't originally planned on coming back for Fall Break because of its proximity to Thanksgiving, but when Allison had said she was coming home, she immediately begged her dad to buy her airfare, too. She unlatched their hands momentarily to tuck an errant strand of corn-silk hair behind Allison's ear.

Their hands found each other again. Allison stared down at where they connected, and she let herself enjoy the feeling of Reagan's fingertips brushing against her own. "Do you want to come over?" she asked. She looked up into bright blue eyes. "My dad's on a business trip, so it's just my mom, Lucy, and me hanging out tonight," she explained. "I'm sure my mom wouldn't mind setting an extra seat at the table. She loves feeding people."

Reagan's mouth quirked. "As much as I'd love to, I'm vegan," she reminded her. "I don't want to inconvenience your mom like that. Or go hungry while you all wolf down giant hunks of some poor, dead animal."

"Don't worry about it," Allison chuckled. "She'll be so thrilled to see you she won't even care she'll have to make a whole other meal for you."

"I don't know…" Reagan hesitated.

"Please?" Allison batted her eyes for extra effect.

Reagan's heart hammered in her chest. She was in trouble. Deep trouble.

"Are you sure your mom won't mind?" Reagan worried out loud.

Allison nodded. "I asked her about it this morning at breakfast."

"Oh really?" Reagan pursed her lips.

Allison ducked her head. "Don't tease me, Rea. I'm really trying here."

"Okay," Reagan conceded. "But one question."

Allison looked up again. "Sure."

"Does your mom know you tortured me in high school?"

Reagan's word choice caused Allison's stomach to tighten. "Uh, no? Why?"

Reagan's features scrunched together. "So why does she think we stopped being friends? Growing up, I used to spend every afternoon at your house."

"I don't know if she thinks about it, honestly."

"I suppose." Reagan made a thoughtful, humming noise. "Why *did* we stop being friends, Allie?"

Allison shook her head. "I've thought about it. I honestly have, and I don't know. I guess people just grow apart. Become different people. But I'm glad we've grown back together, though." The last part came out almost shyly.

Reagan smiled warmly and took Allison's hand in hers. She brought their enjoined hands up to her lips and brushed her mouth against the back of Allison's knuckles. "I am, too."

The public show of affection was starting to make Allison uncomfortable. *Baby steps*, she told herself. She slipped her hand out of Reagan's grip as unobtrusively as possible, but she immediately missed the contact.

+++++

"Well, well," Jill Hoge clucked. "If it isn't Reagan Murphy. Allison said you were back in town, but I told her I wouldn't believe it unless I saw you for myself."

Reagan ducked her head, feeling uncharacteristically bashful around Allison's mom. Jill Hoge was an attractive woman. It was obvious from where Allison got her all-American good looks. "Yep. Just back for Fall Break. Like Allie."

Jill beamed. "How lucky that your schools' breaks overlapped." She turned her attention to her daughter. "Allison, your sister needs to be picked up from soccer practice."

"*Mom*. We just got here."

"I know. And I'm busy making dinner. The least you can do is help me out by picking Lucy up from the school."

"Fine," Allison grumbled. She glanced sideways at Reagan. "Will you be okay here? Or do you want to come with?"

"Reagan can help me with dinner," Jill answered for her. "Allison told me that you're vegan. I'm afraid I wasn't quite prepared for that, but if you don't mind, I've got some things for salad in the fridge and I can do a meatless spaghetti. You'll have to let me know if you can have the noodles."

Reagan smiled and nodded. "Certainly. It's the least I can do."

Allison hesitated but her mom ushered her out the front door. She looked once more in the direction of Reagan. Her mom had already placed a cutting board in front of her and had handed her a large knife. Allison bit down on her bottom lip. She had the strangest urge to cross the room and kiss Reagan soundly on the mouth. She slipped out the front door instead. Not all urges should be acted upon. Especially not in front of your mother.

+++++

Jill Hoge stirred marinara sauce in an oversized pot. "I know it's not my place to pry, but you and Allison were so close growing up and then suddenly you weren't. I never did understand what happened between you two."

Reagan focused her attention on the tomato she was currently cutting. She honestly didn't know how to answer the question, and she didn't want to make the hospitable woman uncomfortable by telling her about Allison's high school cruelty. It wasn't her place. "I'm not really sure what happened either, Mrs. Hoge."

"Well, regardless. I'm glad the two of you have reconnected. She doesn't have many close friends besides maybe Carly and Beth from next door. I worry about her sometimes," Jill noted wistfully. She wiped her hands on a kitchen towel. "She's so much like her father – such a serious personality. Maybe you can get her to loosen up."

Reagan smiled to herself. "I'll do my best."

"You'll do your best at what?"

Reagan and Jill both looked up from their respective tasks to see Allison standing in the kitchen doorway. She had a hand resting on one cocked hip. The familiar, intimidating stance nearly gave Reagan another high school flashback.

"I was just telling Reagan how happy I am that you two are friends again, dear," Jill revealed. "And she's promised to make you not take yourself so seriously."

Allison's mouth quirked and her rigid stance softened. "Oh she has, has she?"

"Yeah, I'm apparently supposed to *loosen* you up," Reagan added with a sly smile.

Allison made a noise in the back of her throat. Maybe having Reagan over for dinner wasn't such a good idea.

"Reagan!" Lucy Hoge shoved past her sister and clomped loudly into the kitchen. "I haven't seen you in forever!"

Reagan looked momentarily startled, but collected herself enough to wave. Lucy and Allison were separated by nearly 7 years. She was surprised the girl remembered her at all.

"Lucy. Go shower," her mother admonished. "You're tracking mud all over the house."

The youngest Hoge woman stuck out her lower lip and slumped her shoulders. "Fine," she grumbled before she stomped upstairs, leaving a trail of dirt chunks behind her.

Allison sidled next to Reagan and popped a piece of cucumber into her mouth. Reagan playfully slapped at her hand. "Stop it," she complained. "Save some for the salad."

"You and my mom seem to be getting pretty chummy," Allison observed.

"Your mom's nice. She makes me wonder what my mom…" Reagan trailed off and shook her head, catching herself.

Allison's smile slipped into a concerned frown. "You know if you ever want to talk about her, I'm a good listener."

"Everyone thinks they're a good listener," Reagan self-consciously wiped at her eyes. "It's like how everyone thinks they're a good kisser."

"Well, I'm a good kisser, too," Allison said without thought.

"I know you are," Reagan grinned broadly.

Allison coughed uncomfortably. "Uh, anyway. I should go set the table."

Reagan watched Allison grab a stack of plates and a handful of silverware before stumbling through the swinging door that led to the formal dining room. She privately gloated in her ability to render the normally in-charge girl so visibly uncomfortable with just a few words.

She wanted to grab her by her slender hips and pull her in for a teasing embrace, to nip at her bottom lip until Allison submitted and begged for more. But she knew this was definitely not the place or the time to continue exploring whatever it was that was building between the two of them. Being so openly affectionate might have been okay in the anonymity of New York City or behind the closed doors of a Providence hotel room, but certainly not in Allison's parents' kitchen in northern Michigan.

A knock at the back kitchen door alerted Reagan. Forgetting that she was a guest in the Hoge's home and not in her own, and with her mind still clouded with imagery of backing Allison up against the kitchen counter, Reagan opened the door.

"Murphy?"

Reagan's hand froze on the door handle. On the back porch stood Allison's high school friends, Beth and Carly Richards. They hadn't been friends in high school, but she certainly knew of them. It was a small school, and they had been two of her most dedicated bullies. "Oh, uh. Beth. Carly. Hi."

Allison's laughter could be heard in the next room. "Hey, Rea, have you finished making that salad yet?" The swinging door that separated the kitchen from the dining room flew open and Allison appeared. She stopped in her tracks so abruptly that the swinging door hit her ass. "Hey guys. I, uh, I didn't know you were home."

Beth looked at Allison and then Reagan. "Yeah," she said, her face unreadable. "We're both home for a long weekend. Needed to do some laundry."

Carly, never one to pull punches, pointed at Reagan. "What is

Reagan Murphy doing in your kitchen, Allie?"

Reagan pulled herself together, straightening to her full height – all 5 feet 2 inches. "I'm making a salad for dinner," she stated boldly.

Carly glanced at her twin sister. "I thought we weren't friends with her."

"Carly," Beth hissed, clearly embarrassed.

Jill Hoge interrupted the increasingly awkward moment when she came into the room. "Girls! So nice to see you!" she greeted cheerfully. "It's like a high school reunion in here. Can you stay for dinner? Allison," she barked, not waiting for either Beth or Carly to respond, "go set two more spaces at the dining room table."

Allison still looked like a deer in headlights, but she nodded and grabbed some more plates and utensils before escaping into the dining room once again.

"How have you been?" Beth asked, continuing to eyeball Reagan.

Reagan busied herself throwing the last toppings into the salad bowl. She grabbed two wooden spoons and began tossing its contents. "I'm fine, thank you," she clipped.

She felt unnerved. Clearly Allison had not mentioned to Beth and Carly that they'd reconnected, even after the disaster of last Spring Break. She tried to keep her anger in check; she didn't know if she should be upset with Allison for keeping her a secret – she didn't know if Allison still even talked regularly with anyone else from high school, after all. But something about the way Allison had looked when she'd seen her old friends made Reagan feel like a dirty little secret.

+++++

Allison stood in the kitchen by herself, finishing cleaning up after dinner. The rest of the dinner company, her mother and Lucy included, were in the living room picking out a movie. Somewhere in the middle of dinner the weather had taken a turn and torrential rains and erratic winds rattled the kitchen windows. Allison grabbed an oversized bowl from a lower cupboard and threw a bag of microwavable popcorn into the microwave. Her mom had insisted after the meal that everyone get cozy and had instructed Allison to pick up after dinner and make snacks for the movie. She silently soldiered the bulk of the chore that her sister had somehow evaded, knowing that she deserved whatever punishment the night dished out.

Dinner had been less awkward than she had imagined it being. No one had made any more uncomfortable statements or questioned Reagan being there, but she couldn't deny the wounded look on Reagan's face. Beth and Carly had made it no secret when they'd shown up unannounced that they were confused by her presence at the Hoge household.

Allison shook her head. Why was she always messing things up? Why was she such a screw-up when it came to Reagan?

The house phone rang and Allison picked up the phone when she recognized the number on the caller ID. "Hi, Dad," she greeted. She cradled the phone against her shoulder and emptied the contents of the finished popcorn into the large bowl.

"Hi, sweetheart," the man returned. "How are you? How was your flight?"

"I'm good. It was good."

"I'm sorry I'll miss you while you're home. If I had known you were planning on coming back for this break I wouldn't have scheduled all of these out-of-town meetings."

Allison bit the tip of her tongue. Part of the reason she'd agreed to come home for Fall Break was knowing that he'd be away on a business trip.

"Allison, I'm not sure how to approach this situation," her father continued gravely, "but your Aunt Marie called to say someone told her you were looking very...*friendly*...with Reagan Murphy at the sandwich shop this morning." He paused and an uncomfortable panic settled in Allison's stomach. "We've talked about this before," he said in a low voice.

"That's absurd," Allison said. She tried to keep her voice even despite how her heart raced. What exactly had this person seen? "Someone is horribly mistaken or they're just trying to make trouble."

"Were you out with Reagan Murphy?" her father challenged.

"Yes. We were having coffee. There's nothing suspicious about two friends from school spending time together over Fall Break."

"I don't think you should be spending time with that girl," Rodger Hoge said sternly.

"Dad," Allison sighed, "it's just Reagan. I've known her forever.

It's really no big deal."

Her father snorted in disbelief. "I hardly think it's not a big deal. You know about her family's history. What kind of mother does that? Just abandons her young daughter and husband like that?"

"Dad, that's not Reagan's fault," Allison defended. She tried to keep her voice down, knowing that the girl in question was just in the next room, but the heat in her tone was palpable.

"You've worked so hard to build a solid reputation in this town, Allison," her father said with a deep sigh. "I'd hate to see this girl and her family drama tarnish it." The tone of his voice let her know this wasn't something up for discussion. He had made his decision.

Hot, sharp tears pricked at the corners of her eyes, but Allison refused to let them fall. "Yes, sir," she submitted. "I understand."

"That's my good girl." The warning, menacing tone was gone, and the smile was back in his voice. "Tell your mother and Lucy I say hello. I'll be home as soon as the details on this new contract are finalized."

Allison slowly hung up the phone, feeling numb.

"Allison?" her mom called out from the living room. "Did I hear the phone?"

"Yeah, Mom," Allison stated with faux-cheerfulness. "Just a wrong number," she lied.

She grabbed the popcorn bowl, nearly forgotten with the unsettling phone conversation, and stiffly returned to the living room. She handed the bowl to her mom who sat on the couch between Lucy and Carly. Allison hovered, not sure where to sit down. Beth had claimed the recliner in the corner, and Reagan sat by herself on the loveseat. She could squeeze onto the couch, but that would look strange if she let Reagan have the loveseat all to herself. *Loveseat*, she scoffed to herself. *Who even invented that name anyway?* She chose the floor instead.

"I've got room over here, Allie," Reagan said, patting the vacant spot beside her.

"I'm fine," she responded without looking away from the television.

She didn't need to look back at Reagan to know that her feelings were hurt. She could practically feel the disappointment radiating off of her. But this was for the best. She wouldn't be able to sit next to Reagan without wanting to reach out to her, touch her, or hold her hand. This was the simplest and safest solution, even if it stung.

+++++

When the movie credits began scrolling down the television screen, Jill Hoge patted the two sleeping girls sitting on either side of her. Both Carly and Lucy had fallen asleep sometime during the 90-minute film. "I think it's time for bed," she murmured.

Carly's eyes fluttered open. "Is the movie over?"

Beth laughed at her sister's frazzled appearance. "C'mon, Car." She rose from the easy chair and jerked her head towards the front door. "Let's get you home before you pass out on the carpet."

Jill stood up from the couch and looked at her eldest daughter. "Allison," she asked, stretching her arms above her head, "say goodbye to your friends and then help me drag your sister upstairs. You know how she can get."

Allison made a face when she saw her teenaged sister lightly snoring on the couch.

"Reagan, dear," Jill stated kindly as she began to heft Lucy to her feet. "Why don't you spend the night tonight? I know you're perfectly capable of getting yourself home, but this storm looks pretty nasty."

"That's really kind of you to offer, Mrs. Hoge," Reagan said graciously, "but I'll be fine. My dad just put new wipers on the car."

"Oh, stop it," Jill smiled warmly. "You know very well you're always welcome here. Besides, if you stay tonight," she continued, "in the morning I'll make you one of my famous breakfasts."

Reagan looked at her feet. Being around motherly types always made her uncomfortable. "Uh, thanks. I guess I can stay. I just need to call my Dad and let him know."

Jill smiled at Allison's other friends. "Beth and Carly, you two are more than welcome to come over for breakfast in the morning, too."

"Thanks, Mrs. Hoge. If I can drag Carly out of bed that early, we'll be here." Beth gave the house full of women a curt wave. "Goodnight everyone."

Allison walked Carly and Beth to the front door. "Do you guys want to borrow an umbrella?"

Beth shook her head. "It's just rain. We won't melt."

Carly looked out the front window. The sky was impossibly dark, but she could see the ferocious, slanted rain coming down in full sheets, settling in massive puddles. "Speak for yourself. I might want to borrow a kayak, too."

"We're just next door, Car," Beth laughed.

"See you guys in the morning?" Allison said, her voice lilting up with the question.

Beth gave her old friend a stern look. "Yeah. Cause you and I need to talk," she said lowly.

A tight knot formed in Allison's stomach. First her dad, now Beth. "About what?" she asked, feigning innocence.

"Like why Reagan Murphy is currently sitting in your living room? How and when did *that* happen?"

Allison pulled at her ponytail anxiously. "It's, uh, it's a long story."

"Well I love a good yarn. Tomorrow, lady. I'm serious." Beth stared hard at her friend. "This kind of stuff doesn't just happen."

Allison nodded glumly and watched her two friends run through the heavy downpour to their parents' house next door.

"Allison?" Jill called out. "Help me with your sister and then help Reagan make up the guest bedroom. There's fresh linens in the upstairs closet."

Allison grudgingly re-entered the living room to help drag Lucy to her feet. The teen let loose a loud snore, but didn't wake up. Lucy was a famously heavy sleeper and had had problems with sleepwalking as long as Allison could remember. Allison teetered slightly as she ascended the stairs to the second floor. Even with her mother's help, her sister made for an awkward and cumbersome burden.

Reagan plopped down on the couch while the first floor emptied. Beth and Carly had left to go home, and Allison and Mrs. Hoge were upstairs with Lucy. She flipped on the television, but finding nothing of immediate interest, turned the set off again. She looked up when she heard footsteps on the carpeted staircase.

Allison descended the stairs, her hands full of blankets and a pillow. Reagan looked critically at her as she made her way over to the living room. "Why did Carly and Beth look so surprised to see me here? Are you keeping our *friendship* a secret from them?"

Allison looked wildly uncomfortable. She dropped the blankets and pillow on the couch. "Er..."

Reagan shook her head hard. "Never mind," she snapped. "I suppose the pressure to keep up appearances was too much for the truth. I shouldn't have expected anything less from you."

"It's not like that, Rea, I promise."

"Allison?" Jill's voice floated down the stairs. "Are you two okay down there?"

Allison's eyes flashed momentarily with panic. "Yeah, Mom," she answered loudly, turning her gaze toward the staircase. "Just making sure Reagan has enough blankets. I'll be up in a bit."

Allison spun back to continue their conversation. Reagan obviously had different ideas of how she wanted to spend the evening, however. Allison watched helplessly as she stormed towards the front door. She stopped before opening the door.

"Good night, Allison," Reagan snapped bitterly. "Please be sure to thank your mom for her hospitality."

Allison lifted a hand to silently halt Reagan's hasty retreat. "Wait," she quietly pled.

Reagan spun around. "What is it?" she scowled. "What could you possibly want from me? Because apparently even friendship is out of the picture."

Allison left the living room and wordlessly padded toward her.

Reagan tensed when she felt Allison's hesitant hands move to her hipbones. Her eyes went wide when she saw Allison wet her lips. "Allison," she whispered, "what are you..."

"Shhh..." Allison commanded, as she closed the distance between their faces. "You'll wake up my Mom and Lucy." She dipped slightly and tentatively brushed her lips against Reagan's mouth. She worried that Reagan might reject her and still run away to her Dad's house. But she wasn't kissing her to make her stay – although she wasn't above using manipulation to get her way. She was kissing Reagan because she *wanted* to kiss her.

Reagan pulled away. "Allie," she sighed, shaking her head sadly. "I-I can't handle more rejection. Just...leave me alone if you can't even be honest with your supposedly closest friends."

Ignoring the unstated question, Allison interlaced her fingers with Reagan's, and led her towards the staircase. "Come upstairs for a minute." It wasn't a request.

Reagan swallowed hard. Allison's hazel eyes looked impossibly dark in the dim lighting of the living room.

+++++

CHAPTER THIRTEEN

Reagan's back was pressed tightly against the back of Allison's bedroom door. No sooner had she closed the door behind her, Allison had pushed her back against the entryway. Allison's hands flew up to the lapel of Reagan's jacket and crushed her open mouth against her lips. Reagan's hands instinctively traveled south to cup Allison's finely sculpted backside. Allison quietly moaned into Reagan's mouth and her fingers moved to the front button of Reagan's jeans.

"Whoa," Reagan panted, pushing Allison's hands away from her zipper. "What…what are you doing?"

Allison took a step backward and her lower lip quivered. "Am I doing it wrong?"

Reagan's lips twitched. "No, you're doing *everything* right," she observed. "I'm just confused about what this is. One minute you won't even sit next to me, the next you're trying to take off my pants."

Allison's face grew grave. "I just want to show you how much you mean to me."

Reagan's eyebrows rose up to her hairline as if the words didn't make any sense. "*Show* me?"

Allison dipped her tongue into the cleft of her bottom lip. "I know I was a jerk tonight," she said quietly. "And after all I've put you through this past year, I know I don't deserve you." Her hazel eyes slowly trailed over Reagan's figure. "But I really need you to stay with me tonight."

Reagan felt conflicted. Allison's actions had been confusing since they'd met up that morning. One minute they were holding hands, the next Allison was ignoring her. But that wasn't anything new; Allison's actions were generally confusing. Ever since they'd reconnected, she'd been nothing but hot and cold.

Allison brought a hand to the side of Reagan's face. Reagan's eyes shut and she breathed out through her nose. She cursed her betraying body. She wanted to be stronger and not give in so easily. But it seemed as if all Allison had to do lately was touch her in a familiar, intimate way, and her resolve fell apart.

"You know I have a hard time verbally expressing myself." Allison's hand dropped down to Reagan's hip.

Reagan opened her eyes. "Why don't you write me a letter?"

"Right now?"

"It would save you the postage," Reagan uncomfortably joked. When Allison flicked on her 'serious' persona, it could be overwhelmingly heavy. She felt like there was an elephant sitting on her chest.

Allison's teeth tugged at her bottom lip. "And you'll stay?"

"If it's a good enough letter."

"No pressure or anything, huh?" Allison sighed. She took Reagan's hand and led her to her bed. The double-sized mattress was still covered by the quilt she had had on her bed since adolescence. Her grandma had made it for her on her 12th birthday. Reagan sat down on the bed while Allison sat at her childhood desk. She opened a drawer and pulled out a piece of blank computer paper and found a pen.

"No peeking," Allison admonished. She moved her arm to cover up her writing like a school kid protecting her test answers from prying eyes one desk over.

Reagan shook her head. "Never. I like surprises."

"Shh...I need to concentrate."

"Right. Shutting up now." Reagan scooted back on the bed until her head propped up against the wooden headboard. She watched Allison stare at the sheet of paper for a moment longer before she continued writing.

Allison sighed and sat up straighter. She set her pen back on the desk. "I think it's done." Her eyes trailed over the words, giving them a second estimate. She carefully folded the piece of paper in half and handed it to Reagan. "I hope you're not expecting Shakespeare. This was on short notice."

"I'll try to keep that in mind when I make my final assessment," Reagan noted matter-of-factly.

"Great," Allison grumbled. "Now I feel like I'm getting a grade for this."

Reagan laughed. "Got any red pens?"

Allison swiped at the piece of paper Reagan held, trying to take back the note. "If you're not going to take this seriously," she growled, "then forget the whole thing."

Reagan pulled the paper away and pressed it against her chest and out of Allison's reach. "I'm sorry. I'll be serious."

Reagan's eyebrows knit together as she read the carefully scrawled handwriting.

Dear Reagan,

These past few months have been one of the most fun-filled yet also the most confusing times in my life, and I have you to blame for all of that. We have so much fun together and my mom was right about you – you do get me to loosen up (get your head out of the gutter, Murphy); when I'm with you, I can't help but be happy. And believe me, I've tried to stop it from happening. Because the way I feel for you scares me – and not just because you're a girl (although that certainly does play a part). It's scary because I've worked hard all my life to be in control. To keep a check on my emotions. To not let anyone get too close for fear of becoming vulnerable. I don't want to get hurt and I don't want to hurt you anymore either, but I just can't stay away. I don't <u>want</u> to stay away. I hope you'll spend the night with me. I hope you can't stay away either.

Yours,
Allison Anne Hoge

Allison chewed on her thumbnail. She'd always been good with words. But that didn't mean she knew how to communicate. She looked expectantly at Reagan, trying to decipher the emotions on her face as she read over the impromptu letter. She felt nervous, like waiting on the results of some medical test. "So?"

Reagan refolded the letter. "You're a good writer, Allie. It started out slow, but really picked up by the end."

"Thanks for that evaluation," Allison said crossly. She felt disappointed. She felt like she'd just poured out her heart, albeit in a hastily written letter, and she'd expected a different response.

Reagan patted at the space on the mattress beside her. Allison rose from her seat at the desk and resettled next to Reagan on the bed. Reagan took one of Allison's hands in her own and brought it to her lips. "I've never...I mean...not with a girl." Her piercing blue eyes seemed to waver as she took in Allison's angelic face.

Allison wanted to look away, but found herself unable. "I'm not exactly an expert either." The words got stuck in her throat temporarily.

"Well, no. I didn't think you'd ever slept with a girl before," Reagan quietly chuckled. "But I imagine you've had, um, experience with guys?"

"Well, even in that department I don't have a lot of experience." Allison felt her face flush warm with embarrassment. "Like I said in the letter, I don't let a lot of people get that close."

"What about in high school. I thought you'd—"

"Rumors," Allison interrupted, trying not to let her past annoy her and ruin this moment. "Hearsay."

"Oh, good," Reagan gushed in relief. "Because I'm so worried that I'll do something wrong and totally turn you off, or not know how to do something, and you'll laugh at me, or I'll do it and it wouldn't be good and you'll–,"

Allison silenced Reagan's anxious ramblings by pressing her lips solidly against her moving mouth. Reagan's hand ran up the side of Allison's face and experimentally slid through her silken hair. Allison tensed slightly before her body relaxed, and she gave in to the gentle pressure Reagan exerted on her lips. Although they'd kissed before, they'd never been with each other like this. It felt like for the first time they were on the same page – if not emotionally, at least physically.

Allison's hands snaked under Reagan's shirt and hesitantly found their way to her naked midriff. Her fingers glided along the warm, smooth skin there, marveling at the tautness of her abdomen. Reagan jumped slightly, feeling Allison's chilly fingers come in contact with her naked flesh.

"We don't have to," Allison breathed, feeling Reagan's stomach muscles tense under her touch. In truth, the pep talk was for herself just as much as it was for Reagan.

Reagan stared up at Allison beneath heavy eyelashes. The concern and warmth she saw in Allison's slightly squinted eyes took her by surprise. "I want to," she whispered.

"We'll go slow," Allison murmured, stroking her fingers along the side of Reagan's face. "And we can stop at any time, okay?"

Reagan nodded. "Okay."

Allison toyed with the bottom hem of Reagan's shirt. She raised an eyebrow, silently asking permission. When Reagan raised her arms above her head, it was all the consent she needed. Allison slipped the garment up, revealing the tan and toned torso she'd come to admire weeks ago in a Providence hotel room. She dragged the shirt further up and her fingers brushed along a slightly visible ribcage until she succeed in removing Reagan's shirt altogether.

She took in the sight of Reagan's slender upper body, the thin and feminine arms, the visible clavicle, and the way Reagan's chest heaved and swelled with every deep breath. Allison licked her suddenly dry lips. She ran her fingertips down the sides of Reagan's bare arms and watched how the simple action caused Reagan's eyes to shut and her breath to come in ragged bursts.

She traced her fingers along Reagan's breastplate. She watched each deliberate movement, intent to etch this moment in her mind in case it never happened again. She dipped her head and peppered light kisses along Reagan's clavicle. She heard the content sigh and observed how Reagan's head fell back to give her more room to work.

While her mouth remained busy with its task, her idle hands slid up the flat plane of Reagan's stomach and hovered just above the sheer material of her bra. When her palms finally made contact and her fingers curled to cup their weight, Allison's eyes slammed shut and she breathed out hard through her nose. She was touching another woman's breasts. She was touching Reagan Murphy's breasts. The recognition made her a little light headed.

Her fingers curled over the bra's flimsy edge and her fingertips made contact with the softest skin she had ever touched. She bit back a telling groan. She was inexperienced to be certain, but she didn't want to sound like a high school boy who'd just rounded Second Base for the first time. It was hard to keep herself tempered, however; Reagan's breasts were a revelation.

She looked up at Reagan. Her eyes were still shut and her lips were parted. "Is this still okay?" she asked.

Reagan's eyes snapped back open. "Of course."

"You just look a little...I don't know...scared?" Allison dropped her hands to her lap.

"Well of course I'm scared," Reagan responded honestly. "But that doesn't mean I want you to stop." She grabbed Allison's hands and moved them back to her breasts.

This time Allison couldn't curb the noise that rumbled out of her throat. She squeezed the firm flesh and roughly palmed Reagan's breasts. She pressed her mouth where neck meets shoulder and lightly bit down. Reagan whimpered, but made no attempt to stop her.

Hands left the cups of Reagan's bra and traveled up to her shoulders. Allison ran her fingers underneath the two bra straps and along more warm skin. She slid the straps down Reagan's shoulders and ran her palms the full length of her arms.

Reagan reached behind her back and unfastened the eyelet catch, the only thing keeping her bra still in place. She brought her arm up pinning the hanging garment between her forearm and her naked breasts.

"Please," Allison whispered. Her eyes went from Reagan's chest to her eyes. "Let me see you."

Reagan took a quick breath before dropping her arm to the side. No longer fastened or held up by its straps, her bra fell into her lap, exposing her breasts to Allison's hungry gaze.

"You're so beautiful, Rea," Allison breathed. She tentatively reached out a hand and ran her fingertips along the now exposed flesh of Reagan's breast.

Reagan audibly swallowed. She watched and felt Allison's light but purposeful touch. She watched pale fingers experimentally circle the rosy nipple, making it harden and pebble. Reagan bit down on her lower lip. These slow tactics were *killing* her. "I want to see you, too," she managed to choke out.

Allison's eyebrows furrowed together. More so than stripping Reagan and all of the intimacies that would follow, this is what she feared the most – letting herself become vulnerable. She knew they couldn't share this moment very well if she remained clothed, but that didn't make this any easier on her.

She reached for the bottom hem of her own shirt and cast a furtive glance in the direction of her bedroom door. The door was unlocked, but she feared that standing up to lock the door would disrupt the moment too much. Why did she never remember to lock doors behind her? Despite the nervous rumbling in the pit of her gut, Allison took off her shirt and cast it to the side.

Reagan immediately reached for the back clasp of her bra, the final barrier between she and Allison being topless together. Allison grabbed onto Reagan's wrists, stopping her. Reagan's face revealed her confusion and concern.

"Slow," Allison gently reminded her. She released her tight grip on Reagan's wrists.

Reagan nodded wordlessly. With more care this time, she slowed her movements. Allison could feel Reagan's fingers tremble as she unfastened the garment and slipped it from her body. It pacified her own anxieties to know that Reagan was just as nervous, if not more.

Allison placed a hand on Reagan's shoulder and gently pushed her onto her back. She crawled on top of Reagan's body, working hard to stifle the groan that came to her lips upon feeling bare breasts brush against her own. She shifted her weight, careful to not squish Reagan beneath her. She parted Reagan's thighs and nestled a knee between them. The warmth she discovered there, even radiating through the layers of their pants, made her inwardly groan.

"*Slow, slow, slow,*" Allison chanted to herself in a silent mantra. Every cell in her body screamed at her to take what she wanted. To take what she felt belonged to her. To take what had been denied for too long. She wanted to bury herself inside of this girl. The aggressive and possessive feelings scared her.

Reagan could feel Allison's muscles twitching and straining as if short electrical pulses were assailing her body. "Are-are you okay?" she asked as Allison moved her mouth from her lips to her neck.

"Uh huh," Allison murmured into lightly perfumed skin. She nipped at Reagan's jugular, causing her to groan and involuntarily thrust her hips upward. Allison's brain screamed when she felt Reagan's hipbone bump into the juncture between her own thighs. "*Oh God, I'm dying.*"

Allison captured Reagan's hands, tangling the brunette's fingers with her own, and pulled her arms above their heads. Her mouth continued to travel further south while she pinned Reagan to the mattress, and she was rewarded with quiet mewls of appreciation. She nibbled along Reagan's breastplate as though devouring the most delicious meal. She skipped past her pert breasts and momentarily released her hold on her hands so her tongue could pay more attention to her slightly jutted ribcage.

Reagan wiggled beneath her partner; Allison had inadvertently found one of her ticklish spots. As she squirmed, Allison's strong upper thigh connected between her own thighs. She audibly gasped when her clit rubbed against the muscled appendage and she instinctively ground herself onto Allison's leg to receive more friction.

"S-Slow," Allison stuttered a reminder. Showing unreasonable willpower, she pulled her thigh away from Reagan's heat.

Reagan groaned in disappointment and frustration. "Please, Allie," she rasped. Her hips thrust upward, hoping to garner some kind of contact, but Allison merely moved her body with the undulations rather than reward her for her impatience.

Allison smiled down at her impetuous bedmate. "It's not time for that yet," she quietly chastised. She lowered her head down to Reagan's perky breasts and grinned. "It's not just about you, you know," she murmured, darting her tongue out against pebble-hard nipples. "I've been thinking about this for too long to dive right in."

"You-you've been thinking about this?" Reagan stuttered.

Not answering, Allison pulled another gasp from Reagan as her tongue flicked against a sensitive nipple. One hand rolled the other nipple gently between her thumb and forefinger while her mouth danced over the other straining breast.

Reagan arched her back into Allison's hot mouth, and she wrapped her fingers around blonde, wild locks. She pulled Allison's face down, mashing her against her breast, wordlessly encouraging her for more. But Allison maintained her steady, gentle ministrations, not increasing the pressure of her fingers or her tongue. She ran lazy circles around Reagan's nipple with the tip of her tongue while her fingers continued to gently tweak the other sensitive bud.

Reagan sighed contentedly when Allison rotated her mouth to the other breast. She sucked the hardened nipple into her mouth and lightly bit down on the small bud. Reagan whimpered and rolled her hips suggestively.

Allison released her lip-lock on Reagan breast and smiled warmly. "Patience," she ordered before returning her attentions back to Reagan's breasts.

Reagan slid one hand under the waistband of Allison's jeans and found her way between her parted thighs. Her fingers easily slid through the arousal. Both women moaned when Reagan's fingers slipped over Allison's outer lips and brushed against her slightly protruding clit.

"Fuck," Allison uncharacteristically swore as Reagan gently slid the tip of her finger along her wet slit, pulling more arousal from her. "That's not fair," she practically cried.

Reagan grinned coyly before sliding a single digit up into Allison's hot core. "Slow, right?" she quietly taunted.

Allison moaned, momentarily forgetting Reagan's naked breasts as her finger slid deeper into her wet pussy. "Reagan," she panted uselessly in protest. She tried to clamp her thighs together to make it harder for her to thrust inside her, but with Reagan's body straddled between her legs, she could barely deny her access.

Reagan sat up in bed. With her free hand, she unzipped Allison's jeans and pulled them down her slender hips. "You should know by now," she smiled, "I always get my way."

Reagan slowly pulled her single finger out of Allison's tightness; the digit was thoroughly coated with thick arousal. With little thought, she brought it to her lips. She moaned, her tongue dashing out to taste Allison for the first time.

"Off," Allison wheezed, clawing at the jeans that had her thighs pinned in position. "Get these off." Watching Reagan licking her arousal off her fingers was too much.

Reagan smirked. "What happened to slow?" she taunted, still licking her lips.

With effort, the two managed to peel Allison's jeans the rest of the way off. Her underwear soon followed. Reagan pushed her finger back inside, and she felt Allison clench around her. Her wetness clicked, filling the quiet bedroom with the sound of her heightened arousal.

Allison slumped forward slightly, her legs parting until she felt a slight twinge in her groin muscle. She rested all her weight on her knees and held herself stable with one hand on Reagan's shoulder. Although she had wanted to tease and delay Reagan's satisfaction, she wasn't masochist enough to deny herself an orgasm.

Reagan smiled mischievously and used her legs and free hand to propel her further down the bed until her face was level with Allison's parted thighs. "Where-where are you going?" Allison panted, unable to fully concentrate with Reagan's finger buried inside her. A low groan escaped her lips. From this position, it looked like she was sitting on Reagan's face.

Allison tossed her head back and screwed her eyes shut when she felt Reagan thrust hard inside her. Blindly, she reached down with one hand and cradled the back of Reagan's head, pulling her up deeper into her pussy. Reagan sucked hard on her sensitive clit while thrusting her finger deep into Allison's wet core.

"Reagan," Allison called out in a strangled voice. She wanted to scream out her name, but she had just enough mental presence to remember that her mother and sister slept just beyond the unlocked bedroom door.

Reagan grunted beneath her, sending an unexpected vibration up through Allison's body. She felt like Reagan had just touched a vibrator to the tip of her clit, and she sucked in deep breaths as her orgasm rocked through her. "Ahhh, fuck," she strained out, her head slumping forward.

Reagan continued to suckle on her clit until Allison pushed the palm of her hand into her shoulder, forcing Reagan's head down into the mattress. "S-Stop," she commanded, looking down at the surprise in Reagan's eyes. "T-too much. Too sensitive." She attempted to move, but found her upper thighs unstable. On shaky legs, she finally repositioned her body so that she once again lay next to Reagan under the sheets.

Reagan propped herself up on one elbow. "Was that okay?"

Allison gave her a lazy grin. "God, Rea," she breathed. "You're a natural."

Reagan released a deep breath. "Good cause…you know…I was nervous."

Allison turned on her side and smirked. "After a year of foreplay, I'm surprised I lasted as long as I did."

Reagan blushed slightly in the darkness of the room. She still had

Allison's arousal on her fingers and face and didn't quite know what to do next. What was the proper protocol for these kinds of things? Was Allison going to reciprocate now or should she excuse herself to the bathroom to clean up? And would Allison take offense to that? Would she think that Reagan hadn't *enjoyed* what they just did if she washed away the evidence?

Allison's eyes narrowed to slits. "You look like your brain is working overtime." Her hands wandered under the sheets and found Reagan's hipbones. She slipped one hand around Reagan's waist and pulled her closer. "I hope you don't think we were done." She nuzzled her nose into the crook of Reagan's neck and breathed in deeply. "After all, what kind of person would I be if I enjoyed myself and left you unsatisfied?"

"A boy?"

"Touché," Allison chuckled. "I'd better do something about that then." She licked along the outside of Reagan's earlobe. She breathed heavily into her ear. "I wouldn't want you mistaking me for a guy."

Reagan swabbed her tongue against her bottom lip, tasting Allison's arousal again. "I'm pretty sure there's no way I'd be able to make that mistake."

Allison licked along Reagan's collarbone, tasting the thin sheen of sweat that had collected on her skin. "God. I want to lick every inch of you," she quietly growled. "I want to taste you all over."

"Do you have to start all over from the beginning?" Reagan asked, her voice slightly quivering. "I mean, can't you just, uhm…"

Allison smirked and raised her eyebrows. "Anxious, much?"

Reagan returned the smirk with a coy smile of her own. "No," she shook her head, "just horny."

Allison chuckled deeply. "You just said the magic words." She slid under the blankets. Reagan's eyes flipped wide open when she felt nimble hands unfastening the top button of her jeans and pulling down on her zipper.

"No imagining I'm someone else while I'm down here," came Allison's muffled command.

Reagan lifted her backside off the mattress and helped Allison remove her jeans and underwear. Her hand went to the moving, sheet-covered lump between her parted thighs. "N-no," she stuttered when she felt Allison's tongue swab across her clit. "Nothing to worry about there." She groaned into the darkness of the bedroom.

Allison's fingers spread her open, and she slowly licked along every crevice and fold. She moved along the insides of Reagan's quivering thighs, sucking the spilled arousal from the tender flesh.

Reagan whimpered when she once again felt Allison flick just the tip of her tongue against her sensitive clit. She wanted to grab onto her face and reposition her exactly where she needed pressure, but worried that Allison might punish her more for showing such impatience once again.

Reagan pushed the sheet down, revealing Allison's head and strong, naked shoulder blades. Allison paused momentarily and looked up. "What's wrong?"

"Nothing," Reagan gasped, rolling her hips slightly. "I just want to see you."

Allison flashed a quick grin before returning her attentions to Reagan's pussy. She trailed a single digit up and down her seeping slit, collecting her arousal and spreading it around. She dipped her finger inside, just to the first knuckle before drawing it back out. She repeated the motion, causing Reagan to breathe hard.

"You feel so good," Allison murmured reverently as she stared at Reagan's swollen pussy. She continued to dip a single finger slowly in and out; every thrust became deeper and harder, causing the breath in Reagan's throat to hitch, yet Allison continued to penetrate her with painfully slow and deliberate movements. "You wrap around my finger like you never want to let go."

Reagan's sex became increasingly saturated with every penetration. The musky scent of sex lingered in the bedroom and the sound of Allison's thrusts clicked in her ears. "God, Rea," Allison moaned as if in pain. She slid a second finger inside. "You're so wet for me."

Reagan gasped when she felt Allison's fingers fill and stretch her. She thrust her hips upward, meeting every downward thrust.

"Mmm...do you like that?" Allison purred as she watched Reagan's hipbones rise and fall.

"Allison," Reagan panted desperately. The mattress started to creak and groan. "Please, I need your mouth on my-my clit," she begged. Her thighs fell apart and her knees slightly bent, opening herself completely.

Allison wet her lips and dipped her head back down to Reagan's sex. She rolled her tongue in circles around Reagan's engorged clit, pulling a quiet hiss from her. She moved Reagan's clit back and forth with just the tip of her tongue while continuing to slowly push her fingers in and out of her core.

Reagan gripped onto the bottom sheet tightly, pulling handfuls of Egyptian cotton into her palms. "Allison," she gasped again, pulling the elasticized fitted sheet away from the sides of the mattress. "Yes, right there."

She groaned loudly when Allison sucked her tender clit into her mouth. "Oh fuck, yes," she moaned, no longer caring that Allison's family slept just beyond the bedroom door. "Your mouth. God, yes. Uhn, don't stop," she continued to encourage her as she clamped her eyes shut. "I'm so close, Allie. I'm so fucking close."

Reagan could feel the sweat pooling in her shallow belly button. As Allison's talented mouth and fingers continued to push her closer and closer to climax, her body temperature continued to rise. Her hands traveled across the front of her body, pressing into her lower abdomen, fluttering over her belly button, dancing up her ribs, and coming to rest on her aching breasts.

Her hardened nipples felt like small pebbles in the palms of her hands. Allison's free hand wandered up her body and rested on one of her breasts. She squeezed Reagan's hand, causing her to grab more soundly onto her own breast. Together, they kneaded Reagan's pliable flesh.

Reagan released her hold on her breasts, and her hands and arms went above her head to grasp tightly to the sides of the wooden headboard. The head of the bed groaned and strained under the pressure. Allison withdrew her sticky fingers from Reagan's core and twisted and tweaked her tender nipples. She rolled the sensitive buds between her fingers, pulling on them hard, earning herself yet another loud groan.

Allison shifted her weight, pulling herself up on her knees and lower limbs. She buried her face deeper into Reagan's clenching core, licking hard at her clit.

"Oh, shit!" Reagan called out, feeling a sharp stab of pleasure attacking her insides.

Allison returned two fingers to Reagan's tightening sex. She pushed her digits in hard, forcing her way through the telltale tightness. She lapped at Reagan's swollen clit, suckling it more slowly and tenderly.

Reagan released her hold on the headboard, and one hand went between Allison's clenching shoulder blades. Her back felt damp with sweat.

Reagan felt a slow-building pressure creeping around inside her lower abdomen. She had climaxed before with other partners and from her own ministrations, but this felt new. "Ah-h-h-h-h..." she groaned out as an intense, yet soothing orgasm washed over her entire body. She felt like a flower opening up to bloom for the sun. She felt like she was sinking inside a warm bath while a hot shower simultaneously beat down from above.

Allison climbed back up the bed and wrapped her arms around Reagan's damp body. "So?" she murmured into her ear. She could smell the slight scent of sex and sweat on Reagan's warm skin. "What did you think?"

Reagan snuggled herself deeper into Allison's yielding flesh. "You were right," she breathed. She could hear her heart in her ears. "Slow is good."

+++++

Allison traced her fingertips along the delicate bones of Reagan's hand. Outside, the sky was still dark, but she couldn't fall asleep. Reagan twitched beside her, but she didn't wake up. Allison continued her light circles on the insides of her wrists. Reagan's lips parted slightly and a quiet sigh slipped out.

She stilled her movements and watched the gentle rise and fall of Reagan's chest as she slept beside her. Allison closed her eyes when a sensation washed over her. She felt so happy, so satisfied, and her heart was so full, she felt as if her chest might burst. But as happy as she was, she was also terrified. She could mess this up. She could lose this perfect feeling.

"Allie?"

Allison opened her eyes at the sound of her name and found bright blue orbs staring at her.

"What's wrong?"

Allison gave Reagan a weak smile. "Everything's fine. Go back to sleep."

Reagan furrowed her brow and looked unconvinced. "Are you sure?"

Allison placed a soft kiss on the tip of Reagan's nose. "Everything's perfect," she breathed. "I promise."

+++++

CHAPTER FOURTEEN

Reagan awoke to a sharp pain in her side. A small, yet surprisingly strong foot connected with her lower ribs, shoving her out of bed. She flailed her arms and landed solidly on the carpeted floor. She swung her legs and feet out wildly from her new position on the floor, but only managed to become more tangled in the sheets that had slid off the bed along with her body.

"God, you're a sound sleeper," came a feminine voice above her.

Reagan pulled the cotton sheet away from her face to see Allison smirking down at her. Her golden hair was pulled back in a messy bun. She wore a fitted t-shirt with her college's name tight against her breasts and tiny sleep shorts.

"That's some alarm clock," Reagan complained bitterly as she continued to struggle with the stubborn blankets.

Allison stifled a laugh. "I tried to wake you up nicely, but you just kept slapping my hands away and moaning incoherently."

Reagan pulled at the sheets and finally succeeded in prying herself free. "I think *you* were the one doing the incoherent moaning last night."

Allison frowned. "Downstairs," she ordered. "Now. We have to make it look like you slept in the guest room. My mom will be up any minute now."

Reagan's mouth opened wide. "But..."

"Listen, Rea," Allison interrupted. She walked over to her bedroom window and pulled the blinds up, allowing more morning sunshine to stream into her room. "My mom might be cool. One might even call her open-minded, especially compared to my dad, but instead of her walking in on us like this, I'd like to give her *some* warning before I can even think about telling her –,"

"That I ate you out last night?" Reagan interjected with a smug smile.

Allison blushed, but tried to cover it up by rolling her eyes. "Just get downstairs. Please?" she pleaded.

Reagan sighed loudly and scowled as she scanned the room for her discarded clothing. Her clothes from the previous night were haphazardly scattered around Allison's bedroom. Allison helped her along by throwing a t-shirt and pajamas pants at her head. Reagan caught the clothes and quickly pulled the top on over her naked upper torso. "Fine," she grumbled, not looking happy to be putting clothing back on.

She hopped up from the floor and pulled the pajama pants on. She looked down and grimaced. Not only were they too long for her short legs, but they also had ice-skating polar bears on them. "You *so* owe me," she grunted.

Allison knew it was completely wrong of her to demand that Reagan act as though the previous night hadn't happened, but she wasn't prepared to deal with the consequences of their actions. Yes, she had been the one to initiate sex. Yes, she had had an amazing night. But now, the morning after, she couldn't help but feel rattled by how bold she had been in bed. The fact that she'd had sex with a girl wasn't paramount on that list of reasons to feel unsettled. Instead, she felt more embarrassed by how aggressive she'd felt with Reagan.

Reagan's head popped back up when she felt familiar hands back on her hips. Allison's palms came in contact with a small strip of naked skin between the top of the too-large pajama bottoms and the bottom hem of the v-neck shirt. Reagan's skin felt warm and soft, triggering memories of what had happened between them just a handful of hours earlier.

Allison placed a gentle kiss on Reagan's twisted mouth and pulled back with a small smile. "And believe me. I can't wait to settle up my debts."

++++++

"So do you girls have any big plans today?" Jill Hoge asked as she whisked the batter for her world-famous pancakes. The metal utensil clicked against the glass mixing-bowl.

The two girls glanced briefly at each other. Allison raised an eyebrow at Reagan who merely shrugged in response. Reagan had made it downstairs just in time to throw some blankets on the guest bed to give the appearance that she had spent the night sleeping downstairs, rather than upstairs with her arms and legs wrapped around Allison. Allison's mother had descended the second-floor staircase shortly afterwards; and now she, the two girls, and Lucy stood around the island in the kitchen.

"I've been promising Lucy we'd go to the pumpkin patch this weekend," Jill continued. She sprinkled some cinnamon into the liquid mixture. "You know the one, Allison, with the hayrides and the apple picking?"

"Oh, yeah. I remember that place." Allison nodded. She flashed a quick smile at Reagan. "Have you ever been to a pumpkin patch? That seems like something you'd be way into."

Reagan shook her head. "I actually haven't," she remarked. "We always got our pumpkins each year from a stand out on the highway."

"Oh, you *have* to come with us!" Lucy insisted in a high-pitched voice. She bounced slightly on her stool. "Mom, tell Reagan she *has* to come."

A knock at the back door interrupted their conversation and all eyes went to the kitchen door where Carly had her hands and face pressed up against the window. Her nose was angled to one side and her lips and cheeks looked warped from being squished against the pane of glass. Lucy giggled and immediately hopped off her stool to let her inside.

Lucy laughed again when she opened the kitchen door. "You know Mom's gonna make you clean that window now," she snickered, pointing at the smudge spots Carly's face had left behind.

Carly strode into the back room, followed by her twin sister. "It's totally worth it as long as I still get breakfast," she beamed, rubbing her hands together eagerly.

Jill checked the turkey sausage on the front burner. "Good morning, you two," she smiled. "Breakfast's almost ready. Carly," she announced, "the Windex is under the sink."

Carly's face fell and Beth gave her sister a playful nudge. "You thought she was kidding about that, huh?" she giggled.

Reagan felt suddenly uncomfortable surrounded by so many people, hostile or not. Everyone was acting like this was the most normal thing in the world – Saturday morning breakfast in the Hoge house – and she felt like an extra and unwanted appendage. She reached for a piece of toast from the stack that teetered on a plate in front of her for something to do.

Allison playfully slapped Reagan's hand away. "Wait until the rest of the food is ready," she lightly chastised. "My mom is making vegan pancakes just for you."

Reagan gave her a mischievous smile. "Sorry," she said quietly. "I'm just really hungry. I didn't have popcorn last night, so the only thing I had to eat since dinner was your – mmrrpph."

Her speech was quickly silenced when Allison hastily shoved a piece of toast into her open mouth. Reagan smiled around the toast and began to chew noisily, smacking her lips. Allison looked flustered, and her hazel eyes darted around the kitchen to take stock if anyone had overheard their conversation. Her friends and family all looked too distracted by the sounds and smells of breakfast to notice them though.

"Lucy," her mother called out, putting the last of the pancakes on a serving plate, "get everyone a plate would you, sweetie?"

The teenaged girl sulked, but wordlessly obeyed her mother's request. Once everyone had a plate and silverware, the group heartily dug into the food in front of them. Jill had made enough food to feed a small army.

"Awesome as usual, Mom," Allison grinned as she bit off the end of a turkey sausage.

"I agree," Reagan echoed the compliment. She washed down a large mouthful of vegan pancake with half a glass of orange juice. "Thank you for making breakfast, Mrs. Hoge. It was really kind of you to make vegan options for me."

"It's no problem at all, Reagan," Jill waved off Reagan's gratitude. Reagan made a mental note of the action. It seemed both Allison and her mother had a gift for deflecting compliments. "What kind of person would I be if I made you go hungry while the rest of us enjoyed breakfast?"

"Oh, Mom!" Lucy squealed suddenly. Her high-pitched voice

caused Reagan to drop her fork and it clattered noisily on her nearly empty plate. "Can Carly and Beth come to the pumpkin patch with us, too?"

Jill laughed at her daughter's enthusiasm. "Lucy, they might have other plans today," she gently reminded.

"That's that pumpkin patch just outside of town, right" Carly stated excitedly. "I'm totally in. How about you, Beth?"

Her twin sister nodded. "I could totally go for an apple donut."

Jill smiled kindly at Reagan. "Okay, so that just leaves you, Reagan. How about it?"

Reagan felt everyone's eyes suddenly burning into her. This family bonding stuff was right up her alley, but the fact that it was with the Hoge family and Allison's high school friends made her uncomfortable. But, if she got to spend another day with Allison, she reasoned, then who was she to deny herself some fun?

Reagan flashed the group a brief smile. "Okay," she caved. "Count me in."

+++++

"Ahhhh!! I *love* Fall!" Lucy squealed as their car pulled into a makeshift parking lot. The fallow field was crowded with other vehicles, and families walked hand-in-hand around the impressive working farm. As soon as her mother parked the SUV, Lucy's seatbelt was off and she jumped out of the passenger-side door.

"Lucy!" Mrs. Hoge called out after the teen as she rushed toward the ticket booth. "Don't get lost!"

Reagan smirked at Allison, who sat beside her in the backseat. "I take it your sister's a big fan of Fall?"

Allison unbuckled her seatbelt. "She's not the only one," she revealed with a shy smile. "Even I've got to admit that there's something about apple cider and pumpkin seeds and scarves that makes me a little weak in the knees."

Reagan leaned in close, causing Allison's heartbeat to accelerate. "I know what else will make you weak in the knees," she boldly murmured.

Allison shuddered. "Don't, Reagan," she breathed. "Not here in front of everyone."

Reagan's hand slid onto the Allison's taut thigh and subtly moved up. She could feel the heat emanating under Allison's jeans. Sitting so close the entire ride without being able to touch had been acute torture. She'd never been with someone who she wanted to touch *all of the time*. It was new and a little overwhelming. After restraining herself around Allison for so long, it felt like the floodgates had been opened after last night. "What's wrong?"

A sharp rap on the backseat window startled Allison. She instinctively slapped Reagan's hand away and looked up. Beth's smiling face beamed back at her, no sign on her face that she'd seen the intimate interaction. She and Carly had ridden up in her vehicle since there wasn't enough room for all of them in the Hoge's car. "C'mon, you guys." Her muffled voice reverberated through the back window. "Your mom got us all tickets for the hayride."

"We'll be right there," Allison responded.

Reagan took her time taking off her seatbelt. "So I take it I'm not allowed to touch you anymore."

Allison flashed Reagan a pleading look. "I'm not embarrassed to be seen with you Rea, I promise. But I still need some time to adjust to what happened last night."

"You're the one who wanted to have sex," Reagan pointed out.

Allison flushed. Why did that word sound so abrasive to her sensibilities? "I know I did," she admitted, unfastening her seatbelt as well. "Just please. Give me some time."

Reagan mumbled something under her breath and exited the car. Allison scrambled after her. "Rea, wait."

Reagan ignored her and continued stomping towards where their group had collected in a line waiting for the hayride. She only stopped when Allison successfully snagged her by the elbow.

"You've giving me whiplash."

Allison immediately dropped her hold. "I'm sorry. I didn't mean to grab you so hard."

Reagan shook her head. "I mean this Hot-and-Cold, Stop-and-Go attitude, Allie."

Allison worried her bottom lip. "Can we just enjoy the day? We don't get to see each other too often."

Reagan released a heaving sigh and ran her fingers through her loose hair. "Fine," she conceded. "We can put this sleeping-together-thing on the backburner." She leveled her eyes on Allison. "But we *are* going to talk about this, Hoge. You can't run away from it forever."

Allison swallowed hard and nodded. "I know."

+++++

"Good afternoon, everybody," came the cheerful voice over a scratchy P.A. system. "I'm Farmer Jeff," the man behind the wheel of the green tractor introduced himself, "and welcome to Harvest Acres. In just a little bit we'll be going deeper into the farm, past the apple orchard and into the pumpkin patches. Once we get there," he continued, "I'll stop the tractor and y'all can go pick your own pumpkins. So for now, just sit back and enjoy the ride."

The P.A. cut off and the engine of the John Deer tractor revved loudly. The speakers crackled before a muffled John Denver song blared out of them. Farmer Jeff fiddled with the controls to the giant tractor. The attached trailer lurched forward, and the group inside banged into each other. Finally, the farmer manipulated the tractor into the right gear and slowly inched the farm vehicle forward.

"This is fun," Reagan observed as they bounced along the dirt pathway. The small group cruised slowly past a large red barn and turned down a narrower road through an orchard of apple trees.

Allison shifted uncomfortably in the trailer. "I've got hay poking my ass," she complained. Rather than traditional seats in the tractor-trailer, the group sat on stiff bales lined up like benches. She wiggled to find a comfortable spot.

Reagan laughed. "I'm sorry. I'd offer to switch seats, but my butt is probably getting it just as bad as yours."

Allison glanced quickly at the people sitting near them. Everyone else in their group looked preoccupied with the rustic surroundings, and the loud roar of the tractor pulling their trailer drowned out their conversation. Allison leaned a little closer to Reagan. "I suppose I could always just sit on your lap."

Reagan felt her face grow hot and she looked away from Allison's achingly beautiful face and pretended to be interested in the hay bale she sat on instead. Allison wasn't playing fair. She was supposed to keep her own affection at bay, but apparently Allison could do whatever she wanted.

When the tractor finally stopped, Reagan waited for the others in their group to descend the small steps that Farmer Jeff had brought out for the riders. When she descended the steps and exited the hay-filled trailer, she looked out into the vast field of pumpkins.

"Wow," she breathed, her voice reverent when Allison walked up beside her. "That's a lot of pumpkins." She had really only ever seen the orange vegetable in small piles in front of grocery stores or in pairs on the front stoops of homes.

Allison smiled warmly and slid her hand into the other girl's. "C'mon, Rea," she grinned. "Let's go find you a pumpkin."

Reagan skimmed her fingertips over the tall stalks of the wild flowers that sprouted amongst the pumpkin. The brittle stems moved like plucking the strings on a harp. "I don't even know where to start."

"What kind of pumpkin do you want?" Allison asked. She and Reagan walked down a tilled aisle of earth, side by side. "Tall and thin? Short and round? Long stem, short stem?"

Reagan blinked and shook her head, looking overwhelmed. "So many questions. It feels like I'm filling out an online dating profile."

Allison frowned. "You have one of those?"

"I, uh, no?" Reagan's voice pitched up. "Not anymore?" She looked a little like a deer in headlights.

Allison crouched down beside a cluster of pumpkins still on the vine. She brushed at a clump of dirt clinging to the side of a small gourd. Reagan stopped to stoop beside her, balancing her weight on the balls of her feet.

Allison didn't know what to say. They were just a handful of hours removed from having slept together. Sex had changed everything. She didn't know what to feel or how to act around Reagan now – not that the past year or so had been easy sailing in the first place. But she recognized that jealous gnawing in the pit of her stomach. She didn't want Reagan dating random people she'd met online. But did that mean she wanted Reagan to date her instead? It was all very terrifying, and she had no one to talk to about it.

"I never got the chance to thank you for last night," Reagan murmured.

Allison looked up with startled eyes. "Um, you're welcome?"

Reagan picked up a small chunk of dry, packed earth. She squeezed it between her fingers and it crumbled apart. She only stopped playing with the dirt when Allison reached out and tucked a lock of her hair behind her ear.

Reagan smiled at the unexpected gesture, and her infectious grin drew Allison's attention to her mouth. As Allison admired Reagan's generous lips, she couldn't help but recall how that same mouth had become so intimately familiar with her body the previous night. She dropped her eyes and refocused on a pumpkin, hoping she wasn't blushing too visibly. "You're beautiful, you know that?"

"You're not so bad yourself, Hoge."

"Way to not take a compliment," Allison countered sourly. She was annoyed. Every time she tried to take a step forward, she felt like Reagan was dismissing her efforts. She didn't know why Reagan couldn't see that this was hard for her; she was doing her best.

"How can you say that after all you did to me in high school?"

Allison swallowed hard. "I have no good excuses for what I did to you back then." She traced lines in the dirt. "All I can say is how sorry I am that it ever happened."

"I think I've made a decision."

At Reagan's words, Allison looked back up. She didn't know to what she was referring, but she worried it had something to do with them.

"I want a giant, round pumpkin with a medium-sized stem."

Allison finally returned Reagan's smile. "Then you shall have one."

Reagan managed to claim one of the largest pumpkins in the field for herself. Its skin was tough and weathered, deep creases decorated its exterior, and a thick stalk stood up from its top. Visitors to the farm could pick whatever they could carry. Allison smirked from her position alongside Reagan. She watched her struggle, nearly breaking into a sweat as she lugged the oversized gourd from the fields to the waiting tractor. Allison had chosen a significantly smaller pumpkin with light yellow spots on its outer shell. "Go big or go home, I suppose," she muttered beneath her breath.

"So, what's next?" Reagan asked as she hefted her large pumpkin onto the back of the trailer.

Allison grabbed her hand to give it a quick squeeze. Her hand felt slightly gritty from the dirt on the pumpkin. "I knew you'd be into this," she smiled.

Reagan's face looked youthful and truly happy. The warm sun shining down bounced off her playful eyes and her long, brunette waves. Allison had an overwhelming urge to lean in and kiss her upturned mouth; but she just squeezed her hand harder instead.

+++++

"Welcome to the Amazing Corn Maze," a teen boy in faded jeans and flannel shirt droned. It was clear that he had already given this same introduction a hundred times that day and was waiting for the end of the workday. "Please do not pick the corn or stray from the paths," he continued, his eyes looking bored as he flicked over the small group of six. "In teams of two, your mission is to find the exit before anyone else. If at any time you find yourself completely lost and need assistance out of the maze, just push this button." He held up a small black box that vaguely resembled the beeper one receives at busy restaurants. "Once you hit the button, someone from our staff will come retrieve you and guide you to the exit. Any questions?" The teen boy barely paused. "Good. When you hear the air horn, the race is on. Have fun," he stated without emotion.

"You guys are *so* dead!" Lucy taunted as the farm employee disappeared. "Mom and I are totally gonna win this!" She set her jaw in a hard look of determination.

"I don't think so," Beth grinned. "Carly and I used to be Girl Scouts. We'll totally find out way out first." She locked arms with her sister.

"I'm making a rule right now," Allison said with a serious face. "No setting rope snares and booby traps in the maze."

An air horn echoed through the air, causing the small group to collectively jump. Lucy squealed and took off running in one direction with her mother chuckling behind. "Not too fast, Lucy," she called.

Reagan grabbed onto Allison's hand and plunged them deep into the corn maze. The stiff stalks loomed tall above the pair. "Let's go, Blondie," she breathed. "We've got an exit to find."

"Whoa," Allison breathed as Reagan dragged her along a well-worn path. "You really want you win."

"Don't you know me at all?" Reagan exclaimed, looking back briefly. "There's no way I'm losing."

Reagan swore loudly when she and Allison came to yet another dead end. "Damn it," she complained, coming to an abrupt stop. "I didn't think this was going to be so hard. Aren't we supposed to be good at this stuff?"

Allison stopped in her tracks a short distance away and raised an eyebrow. "Corn mazes?"

Reagan curled up her lip and shook her head. Her loose brunette locks slightly fluttered. "No, you know – like directional stuff," she clarified. "Don't women have internal compasses or something?"

"I don't know about compasses, but I do know there's something else we seem to be naturally good at." Allison took a step closer, and a glint of surprise and arousal flashed behind Reagan's bright blue eyes. Allison wrapped her arms around Reagan's waist, pulling their bodies closer.

"Th-The maze," Reagan stuttered when she felt Allison's breath burst against her neck. "I-I don't like to lose."

Allison bent slightly and licked the hollow of Reagan's throat. "I thought being with me was prize enough," she rasped into her fragrant skin.

A sharp gasp filled her ears. It took Allison a second to register what exactly had made that noise. She'd been too busy working her mouth from Reagan's neck to her very sensitive earlobes. The gasp wasn't her. And it hadn't come from Reagan. So who..."*Oh God!*" Allison's eyes flipped wide open. She instinctively placed her palms flat against Reagan's chest and pushed hard, forcing her to stumble away.

"A-Allie?" Carly's voice sounded unsteady.

"Carly! Beth!" Allison exclaimed. Her two friends stood awkwardly in the middle of the cornrow, having found their way to the same dead end. "We were just..." She scrambled to come up for an excuse why she had been holding Reagan close and sucking on her ear lobe. "Bugs!" she blurted out suddenly. "I-I thought Reagan had a tick...in...in her ear. And I was, uhm...I was just, uh..."

Beth gave her friend soft smile. "Sucking the venom out?" she offered.

Carly turned and gave Beth a strange look. "Ticks are poisonous?"

Beth took her sister's hand in her own and patted her arm. "C'mon, Sis," she murmured. "I think the exit's this way."

Carly stood still momentarily, her eyes continuing to dart between Allison and Reagan who now stood a few awkward feet from each other. Allison's face had turned a deep red color and Reagan's eyes flashed with a silent anger. "Oh, uh, okay," she bumbled as she allowed Beth to lead her in a new direction.

Allison's hands went to her face when her two friends wandered away. "Oh God."

"What. Was. That?" Reagan enunciated each word around clenched teeth. Her body seemed to twitch as if she couldn't decide between running away in embarrassment or staying to fight.

"I'm so sorry, Reagan." Allison peeked between her fingers. "I-I was surprised, that's all," she muttered miserably, dropping her hands to her sides. "It just came out."

Reagan's eyes closed and she turned her head away. The muscles in her jaw twitched. "Would it *really* be that bad if your friends knew about us?" She opened her eyes again. "I mean, if there is even an 'us' to tell about?"

Allison swallowed hard. "I know them…they can't help but gossip. And if my parents found out, I'd be disinherited. Totally cut off. They pay for my school, my rent, my everything. Is that what you want for me?"

Reagan's shoulder's slumped. "No, Allie. I just want you to be happy."

Allison cringed when Reagan's arm lashed out at her suddenly. She didn't know why she thought she was going to hit her. Maybe because she knew she deserved getting smacked. But rather than the blow landing, Reagan merely snatched the black box from Allison's hands.

Reagan stared with disbelief. Allison's recoil had not gone unnoticed. "You thought I was going to…" She shook her head bitterly and sucked in a deep breath. "Never mind," she stated, the pain thick in her wavering voice. "Let's just forget the whole thing. It's not worth it."

Reagan pressed the button on the box and dropped her head in defeat.

+++++

The ride back to town had been quiet. Although Allison and Reagan had once again shared the backseat of the SUV, they ignored each other, staring out their respective sides of the vehicle's back windows. Lucy's bubbly voice, however, had more than made up for the tense silence that blanketed the backseat.

When the vehicle pulled into the driveway of the Hoge's home, Reagan scrambled out of the backseat before Allison's mother had even turned off the engine. "Reagan," Jill called out the open window as she saw her scamper out the backseat. "Is everything okay, dear?"

Reagan bit her bottom lip and her eyes flickered to the backseat where Allison sat. She looked stonily out the back window, away from her. "Yes, Mrs. Hoge," she claimed. "I'm just eager to see my Dad. I'm supposed to be home visiting him, after all."

Lucy poked her head around her mom. "But we haven't even carved the pumpkins," she pointed out. "And then we're gonna bake the seeds!"

Reagan's hands went to the back pockets of her jeans, and she looked away from Lucy's pleading gaze. "Sorry, you guys," she mumbled uncomfortably. "But I really have to go. Go ahead and carve my pumpkin for me." She flashed Mrs. Hoge a brilliant, yet brief smile. "Thank you so much for inviting me to come along with your family today. It was very kind."

Before anyone could protest further, Reagan turned on her heels and stalked away in the direction of her parked car.

Lucy immediately turned in the front passenger seat to glare at her older sister. "What did you do *now*, Allie?" she accused.

Allison remained silent and ignored her sister. She bit her bottom lip and continued to stare out her window at nothing in particular. Her eyes filled with tears until the trees outside became just blurry green blobs.

+++++

CHAPTER FIFTEEN

Allison looked over the contents of the menu at the deli even though she wasn't hungry. It gave her something to do so she wasn't continually checking her phone for the time or for missed calls or texts from Reagan. But just like the last time Allison had messed up, Reagan was ignoring her. If they never came back to their hometown, maybe she wouldn't keep doing this. The major difference this time, however, Allison hadn't denied Reagan's existence. This time, she'd denied her own emotions and feelings for her. And of the two offenses, the latter felt infinitely worse.

"We apparently have some serious catching up," Beth said as she unceremoniously sat down in the chair across from her. "How long have you and Murphy been sleeping together?"

Allison felt her face flush. Her eyes darted nervously around the sandwich shop to see if anyone had overheard Beth's outburst. "Do you have to put it like that?" she asked, dropping her tone.

"It's the only way I'll get an answer out of you, Hoge," Beth chuckled.

Allison took a deep breath. This was it. This was her moment to stop being a coward. "Reagan and I had sex."

Beth rolled her eyes. "Well, duh. I gathered as much from that little show in the corn maze. I figured if you all hadn't had sex yet, it was just a matter of time."

"I just need to know that you're not going to tell anyone," Allison said, locking eyes with her old friend. "Not yet, at least. I need some time to figure this thing out."

175

"You mean if you want a relationship with Reagan Murphy."

"Yeah, I guess so." Allison picked at a napkin. "But other things to."

"Like if you're gay?"

Allison looked up from the table. She met Beth's concerned gaze and nodded.

"Well, don't worry about Carly. She actually believed your lame tick story." Beth chuckled. "She's pulled out all her winter scarves and won't leave the house without her neck covered up."

"And Vanessa?"

"Vanessa's a bitch," Beth spat out. "And this...whatever *this* is, isn't any of her business."

"Why are you being so cool?"

"I'm not a Neanderthal," Beth defended herself. "And I have a gay cousin," she revealed. "He tried to commit suicide when the family came down hard on him," she said in a quiet voice. She looked up, her eyes unusually fierce. "I love you like a sister, Allie. I don't want to see that happen to you."

"I appreciate your concern," Allison said genuinely, "but I'm not gay. At least, I don't think I am." She sighed heavily. "I don't know anymore."

Beth's mouth quirked. "You just like having sex with girls?"

"Not *girls*," Allison said in a lowered voice. She looked around, nervously. Why did everyone insist on having these conversations with her so loudly and in public?

"So just sex with Reagan Murphy?"

Allison covered her face with her hands and peeked through her fingers. "Oh, God," she groaned. "I know, I know. What am I thinking?"

Beth shrugged. "I always thought she was nice." She looked thoughtful. "A little weird, a little quiet, but nice."

"She *is* nice," Allison confirmed, dropping her hands from her face. "Almost *too* nice. Half the time we spend together I can't believe she could ever forgive me for what a bitch I was in high school."

"And the other half you're making out?" Beth guessed with a broad grin.

Allison dropped her eyes to the table and cleared her throat uncomfortably.

Beth laughed. "Girl, it's okay. I really don't need to know those kinds of details," she teased. "Do you guys ever talk about high school?"

Allison looked up and shook her head. "Kind of. I mean I've apologized to her about a billion times for it. But no matter how many times I apologize, I always seem to do something else to mess things up between us."

Beth nodded. "I'm certainly not an expert in relationships, let alone one with another girl," she noted, "but I think you have some serious groveling to do in your immediate future."

Allison raised a questioning eyebrow.

"Apologizing to Reagan for what happened in the corn maze?" Beth clarified with a mischievous smile.

Allison's eyebrow dropped back in place. "Oh shit."

+++++

Allison Hoge didn't apologize. Allison Hoge didn't grovel. And she most certainly didn't beg for forgiveness. She felt like a fool. That's why, when she found herself standing on the front porch of Reagan's father's house, holding a bouquet of flowers, she had no idea what to do next. This wasn't her life. This was a movie – a *mockery* of what she'd become.

"I suppose I should knock on the door," she mumbled. She shook her head. "Great. And now I'm talking to myself."

She lifted a lightly clenched fist and rapped her knuckles against the front door. Taking a single step backwards, she waited. Like a fool.

Within seconds, the front door swung open. Allison's father stood in the doorway. "I was wondering how long you were going to stand out there," he said in his deep voice.

"Mr. Murphy," Allison tensely greeted.

"Allison," the man stiffly replied.

"I'm not sure what Reagan told you..."

"My daughter and I have no secrets from each other," the man said curtly.

Allison fought against the urge to run. She could do this. She could handle this. She straightened her shoulders.

"She might be living in the biggest city in the country and be

177

independent and all that, but she'll always be my little girl. Her happiness is my priority."

"I just want to make her happy, too."

Mr. Murphy regarded the girl on his front stoop. It was no secret that Allison Hoge had bullied his daughter relentlessly throughout high school. He honestly couldn't pretend to understand why Reagan had so eagerly entered into a friendship with her, let alone why she would want to pursue a romantic relationship. But that wasn't his decision. He trusted his daughter.

"She's upstairs in her room. For you sake, I hope you have a brilliant apology prepared."

Allison climbed the stairs slowly, one at a time. She couldn't help but feel like she was being sent to a firing squad. Reagan's father's home was just as she remembered it. It even smelled the same. It was comforting and familiar, but it also brought back residual guilt that it had been so long since she'd been within these four walls.

The door to Reagan's childhood bedroom was closed and Allison found herself standing like a fool, once again. She tentatively knocked.

"I told you before. I'm not hungry," came Reagan's voice.

"Well that's good. Because I didn't bring any food with me." Allison waited, her body tense.

She heard the creak of a mattress and bare feet on hardwood floor. The door flung open.

"And I told *you* I wouldn't let you make me feel insignificant again," Reagan said flatly. She was physically exhausted from not getting much sleep the night before and emotionally drained from Allison's waffling.

Allison felt panicky. "I don't like being ambushed," she defended herself. "And I know I can't blame Beth and Carly for seeing us. It was my fault; I shouldn't have been...doing *that* to you when I knew we could have gotten caught." She worried her bottom lip. "But maybe a part of me *wanted* to get caught."

"Why?"

"Because then I wouldn't have to actually say the words."

"That you had sex with Reagan Murphy?" Reagan wrinkled her nose and frowned.

"No. That I think I'm gay." Allison was quiet a moment, letting the words settle in the air. There. She'd said it. But what did it mean? "Believe me when I say I'm not embarrassed by you. I don't know how to get that through your thick skull."

"Stop shoving me away like I have cooties. That might be a good start," Reagan grumbled.

"So does that mean I'm forgiven?"

Reagan took a step backward into her room. "It's a start."

Allison walked into the bedroom and thrust the bouquet of flowers under Reagan's nose.

Reagan's lips twisted and she took the flowers. "For future reference, I don't really like flowers."

"What girl doesn't like flowers?" Allison asked incredulously.

Reagan shrugged. "I like them growing in the ground – not picked and ready to die in a few days."

Allison pinched at the bridge of her nose. "You are unbelievable," she muttered.

Reagan tossed the bouquet onto her vanity. "Rumor has it."

Allison rested her hands on Reagan's hips. "I can't stop thinking about last night. I didn't know I could enjoy something so much." Her hands tightened on Reagan's hips. She nuzzled her nose against the column of her neck. She pressed her lips against the sensitive skin, and when she began to lightly suck, Reagan made a small noise in the back of her throat. Allison licked the flat of her tongue against the small pink mark she had made.

Reagan felt herself panting, but she somehow managed to pull away. "You have to stop."

Allison's features scrunched together. "Do you not like it?"

"I like it just fine," Reagan breathed out shakily. "Maybe a little *too* much."

"It's my body, isn't it?" Allison worried out loud. "I know I'm not as in as good of shape as I was in high school," she frowned. "You must think I'm disgusting."

"Don't be ridiculous," Reagan quickly corrected. "Your body is amazing. I mean, your abs…" She mentally pictured herself licking along her strong stomach, the muscles twitching and flexing under her tongue. She shook herself. "Your body is so hot, it should be illegal."

Reagan's compliments did nothing to appease Allison. The frown stayed on her lips. "Well, what's the problem then?" she demanded.

"Ever heard the phrase no one's going to buy the cow if you're giving away the milk for free?"

Allison frowned deeper and nodded.

"I care about you, and yes, I'm really attracted to you," Reagan said. Her face felt warm and she hugged herself. "But I don't know what your intentions are. Do you want to be fuck buddies or do you want something more?"

Allison winced at her coarse language. She didn't know if she'd ever heard Reagan swear like that before. The word sounded ugly coming from her mouth. "More like what?"

Reagan put her hands on her hips. "Do you want to date me, Allison Hoge?" she asked impatiently.

"I –uh – is that something *you'd* want?"

Reagan's face was unreadable. "That's not what I asked."

Allison rubbed at her face with frustration. "You're really not going to go easy on me, are you?" she grunted.

Reagan's features softened. "I just want us to be on the same page. We keep hinting at what's happening – where this thing is headed – but neither of us has made the plunge yet. That has to stop. We *have* to make a decision."

"I've never, you know, dated a *girl* before," Allison admitted. "I'm not even sure I'd know how to do that."

"You hadn't had sex with a girl before last night," Reagan pointed out. "And that seemed to work out fine."

Allison ducked her head. "I-I have a lot of fun with you," she admitted. "And not just the sex stuff either; although that was amazing, too."

"I have fun with you, too," Reagan agreed. "And I have nothing against us continuing to have fun together, but I'd like to figure out what this is between us, you know?"

Allison licked her lips. "I know. And, don't take this the wrong way, but can I sleep on it before I give you an answer? This is…a big deal for me."

Reagan nodded, but she couldn't deny she felt a little disappointed that Allison didn't automatically know what she wanted.

"Will you lay down with me?" Allison asked, wringing her hands. "No funny business, I promise."

Reagan was surprised. When Allison had said she needed to sleep on it, she hadn't imagined she wanted to "sleep on it" in *her* bed. She nodded silently and the two moved to lay on the bed on top of the covers.

Allison glanced at the closed bedroom door. "Should we lock your door?"

Reagan quirked an eyebrow. "Why? Is my dad going to walk in on something he shouldn't?"

Allison dropped her gaze. "N-no," she stammered. "Did you really tell him about last night?"

"Not in graphic detail," Reagan scoffed. "We're not *that* close. But yes, I did tell him about you and me."

Allison blinked once. "Oh. And how did he react?"

"He was a little confused at first, I think." Reagan paused and looked wistful before continuing. "He obviously knows what our relationship was like in high school. So it took him some time to wrap his head around the idea that my high school tormenter was now my lover."

"Oh my God," Allison groaned. "Don't *ever* say that word again."

Reagan giggled. "Lover?"

"Seriously." Allison rolled her eyes. "Are you a Harlequin romance novel?"

"Well as soon as you admit you want to date me, I'll replace it with girlfriend. Do you like that better?"

Allison chewed on her lower lip. "I might. I don't know." She played with Reagan's fingers and they remained silent for a comfortable moment.

"I had lunch with Beth today. I told her about you. About us."

Reagan looked surprised. "You did? What did you tell her?"

"I admit I met up with her at first to make sure she knew how important discretion is. If my parents found out…"

"I know," Reagan sighed, cutting her off. "You don't have to explain it to me again. I get it."

Allison examined the other girl's face. "But I realized something," she said softly. "After talking to Beth I realized how *relieved* I was that somebody knew; that I didn't have to keep this a secret anymore." She grabbed Reagan's hands and brought her knuckles to her lips. "You're the best thing that's happened to me in a very long time. And I'm *so* sorry I'm not brave enough to shout it from the mountaintops. You deserve so much better than me."

"It's not like I'm an expert at this either," Reagan noted. "I've never thought about having to, I don't know, Come Out. I'm just lucky that I have a dad who loves me unconditionally. Not that *your* parents don't love you," she hastily self-corrected when she saw Allison's frown.

"No. You're right. My parents, especially my dad, love the *idea* of me. Ivy League school. Top of the pyramid." She sighed deeply. "I just hope Lucy doesn't go through the same pressure that I felt when I was her age."

"You seemed to turn out alright," Reagan observed, "even with all that pressure."

Allison snorted. "That's highly debatable. "

"At least you got good genes out of the deal."

"You don't give yourself enough credit, Rea." Allison brushed her fingers through Reagan's thick, dark hair. "You're so beautiful," she breathed reverently.

Reagan averted her eyes.

"Don't."

Reagan flicked her eyes back to Allison's face. "Don't what?"

Hazel eyes stared intensely back at her. "Don't doubt what I say is true," Allison said fiercely.

+++++

Reagan rolled over in bed and threw out an arm, expecting to find Allison beside her. But she found only an empty space, however, and the sheets were cool to the touch. She sat up in bed and rubbed at her eyes. She pulled her hands away from her face when she heard her bedroom door click open. "Where did you go?" she asked in a sleep-confused voice.

Allison stood in the doorway. "I took a shower. I used your things," she said, fidgeting. "I hope you don't mind."

Reagan allowed her eyes to focus on the woman in the doorway of her bedroom. Unlike her own sleep-disheveled appearance, Allison looked meticulous and ready for the day despite wearing the clothes she'd worn the previous night. Her hair was clean and carefully flat-ironed.

She rubbed at her eyes again. "Why are you dressed?" she croaked. "I thought we could have a lazy day today."

Allison's features were unreadable, but she kept rubbing the tip of her thumb over her pointer finger, a nervous habit she'd had since childhood.

Reagan sat up straighter in bed. Something was off. "What is it?" Her chest tightened with dread. "What's wrong?"

"I can't do this, Reagan."

"Do what? Have a lazy day? We're on vacation."

Allison dropped her hands at her sides and began clenching and unclenching her fists. "I can't be with you."

"When did you come to this decision? Before or after using my conditioner? Cause really, I'm not particularly attached to that brand if you don't like it."

"I'd still like for us to be friends," Allison said quietly. She dropped her head and her blonde hair cascaded in front of her face.

"You're being serious right now, aren't you?" Reagan grabbed onto her fitted sheet to keep from launching out of bed.

Allison tilted her head back up. Reagan noticed her eyes for the first time; they were bloodshot and red rimmed as though she'd been crying for a while. "I told you before. I can't be gay." She choked on the words. "My father, my family, would disown me."

"What changed in a single night, Allie?" Reagan implored.

Allison shook her head from side to side. She shut her eyes tight and a few tears squeezed out. "It was just a silly dream to think things could be different – that *I* could be different." She brushed her fingers under her eyes and swept away the wetness. "I'm sorry, Reagan. I'm just not ready for this. I'm not ready to be gay; I'm not ready to be anyone's girlfriend."

"I don't accept this," Reagan said defiantly. She straightened her back.

Allison's eyes narrowed. Despite the situation, she was still Allison Hoge. And *no one* challenged her decisions once she had made up her mind. "You have no choice," she said icily. She spun on her heels and immediately fled down the stairs.

Reagan remained rigid in bed until she heard the front door open and close.

+++++

CHAPTER SIXTEEN

Allison sat at the window seat in the living room of her rented house. Outside, a light snow had begun to fall – the first of the early winter season. The flakes were heavy and oversized and would no doubt result in some serious accumulation overnight if it continued. She pulled her knit cardigan tighter. The windows were old and drafty and she could feel the residual chill from outside every time the wind blew. There were much warmer places to sit in the house, but the window seat was one of her favorite spots, even with the weather.

She blew across the top of her ceramic mug, cooling down the hot tea she'd just poured herself. In a pile next to her was the day's mail. It was mostly fliers and junk mail, but amongst the trash that would soon be in the recycle bin was a legal-sized envelope made of heavy paper stock. Allison had immediately recognized the logo on the return address.

She'd held her breath as she opened the cream-colored envelope. She hadn't needed to read the entire letter. She just needed to read the opening 5 words: *"We are pleased to accept..."*

Getting her undergraduate degree from Brown, combined with her high standardized test scores and 4.0 GPA had all but guaranteed her acceptance into the most elite graduate programs around the country. But for the first time since she'd made the decision to pursue graduate school, the prospect of going to school on the West Coast was no longer an uncomplicated decision.

She fingered the acceptance letter from Stanford and inspected the careful black font that promised full tuition and a generous stipend for living expenses over the course of her graduate career. Allison sighed and let the letter slip from her fingers. Now she all she had to do was count down the days until graduation when she could pick up and move someplace else and start all over again. Again.

Since the drama that had occurred over Fall break, she'd been bombarded with phone calls, text messages, and emails from Reagan. And since that day when she'd woken up in Reagan's childhood bedroom, she'd ignored them.

She had promised they could still be friends, and even though she'd said the words, she didn't really believe it. She couldn't just be friends with Reagan Murphy. It was just a matter of time before Reagan gave up on this charade and moved on. She knew she was being selfish, but how could she be happy seeing Reagan move on and finding happiness with someone who wasn't herself?

Her phone jangled with the text message sound she'd assigned to Reagan's number and hadn't bothered to change back. She picked up her phone and glanced at the screen. *"Where are you?"* She set her phone back beside her on the window seat without responding. She picked up the weekend paper and turned to the crossword puzzle.

She chewed on the end of her pen. 1 Across. "Ride up and Down."

Her phone buzzed again.

"Are you home?"

Allison made a disgruntled noise and tossed her paper to the side. She typed off a response. *"Why?"*

She was acutely aware that this was the first time she'd responded back to any of Reagan's attempts to contact her since Fall break.

"Because I'm at your front door."

Allison leapt to her feet and raced to the front entrance. Without bothering looking out the peephole, she threw the door open. There, with a duffle bag in one hand, stood Reagan Murphy, slightly damp from the snow. Allison clenched the edge of the wooden door, but said nothing.

Reagan stamped her foot impatiently. "I came all the way here; the least you can do is invite me in."

Allison took a step back and opened the door perceptibly wider.

Not waiting for an invitation, Reagan brushed past Allison and into the front foyer. She dropped her duffle bag onto the floor.

Allison stared down at the bag. "You brought clothes?"

"Well I'm not going to sleep in this," Reagan huffed. "And I figured under the circumstances, you'd feel uncomfortable if I slept naked."

"You expect to sleep over?" Allison arched an eyebrow.

Reagan pressed her lips together. "I expect you to be polite, Allison. You'd do that much for an acquaintance from high school, wouldn't you?"

Allison's shoulders slumped forward in defeat. "Why are you doing this to me?"

"Because I care about you. And I deserve to know why you're doing this to us."

Allison's head snapped up. "There is no *us*," she said with heat. "I've told you," she practically growled. "I can't do this anymore with you."

Reagan tried to remain calm. She'd been expecting this – this denial, anger, and stubbornness. But she was stubborn too, and she was angry. "I know," she snapped back bitterly. "You're not gay. Say it enough and maybe one day you'll have yourself convinced."

Allison's body seemed to jump forward on its own accord until she was practically nose-to-nose with Reagan. "How *dare you* presume to think you know anything about me or my situation," she seethed.

"You're in so much denial, you don't even know yourself!" Reagan hollered back.

"I know enough about myself to know that I don't want *you*."

Reagan's face immediately crumbled. "I'm sorry," she mumbled. "I thought…I shouldn't have come." She stiffly bent and retrieved her bag from the floor.

"Reagan," Allison sighed tiredly. She rubbed at her face with both hands. "Don't do this."

Ignoring Allison's words, Reagan tilted her chin up, and like a wound-up toy soldier, marched back outside.

Allison stood in the doorway. "Reagan," she called out after the other girl in an even, emotionless tone.

Reagan remained closed lipped and continued back in the direction of the train station.

"Reagan!" Allison hissed, not wanting to draw attention to them, and still unwilling to move from the front porch. Reagan continued walking away, not hearing or choosing to ignore her.

"Reagan!" Allison finally yelled. "God damn it," she cursed. She took off at a full sprint, barefoot and in the snow. "Reagan!" she called again.

When she caught up, she grabbed Reagan's elbow to stop her. She spun her around to face her. "Why do you have to be so stubborn?" she growled.

The short sprint had her blood pumping and her normally alabaster skin was slightly flushed. Reagan hated how attracted she was to this woman who had done nothing but reject her since they'd renewed a tenuous friendship.

"Are you the kettle or the pot?" Reagan said haughtily.

"In case you didn't notice, it's *snowing*."

"Do I look like I care about the weather report?" Reagan snarled, getting uncharacteristically angry. She felt like such a fool for traveling all this way only to be rejected once again.

"Come back to the house," Allison implored. "It's ridiculous to try to have a conversation out here."

Reagan looked skeptical. "Are we *really* going to talk? Or are you going to get uncomfortable and shut down and ignore me the rest of the night?"

"We'll talk. I promise." Allison linked their hands together and intertwined her fingers with Reagan's. "And I'll make hot tea and we can change into dry clothes."

Reagan looked down at their enjoined hands. Her heart ached inside her chest at how well they seemed to fit together. "Fine."

+++++

Reagan sat as quietly and as still as her body could handle. Allison sat across from her at the small kitchen table with her head in her hands. Reagan observed the elegant, pale fingers press into her hairline. She looked down at her own hands and absently ran her index finger back and forth along the beveled edge of the wooden table. She looked back up when she heard Allison push out a sharp breath from her lungs.

"I may have misled you about something."

Reagan pressed her lips together, but said nothing.

Allison stared at Reagan with hazel eyes red around the edges. It seemed to Reagan that she had aged before her eyes. "You're not the first girl I ever kissed."

Reagan's eyes widened, but she said nothing, sensing that Allison was gearing up for a long, important revelation.

Allison lightly ran the tip of her finger along the rim of her ceramic mug. "It was the summer before our junior year of high school," she started. "I was at team cheerleading camp, and there was this girl on another school's squad."

"Cheerleading camp?" Reagan interrupted. "This sounds like a story from *Esquire* or *Playboy.*"

Allison glared across the kitchen table. "Do you want to hear this story or not, Murphy?" she snapped.

"I'm sorry. Continue."

Allison sighed and her shoulders slumped forward. "Her name was Daria Grey."

"Pretty."

Allison shot Reagan another warning glance. Reagan held up her hands in retreat and mouthed her apology.

"Anyway, I guess we got close while we were at camp. And one night, she kissed me." She swallowed hard. "And I kissed her back."

"Girls kiss their girl friends at that age," Reagan said dismissively. "It's all about exploring and experimentation when you're that young."

"Did *you* kiss any girls in high school?" Allison countered.

"Well, no…"

"When camp was over," Allison continued, ignoring Reagan's commentary, "we wrote letters back and forth for a good part of the school year." She took a deep breath. "And everything was fine until my dad found her letters in the shoebox I kept under my bed."

"Why would he care if you had a pen pal?"

Allison flushed and grimaced. "They were, uh, pretty *intimate* letters."

"O-oh," Reagan said, catching on.

"He immediately tore them up and burned them in the fireplace, and told me I was never to have any kind of contact with her again. He and I never talked about it afterwards, and I'm not sure if he told my mom about it." Allison's voice broke. "It was like it never even happened." She paused, collected herself and brushed at her eyes with the back of her hand. "Around that time I started to date Chad, and then everything seemed forgiven." She bit her lower lip. "But then one of his *spies* saw us – they saw you and me together. He called the night you stayed over at my parents house, when we…."

"Spent the night together?" Reagan supplied for her. She felt her lips tilt in a half smile. She thought it endearing, but a little strange that Allison still couldn't say the words out loud.

Allison swallowed hard and nodded. "He called during the movie. Someone told him they'd seen us holding hands or something at the coffee shop. He told me," she took a sharp breath, "that I wasn't to spend time with you anymore."

"You're not a little girl anymore, Allie," Reagan tried gently. "He can't dictate who you spend time with."

"But that's the thing…he *can,*" Allison insisted. "He pays for my tuition, my rent, all my bills. And until I'm financially independent, he has control over me."

"So why not become financially independent?"

Allison rolled her eyes and sighed. "You make it sound so simple."

"It could be simple."

"I'm so sorry, Reagan." Allison's bottom lip trembled. "I wish things could be different."

"You've really made up your mind about this, haven't you?" Reagan looked down at her hands.

"I don't want you to hate me."

"I could never hate you, Allie. I…" Reagan stopped and swallowed.

Allison looked down at her lap and picked at the fabric of her grey yoga pants. "Do you still want to stay the night?" She sounded defeated. Far from the girl Reagan had known in high school, Allison Hoge was vulnerable and broken. It made her heart ache to see her like this. But she didn't know how to fix her. She could only be patient and empathetic, a talent she didn't think she possessed. She thought about going back outside and divorcing herself from this uncomfortable moment. But she wasn't a runner. She wasn't going to abandon Allison just moments after revealing this.

Outside, the weather had turned from a light snow to a thundering rainstorm. A violent gust of wind rattled the old windowpanes in the drafty kitchen, and an echo of thunder rumbled in the distance. She flicked her gaze toward the kitchen window. Raindrops had accumulated on the glass pane, distorting the view of Allison and her roommates' backyard. "I think the weather's getting worse," she said in a quiet voice.

"Then you should stay," Allison said in an equally soft tone. "My mother would be disappointed in my manners if I sent you out into this weather."

A strange smile passed Reagan's lips. "You and your mom are awfully concerned about the weather and me."

Allison said nothing in reply. Instead, she stood in a single, graceful motion that startled Reagan, and removed her teacup from the table. She set the cup, still full of liquid, into the kitchen sink. She rubbed at her face and sighed. "Are you coming to bed?" she asked with her back still turned to Reagan.

She heard the unmistakable noise of a kitchen chair scraping against the tile floor. Reagan's ballet flats padded lightly, her steps delicate and purposeful. "Are you tired?" Reagan asked.

Allison turned and her breath caught in her throat. She hadn't expected to find Reagan standing so close. She also hadn't expected the sadness in Reagan's bright blue eyes. "Exhausted."

+++++

Reagan stared up at the ceiling fan that slowly rotated above Allison's bed. In the adjacent bathroom she could hear the sounds of water turning on and off as Allison got ready for sleep. She'd tried to contain her disappointment when Allison had scooped up her pajamas and promptly marched to the bathroom to change. It wasn't that she wanted to ogle Allison's naked body; but the fact that Allison was hiding herself didn't bode well. But at least for now, Allison hadn't retreated to the living room couch.

She looked away from the lazy ceiling fan when she heard the bathroom door creak open. Allison teetered uncertainly in the doorway. Reagan sat up slightly on her elbows in bed. "Which side do you want?"

Allison looked away. "The left, I guess."

Reagan shifted beneath the blankets to make room and pulled back the top layer. She frowned when she sensed Allison's hesitance. "It's just sleep, Allie."

Allison visibly swallowed and nodded curtly. She took a deep breath as though summoning her resolve and finally slid into bed next to Reagan.

Reagan rolled onto her side and grabbed Allison's arm to drape it over her waist. "Is this okay?"

Allison breathed out through her nose. "Yeah." The heat radiating from Reagan's body was driving her crazy. Her scent lightly perfumed the air, but Allison felt like she was drowning. There was no way she was going to be able to sleep spooning her like this. "Why is this so hard, Rea?" her voice sounded pained. "Why can't I just lay next to you without wanting to devour you?"

Reagan whimpered in agreement; she pushed her backside flush against Allison.

"Reagan," Allison growled in warning.

"We don't have to do anything," Reagan said. "We can just sleep." The fingers holding onto her hipbones stiffened and dug in. She could feel Allison's short fingernails bite against her flesh.

Allison silently cursed. Reagan wasn't even wearing anything provocative to warrant these feelings – or at least not conventionally so. How anyone could look so temping in a matching flannel pajama set was beyond her. But maybe because the sleepwear made her look so innocent and so unassuming was precisely the reason she felt the urge to corrupt her.

"It doesn't count if our clothes stay on, right?" she asked thickly.

"What?"

"If our clothes stay on, it doesn't count?" Allison seemed to be pleading with her. Without Reagan looking directly at her, she felt a little braver.

Reagan arched her backside against Allison again in a wordless answer.

Allison's breath tickled the fine hairs at the base of Reagan's neck.

"Please, Allie," Reagan pled. "Don't tease me. I can't take it."

A surge of intoxicating power overcame Allison. Experience told her that she craved this, to see Reagan writhing and whimpering because of her. Perhaps it was just one of the myriad reasons she had enjoyed tormenting her in high school. But this – this was infinitely better.

She palmed Reagan's pert, braless breasts over her pajamas. Even through the thick flannel material, she could feel her nipples pebble beneath her ministrations. Allison slid her hand down the front of Reagan's pajama pants and beneath the elastic band of her underwear. Her fingers traveled past tightly cropped and groomed curls and through warm, slippery wetness. With her ring and pointer finger, she delicately separated Reagan's lips and ran her middle finger up the length of her smooth slit.

Reagan breathed out harshly and bit down on her lower lip to keep from crying out and alerting Allison's roommates. She hadn't seen them, but she assumed they were in their respective bedrooms. They really needed to stop doing these things with parents and roommates just in the next room.

"I want to taste you," Allison husked. "I want to suck on you." She licked along the outer shell of Reagan's ear.

Reagan whimpered again, uselessly pressing her back against Allison's front. She desperately wanted to turn around and face her, but worried Allison would stop touching her if she did.

Allison's middle finger ghosted along her outer lips and flirted with her inner folds. Reagan could feel herself getting wetter with every pass and dip. But then the hand shoved inside her pajama pants abruptly disappeared.

Allison rolled onto her back. "I'm sorry." She pulled a twisted cotton sheet to cover her even though she was still wearing her clothes. "This can't happen."

Reagan stared up at the ceiling unblinking. "I know," she said, still a little breathless. The ache between her thighs wasn't going away even though Allison's hand had.

Allison rolled onto her side so she could look at Reagan. "I'm not saying I regret having sex with you," she clarified. "But I can't do that again. It's not fair to you if I can't do this 100%."

"We don't have to be Out and Proud," Reagan said. "I don't need you to hold my hand in public."

Allison shook her head. Salty tears stung her eyes and clung to heavy eyelashes. "Don't sell yourself short," she rasped. "You deserve more than I can give you."

"But it wouldn't always have to be like this," Reagan stubbornly declared. "When you graduate and you don't need your dad's money anymore, things will be different."

"You shouldn't have to wait for me, Reagan," Allison said with heat, angry with herself, angry with Reagan. "I'm too much of a coward," she spat out. "I don't know if I'd ever be able to do this with you."

"And why do you get to make decisions for me?"

Allison growled in frustration. "This isn't up for debate," she snapped. "It's just not going to work."

Reagan opened her mouth to once again protest, but her words were cut off by Allison.

"Do you want to stay friends?"

"Of course," Reagan said in a far more controlled tone.

Allison grabbed onto Reagan's hands and brought her knuckles to her lips. Her own hands smelled like Reagan's arousal. "Then please don't demand something I'm just not capable of doing. If you can't accept that, I can't...I just can't stay friends."

"Not capable of doing *yet*?" Reagan posed hopefully.

Allison's hazel eyes shut tight. "Reagan," she choked out. "Please don't make this harder than it has to be. I need you to be okay with this. I care for you *so much*, and it would kill me if we weren't in each other's lives anymore. I know I can't hide from myself forever. And you've helped push me to accept who I am, but I'm not brave like you."

Reagan sighed deeply. She flexed her fingers and Allison released her hands. "Okay," she conceded. "Friends." She bit down hard on her bottom lip. She felt the top and bottom rows cutting into the vulnerable flesh, but she didn't care. She needed something to distract her so she didn't start to cry. She opted for counting inside her head.

"We should get some sleep," Allison said with a rough sigh. "I'm sure you'll want to get an early start in the morning back to New York."

Reagan rolled onto her side, her back turned to Allison. She felt the other girl moving in bed beside her, getting comfortable. The dark, the silence, the moment, it all felt oppressive.

"I'm sorry you know." Allison's voice cut through the blanketing darkness.

Reagan was surprised she was able to find her voice without it reverberating with emotion. "Let's not, Allie."

Allison clamped her mouth shut tight. Frustrated, angry, and not a little melancholy, she yanked the cotton sheets up to her chin. "Good night."

Reagan stared at the darkness in front of her eyes. She opened and closed her mouth, working the muscles in her throat, but no similar gesture came out. She closed her eyes and willed sleep to come.

+++++

CHAPTER SEVENTEEN

Ashley cruised into the room and threw her school bag onto her bed. "Prez, have you moved from that spot since this morning?"

Reagan groaned and stretched her arms above her head. "I got up once to pee."

"Damn, that's quite an assignment. What class is it for?"

Reagan bit her lip and shut the lid on her laptop. "It's actually not for school. I've been trying to find someone online."

"Oooh," Ashley cooed. "Internet stalking? Sign me up."

"I'm not stalking anyone!" Reagan protested. "I'm trying to find someone from Allison's past."

Ashley gave her roommate and odd look. "Why doesn't Allison look for this person herself?"

Reagan frowned guiltily. "She doesn't know I'm doing this."

"Oh, Prez. You crack me up, you little meddler." Ashley flopped onto her stomach on Reagan's bed. "So who are you trying to find? Allison's biological twin she never knew about? Her estranged Uncle Herman? Her family dog Spot who's been living with another family out on a farm?

"Her first girlfriend."

Ashley sat up. "Whoa. Was not prepared for that. *Girlfriend* girlfriend or friend who's a girl?"

"*Do not* tell anyone I told you this," Reagan warned. Her eyes flashed wildly.

Her roommate held up her hands in surrender. "Who would I tell?"

"I don't know. I'm just paranoid Allison will find out I'm doing this. And if it turns out I can't find this girl, she could get mad at me for nothing."

Ashley quirked an eyebrow. "And what exactly do you think you're doing?"

Reagan looked back at her computer and bit her bottom lip. "Trying to give Allison her second chance."

+++++

Allison tugged at the ends of her blonde hair. "Should I get my hair cut again or should I let it grow out long?"

Reagan wiggled around on her mattress and tilted the lid of her laptop to better appraise her friend. "You're obviously beautiful either way, but I really like it when it's short." Allison would still be stunning completely bald, she silently observed.

"I like it short, too." Allison looked wistful. Cutting her hair had been a kind of rite of passage for her. She'd had it cut just a few weeks before her senior year began. It signified a new start to a new academic year, but it also coincided with the moment when she'd stopped pretending that she wasn't attracted to Reagan.

"I did something," Reagan announced. "And I'm worried if I tell you, you'll be mad at me." She chewed on the corner of her bottom lip.

A million scenarios flashed through Allison's thoughts, most of which had to do with sex, boys, and pregnancy. She deliberately and loudly cleared her throat. "You know you can tell me anything, Rea."

"I found Daria Grey," Reagan blurted out.

Allison was sure she'd misheard her. She pushed the volume key on her laptop. "What?"

"After you told me that story about you and her in high school, I was curious. So I went on Facebook and I found her."

Allison's jaw fell open. "You did *what?*"

"I still don't understand why you don't have Facebook," Reagan deflected. "It would make things so much easier."

"Social media is intrusive," Allison said dismissively. "Get back to the part where you stalked Daria."

"It's not stalking if it's on Facebook," Reagan grimaced. "I messaged her and told her you were a mutual friend. She immediately responded." She took a breath. "She lives in New York. She goes to design school in Brooklyn. And…she wants to see you."

Allison licked her lips. "She wants to see me?" The words fell out quiet and precise.

Reagan stood from her bed and grabbed a post-it note from her desk. When she returned to her laptop and the Skype session, she held up the post-it to her built-in camera. "This is her email address. She's waiting to hear from you."

Allison's eyes ran over the inked address. "Why did you do this?"

"Because everyone deserves a second chance," Reagan said. "I mean, look at you and me." Her grin visibly dimmed. "Maybe you and Daria could have a second chance, too."

Allison wished she was in New York in Reagan's dorm room. She wanted to grab her hand and intertwine their fingers. She knew Reagan had sought out Daria because she thought it would make her happy. She wanted to tell her it wasn't necessary. She wanted to wrap her arms around her and nuzzle her nose into her neck. She wanted to breathe in deeply and swim in the scent that was all her. She wanted to do all this and a million other things, but she decided instead to be polite. "Thank you, Reagan." She glanced at the clock in the corner of her laptop. "Shoot," she said, scrambling to her feet. "I've got a meeting with a professor about my senior project. I have to go."

She rushed around the room and threw a few books and a notebook into her messenger bag. She flashed a wide grin in the direction of her laptop and her friend's face. "I'll text you later, okay?"

Reagan smiled back and nodded. When she ended the Skype session, it felt a little like dying.

+++++

Allison stared at her laptop screen and flexed her fingers. Her email program was open and the email address that Reagan had given her stared back at her. After all this time, Daria Grey still remembered her. After all this time, Daria wanted to reconnect.

She thought back to cheerleading camp so many years ago. Every summer a few weeks before the start of the school year the high school cheerleading squad went to team camp. It wasn't your typical summer camp experience though. For one, there was no actual camping involved. Expecting cheerleaders from around the state to pitch tents in the woods or even live in bunkhouses with primitive bathroom facilities would have been cruel and unusual punishment. Instead, teams were housed at the state university while school was still out for the summer.

Normally teams kept to themselves and didn't engage with girls from other schools. This was the opportunity to work on team togetherness, strategize and choreograph dance and cheer routines, and get guidance from university cheerleaders who functioned as camp counselors. Cheer competitions between squads also took place during the 10-day camp, further building the barriers that kept teams from becoming too friendly with each other.

Daria's squad was from the Detroit area – a private, suburban school with a privileged student body far removed from city life. Students were aggressively recruited from the Metro area for their athletic and academic prowess. Rumor had it attractive girls were recruited as cheerleaders, too. It was the kind of school Allison imagined her own parents would have sent her to if they lived there rather than their small hometown with its single school district.

The girls on Daria's squad were notorious snobs with a biting ferocity that showed up in their precise, crisp routines. For someone who came from a small, remote town, they were Cheerleading Royalty – awe inspiring and not a little intimidating. That's why, when Allison was brushing her teeth one evening in the dormitory bathroom, it took her by surprise when Daria Grey, head cheerleader, said hi.

For the rest of the week, they continued to bump into each other like that. At some point Allison had lost track of which meetings were true accidents and which were premeditated meet-ups. 9:27pm: that's when they brushed their teeth each night. 9:29pm: that's when Daria kissed her. It was some time before Allison could taste mint without thinking of Daria's lips.

At the end of camp they hadn't exchanged phone numbers, and the Internet wasn't quite a thing yet in her hometown – dial-up modems and other prehistoric infrastructure had delayed the technology. But they'd exchanged postal addresses. There was never any thought that one day they'd visit each other; Detroit was at least a

7-hour drive and Allison's parents would have never allowed it. The only time she'd been to the city had been for a church conference.

The letters were good enough though. The letters were safe. At the time, she'd felt a little like John-Paul Sartre and Simone de Beauvoir. Daria's letters contained all the romance and intensity high school boys seemed to lack. She had found in Daria a confident, someone who understood the pressure of being perfect because she lived that life herself. She wrote about more than just her daily life. She wrote about her dreams and her plans for the future, to get away from Michigan and her parents. She wrote about all the things Allison wished she was brave enough to do. It was kind of like writing in a journal that wrote you back.

It had been a safe place to explore her emotions as well. Being gay wasn't an option – not in her family, not in her hometown. The letters had been the one place where she could be herself without judgment. She should have been more careful. She should have destroyed the letters after reading them. But she'd never imagined her father would look in the shoebox under her bed. Maybe a piece of her wanted to get caught thought. Like with Reagan in the corn maze. Maybe a part of her just wanted someone to notice that she, Allison Hoge, was tired of doing what was expected of her.

+++++

CHAPTER EIGHTEEN

"Stop looking at me, creep," Allison said playfully.

"Then stop being so pretty all the time," Reagan complained. "I'm an artist. I can't help but be drawn to beauty."

Trying to prove that they could in fact be just friends, Allison had come to visit Reagan for the weekend. They'd spent the majority of that morning walking around and just exploring. Now they were doing homework in Reagan's dorm room. Allison sat on the bed while Reagan lounged on the floor. Reagan tried to focus on her Modern Art textbook, but she kept staring at the fine bones of Allison's ankles instead.

"I've been to the Museum of Modern Art before," Allison said. "I hope I'm not one of those contemporary art pieces."

Reagan looked horrified. "Don't speak ill of MOMA. That's blasphemy. Besides, there's nothing contemporary about you – you're an old soul."

Allison smirked. "I'll take that as a compliment."

"You should. You're like a classic piece of art."

"So now you're calling me fat?"

Reagan shook her head as if to rattle her brain. "How did you just turn my compliment into me calling you fat?"

"I've seen the women in those classic art pieces," Allison said with an upturned nose. "Venus de Milo, Botticelli's *The Birth of Venus*, Aphrodite of Cnidus – all those women were fat."

"You're ridiculous," Reagan protested. "They aren't fat; they're beautiful. Also, they're all the same woman – the Goddess of Love."

Allison smirked. "Well I can believe the Goddess part, but that still doesn't give you permission to call me fat."

Reagan jumped on the bed and pounced on Allison. Even though she knew Allison was teasing, she was still losing patience. The two girls squealed and giggled as hands and fingers gripped sides and wiggled against the nooks and crevices of exposed body parts.

They wrestled on the bed, rolling on top of each other, each trying to gain the upper hand. Allison was taller and stronger though, and she successfully managed to pin Reagan beneath her. She held Reagan's hands above her head and pressed her wrists into the pillow. Her pale skin was flushed and she was breathing a little heavy. Blonde hair fell across her forehead; Reagan didn't think she'd ever seen her look so pretty.

"Have you gotten in contact with Daria?" The question had been nagging at Reagan's sanity from the moment Allison had arrived at her dorm Friday night. Until that point, however, she'd been able to shove it from her mind and just focus on having fun and being a good hostess.

The teasing smile vanished from Allison's face. Her hold loosened on Reagan's wrists and she pulled away. "Yes. I emailed her."

Reagan felt her stomach drop. "And?" She hoped her voice sounded normal. She could hear Allison's heavy sigh and could almost picture the annoyance on her face as she rubbed at the bridge of her nose.

"I told her I was going to be in New York this weekend, and she wants to meet up for coffee," Allison said. "I'm not going to do it though," she added before Reagan could interrupt with the predictable question.

"Why not?"

"Why not?" Allison echoed. "Why would I? I'm here to spend time with *you*, not Daria. Besides, I don't even know this girl. I haven't had contact with her in *years*."

"You hadn't had contact with me for years either," Reagan pointed out.

"Yeah, but that's different," Allison argued. "We'd known each other all our lives. I don't know this girl at all."

"But you could get to know her again."

"Why is this so important to you?" Allison demanded shrilly.

201

"I just don't think you should walk away from this opportunity," Reagan explained, not backing down.

"Like I walked away from you?" Allison shot back.

Reagan teetered. "You said it yourself; we're different."

"If I can't do a relationship with you, I can't do it with Daria either." Allison was getting annoyed.

"I never said you had to hop into bed with her, Allie," Reagan scoffed. "But you should at least have coffee. You're not the least bit curious?"

"No."

"You're a terrible liar. It's one of your better qualities."

"Fine," Allison huffed. She threw her hands up in frustration. "If it's so important to you, I'll have coffee with her." She paused, thoughtful. "How do you do that?"

"Do what?"

"Get me to do whatever you want."

"Well, not *everything*," Reagan said, pouting.

Allison gave her a warning look.

Reagan shrugged. "I've got lots of practice with my dad," she explained. "Plus, you're kind of a pushover."

"I am not," Allison denied. "I just have good manners. Manners are important."

"You hardly felt the need to be polite in high school."

"Well, you're not as annoying anymore."

Reagan laughed. "So when's the big date? Call her right now. Make it happen."

"It's not a date," Allison scowled. "It's just coffee." She pulled out her phone and sent a quick text message to see if Daria was free to meet. They had exchanged phone numbers over email, but she had yet to call or text her. She put her phone out of sight, half-hoping the text would go ignored.

"What are you going to wear?"

Allison shrugged. "Does it matter?"

"This cannot happen."

"What?"

Reagan looked suitably offended. "I did not go through all the work of tracking this girl down for you to blow her off."

"One, I hardly call messaging Daria on Facebook 'hard work,' and two, how am I blowing her off?"

"Allison Hoge doesn't do things half-assed," Reagan said. She rose from the bed and grabbed a jacket and her purse. "You need a carefully planned outfit for this, not something you shoved in your suitcase as an afterthought. We're going shopping."

Allison raised an eyebrow. "Oh we are, are we?"

"And without Rodger Hoge's credit card, too," Reagan added.

Allison looked amused. "I suppose it would be inappropriate to use his money for a date with a girl. Might serve the old bastard right though."

Reagan bristled. Hearing Allison call it a date stung more than she had expected. It was okay for her to refer to it as such, but not Allison. "Kind of like when you used it to get me alone in a hotel room so you could take advantage of me."

Allison's jaw went lax. "I did no such thing."

Reagan shrugged it off. "I didn't say I minded."

+++++

The subway car rattled from side to side as it rushed down the track. Allison tightened her grip on the metal pole and tried to keep from knocking into the other passengers. She shouldered her bag a little tighter to her body.

"Are you nervous?" Reagan's voice carried over the roar of the train.

Allison nodded and blew some errant strands of hair out of her face. Her hair was starting to grow longer, but still not long enough to pull it back away from her face. She needed to have it cut, but there never seemed to be time. "A little. I still can't believe she wants to see me after all this time. I can't believe she even remembers who I am."

"You're Allison Hoge. You're kind of hard to forget."

Allison shook her head and looked out the subway window. There wasn't much to look at because they were underground. White tiles and an occasional streak of color rushed by. She didn't understand Reagan's attitude. It felt like she was determined to throw Daria at her – like Reagan was already moving on and that Allison going out with someone else didn't bother her. But other times, especially when she said things like that, she second-guessed Reagan's nonchalance about her reuniting with Daria. Everything she had said that day seemed to have a double meaning.

"Have you two talked much since you first emailed her?"

"Not much, no. End of the semester is always pretty busy though. Finishing up my senior project. Graduation," Allison ticked off. "Figuring out what I'm going to do in the Fall."

Reagan nodded and said no more. She wanted to press Allison with more questions about Daria, but she didn't want to come across as too nosy or jealous. She wondered what Allison would do or say when she saw Daria again after all these years. Would they hug? Kiss? Shake hands? She wondered what they'd talk about. Normal catching-up topics she assumed, but she wondered how long it would take until the conversation inevitably turned to a recounting of their year of letters.

She wondered if Daria had kept Allison's letters. She wondered if she'd bring some to their date so they could re-read them together and bask in their good-fortune to have been reunited. Reagan shut her eyes tight. She had to stop obsessing over this. It wasn't healthy. She exhaled deeply, opened her eyes, and looked at the directional map. She knew where they were and how many stops remained until they reached their destination, but she needed something to look at that wasn't Allison.

When they reached their stop, Reagan reflexively reached for Allison's hand to usher her off the train. It felt so natural just to reach for her. When their fingers touched, Allison looked away from her window and down at their hands. Reagan pulled her hand back.

"This is our stop."

Allison nodded once and followed her off the train.

+++++

"Why aren't you more into this?"

Allison ran her hand over a stack of carefully folded sweaters. She picked up a shirt, but set it back down without really looking at it. "I'm not really into clothes shopping."

Reagan held up a shirt for inspection. "Are you sure you have X-chromosomes?"

Allison pulled a pencil skirt from a rack and held it up to her waist. "It was nice in high school when I didn't have to pick out outfits everyday," she said. "I miss that cheerleading uniform sometimes. I never had to worry about what to wear to school."

"I miss your cheerleading outfit, too." She hadn't seen Allison in a short skirt since her cheerleading days. Legs and an ass like that should never hide behind clothes, but she would have preferred if Allison wore snow pants when she met up with Daria later.

Allison's lips twisted into a wry smirk. She pulled a dress from a rack and held it in front of her. "I guess I'll go try some things on."

Reagan nodded distractedly. She flipped through a rack of short skirts as Allison walked toward the fitting rooms. She would have invited herself along to watch Allison strip in and out of each outfit, but with her dressing for the purpose of going out on a date with someone else, it felt inappropriate. She shook her head. *Date.* That word really upset her. She and Allison had never gone on a date. They'd spent plenty of time together, but Allison had never called them dates. They'd had sex, but they'd never gone on a date.

"Hey, are you okay?"

Reagan looked up from the clothes rack. Allison had reappeared from the fitting rooms in record time. "I'm fine."

Allison cocked her head to the side. "Rea, are you crying?"

Reagan inhaled through her nose and it rattled. "Crying?" She wiped at her eyes. "What? No. Just allergies or something."

"Oh. Okay." Allison looked unconvinced, but she didn't press the issue. "What do you think of this outfit? I think I like the skirt, but I'm not sure."

Reagan wiped at her eyes again. "Turn around for me."

Allison twirled and the knee-length skirt attractively billowed.

"I like it to," Reagan confirmed. "Where are you meeting Daria?"

"Some coffee shop in Manhattan," Allison said, shrugging. "It's not a big deal."

Reagan pressed her lips together to keep from saying or asking more. She felt petty and jealous, and she hated it. She knew it was her own fault for tracking down this girl. It had been her idea, not Allison's. But she couldn't help the way she felt.

Allison ran her palms down the front pleats of the bell-shaped skirt that she wore paired with a short-sleeved cardigan, blouse, and skinny belt. She didn't want to look like she was trying too hard, but she didn't want to look too casual either. Reagan was right about her – Allison Hoge didn't do anything half-assed. "How do I look?"

Reagan couldn't hold back her honest appraisal. "Enchanting."

Allison ducked her head. "Thanks. If you like this outfit, I should probably pay for it and go. I'm supposed to meet up with Daria soon."

Reagan nodded numbly. "Right. Don't want to make her wait."

After paying for her purchases, Allison hesitated by the shop door. "Are you sure you're okay with me leaving?" She was planning on leaving straight from the store to meet up with Daria for coffee. She wore the new outfit she'd purchased and her old clothes were in the shopping bag.

"Yeah. Don't worry about me; I'll be fine. I'm just going to head back to campus."

Allison smiled mildly. "Thank you again for everything, Rea." She kissed the tips of her fingers and pressed them against Reagan's lips. "I'll call you afterwards."

Reagan watched Allison walk out of the boutique and into the sun. The door had just barely closed behind her, signaling Allison's departure, when hot tears began to roll down her cheeks.

+++++

Ashley bounded into the room and tossed her backpack on her bed. "Heya, Prez. What's up?"

Reagan lay on her bed, staring up at the ceiling. "Hey," she replied back, her voice devoid of emotion.

Ashley flopped down on the bed beside her. "Why so glum? Did you and Allison not have a good visit?"

Reagan rubbed at her eyes. "It was fine."

"I recognize that look," Ashley frowned. "You're still pining over her, and she's still sticking to that lame story about not being gay."

"Something like that," Reagan sighed. She continued staring at the ceiling. "I did something, Ash, and I'm not sure if it was the right thing to do or not."

"Oh…vague comments…you certainly know how to tell a captivating story, Prez."

"It has to do with Allison."

Ashley made a snorting sound. "Obviously. It's *always* about Allison."

Reagan rolled onto her stomach. "Be nice."

"This *is* me being nice," Ashley protested. "I'm just concerned about you. If this girl doesn't realize what a great catch you are, then she's crazy."

"That's very kind of you. Unnecessary," Reagan sighed, rubbing at her face, "but kind."

"I'm just keeping you buttered up so you'll room with me after college," Ashley winked. When Reagan remained silent and melancholy, she continued. "Seriously, Prez. You know you can talk to me about this stuff. I'm not gonna judge. Okay, so I probably *will* judge," she self-corrected, "but I'm not going to throw it in your face. I find that talking about stuff helps me process better."

"I found that girl – Daria Grey. And I gave Allison her email address. And now they're on a date someplace in Manhattan."

"You did what?" Ashley squawked.

Reagan shrugged. "It's no big deal."

"So let me get this straight – pardon the word," Ashley quipped. "You're falling in love with Allison, so you helped her reconnect with her old girlfriend."

Reagan stiffened at the label. "Just a girl she knew in high school."

"Whom she had a mad affair via romantic letters with for nearly a year," Ashley pointed out.

Tears sprung to Reagan's eyes again. "God, I'm an idiot."

Ashley shook her head. "You certainly are a piece of work, Reagan Murphy. Grab your jacket."

"What? Why?"

"You're done moping around, and you're done blasting the saddest love songs ever written. Get out of bed because we're tracking Allison down and knocking some sense into her."

"You're ridiculous." Reagan grabbed a pillow and hugged it to her chest.

Ashley wrestled the pillow away and threw it across the room. "And you're a coward."

"I am not," Reagan whined. "I tried." Why couldn't Ashley just leave her alone? All she wanted to do was listen to sad music and eat her emotions. She wished she wasn't vegan. All she wanted was a package of double-stuffed Oreos.

"Try harder."

"It's not that easy."

"Nothing worth it ever is."

Reagan released a long, tortured sigh. "Even if I wanted to," she started cautiously, "how would I find them? Allison said they were meeting for coffee, but there's got to be at least a thousand coffee places on this island. And what if they're not even having coffee anymore?" She felt a panic attack rising in her chest. "What if things went so well they decided to have dinner together? Or maybe they just skipped food altogether and got a hotel room!"

"Give me your phone," Ashley ordered.

Reagan hesitated. Letting anyone hold her phone felt a little like letting them read her diary. Reluctantly, she handed it over.

"Your anti-establishment honey is off the grid, right?" Ashley said, rifling through the contents of Reagan's phone in a way that made her feel violated.

"I guess so," Reagan shrugged, not sure what that had to do with anything. "She doesn't do social networking and loathes text messaging."

"But I bet that chick you threw at her is human like the rest of us." Ashley beamed victoriously and tossed the phone back at Reagan.

Not being naturally athletic, Reagan bobbled the phone like a hot potato before she could look at the screen. She read the status update out loud: "Having coffee with an old friend; Daria Grey checked in at the Manhattan Starbucks on Broadway."

"I can't believe you Friended her," Ashley chucked. "She's the enemy, Prez."

Reagan frowned. "I had to. Her profile was private and I was curious."

Not wasting any more time, Ashley threw a jacket in Reagan's direction, nearly smacking her in the face. "Hustle up. We're gonna get your girl."

+++++

Reagan wished she knew how to read lips. She also wished that Daria Grey's profile picture had been prettier than she actually was in person. Unfortunately Reagan was not a lip-reader. And unfortunately, Daria Grey was stunning.

Reagan had hoped that Daria Grey was Catfish-ing her or that she'd gotten fat after high school. But she couldn't deny that the woman sitting across the table from Allison was strikingly beautiful. She had the kind of clean-cut, girl-next-door look about her common in the Midwest. Her dark brown hair was almost black and fell in carefully tamed waves around her face, falling just below her shoulder blades. Her skin had a reddish, bronzed hue as though she spent a lot of time in the sun, but it was natural looking, not fake-baked or sprayed on. If Reagan had to place the girl's ethnicity, she'd probably guess American Indian. Allison was having coffee with the live incarnation of Pocahontas. How was she supposed to compete with a Disney Princess?

When Daria stood to get a refill, she walked with the practiced grace of a classical dancer. She wore skinny jeans and an off-the-shoulder sweater belted at the waist that emphasized her slender waistline and gently curving hips. Her nose was small and proportionate to the rest of her face. Her lips were tinted a muted shade of red. They weren't bee-stung or the kind Hollywood actresses pine for, but they were generous and seemed to fall naturally into a warm, pleasant smile.

Her eyes were what really struck Reagan, however. Even with the distance between them, Reagan could see how remarkable they were. The large, dark, and slightly almond-shaped eyes made Daria look surprised all the time until they crinkled at the corners when she smiled. And she was doing a lot of smiling. It didn't surprise her though; Allison was the queen of charm.

Reagan leaned close to the plate glass window of the Manhattan Starbucks. "I can't go in there." Her breath fogged a small circle on the glass.

"Why the hell not?" Ashley demanded. "We came all this way, *and* I used my super sleuthing skills. Don't let that be in vain."

"But I'm the one who threw them together!" Reagan hissed. She watched Daria reach across the table and place her hand on top of Allison's. Her stomach dropped and she turned away from the window, not willing to put herself through more torture. "This is wrong," she choked out. "We shouldn't be here."

Ashley continued to unabashedly peer through the window. Her face was practically pressed against the glass surface. "You're not the least bit curious?"

"Of course I am," Reagan admitted. "That's why I did the Facebook thing." She leaned against the window and folded her arms across her chest. "But that doesn't mean we should be here."

New Yorkers dodged around her and Ashley, shooting annoyed looks their way for occupying so much sidewalk space. Normally Reagan would be ducking out of the way and profusely apologizing for taking up so much space, but she was too upset to care. It was the Upper East Side on a Saturday. Why were people in such a rush anyway?

"Besides," she sniffled, hugging her arms around her tighter, "Allison's made it clear that she doesn't want to date me. Not now. Not ever."

Ashley turned away from the window and regarded her friend. "Well then, Allison's an idiot."

Reagan's face crumpled and her shoulders slumped forward in defeat. "What's wrong with me, Ash?" she cried. "Why doesn't she want me?"

"Oh, sweetie." Ashley wrapped her arm around Reagan's shaking shoulders. "C'mon," she hushed in her ear. "Let's go get you good and drunk."

+++++

CHAPTER NINETEEN

Reagan and Ashley stumbled into their dormitory room, both giggling in fits. Manhattan had a lot of coffee shops, but it had even more bars. They both halted just inside the threshold when they saw the figure seated on Reagan's bed.

"Allison?"

The woman in question looked up from her hands. "Hi," she said, almost shyly.

Ashley hovered by the door. She looked back and forth between Allison and her roommate. Their eyes were locked on each other. "I just forgot I have…a thing…a place to be," she mumbled. Neither Reagan nor Allison seemed to be paying attention to her, so she slinked back out of the door unnoticed.

Reagan straightened, immediately sobering. "How did you get in here?"

The corner of Allison's mouth twitched. "The girl working the front desk recognized me and let me in. I'm sure she was breaking a dozen rules."

"You could get away with murder with that smile," Reagan mumbled.

"What?"

Reagan sucked in a deep breath. "How was Daria?"

Allison visibly sat up straighter on the bed. "I, uh, she's fine." She smiled softly and her eyes seemed to lose their focus. "She's just like I remembered her, actually. We talked as though almost no time had passed."

The words falling out of Allison's mouth seemed to blur together for Reagan. Her brain screamed at her: *Why is she here? Why does she insist on torturing me? Why won't she just kiss me?*

"You are the most infuriating person I've ever met." The words were out of Reagan's mouth before she could stop herself.

"If this is your version of being charming," Allison deadpanned, "then you suck at it."

Reagan threw her hands up in frustration and made a disgruntled noise. "See? This is what I'm talking about. I can't even finish a thought without you interrupting me."

Allison laughed. "Fine, I'm sorry. I'm listening. I won't interrupt again," she promised with a sweet smile.

"Seeing you with Daria today—"

"Wait," Allison interrupted again despite her promise. "When did you see me with Daria?"

Reagan grimaced, realizing her slip. "Ashley and I kind of tracked you down."

Allison's hazel eyes widened. "Reagan!"

"I know! I'm crazy!" Reagan bellowed. "And seeing you with Daria made me sick to my stomach."

"Why did you do that?"

"I had to know." Reagan worried her bottom lip. "And I know I'm the one who reconnected you two and that you never would have tracked her down on your own if I hadn't meddled, but I'm actually glad I did. Seeing Daria may have rekindled whatever you had with her, but it also forced me to realize something that might not have come without that push."

She paused long enough to take a deep breath. "I think I'm in love with you, Allison." She stopped and shook herself. "No. I *know* I'm in love with you. And it's impossible to think about how it even happened because of our past. I always have a plan, but loving you is not something I ever planned. Being your friend, yes. But not falling in love with you." It felt like the floodgates had been opened. She'd kept her emotions in check and her heart contained, but now that she'd begun to open up and be honest, she couldn't stop. "And now that I realize what this feeling is – that this perpetual knot in the pit of my stomach when you're around isn't indigestion or bad Indian curry – I don't know what to do. I don't know if it's too late, but I do know that I love you. I love you," she said again, as much as for herself as for Allison's benefit. "It's always been you."

Reagan took another deep breath and filled her lungs with much needed oxygen. She fell silent and warily eyeballed Allison. True to her word, she hadn't interrupted again. But now that Reagan had finished her speech, Allison continued to remain silent.

Worst of all, Reagan couldn't read the expression on her face. Allison had a singular talent for wiping all emotion from her features. No poker player herself, the lack of reaction terrified Reagan. "Please say something," she managed to croak out.

Allison pursed her lips. "Are you finished talking?" she calmly asked.

"Yes." Reagan tried to match the evenness of Allison's tenor, but failed. The one-syllable response got stuck in her throat instead and came out terribly garbled.

Allison ran her hands down the length of her skirt, smoothing down the material. "Well then," she started serenely.

Reagan tensed, expecting the worst.

Allison quietly cleared her throat. "I'd have to say...I agree."

"What kind of response is that?" Reagan squawked.

The corners of Allison's lips curled up to form a Cheshire-sized grin. "An infuriating one."

Allison stood from the bed and crossed the room until she was standing directly in front of Reagan. Reagan seemed to sway until Allison rested her palms on her shoulders. Hazel eyes stared down into bright blue eyes.

"I want to thank you for helping Daria and I reconnect," Allison started. "Seeing her again made me realize that I've been pretending to be someone I'm not for a very long time."

"Uh, you're welcome?"

Allison laughed and shook her head. It sounded like the delicate tinkling of bells. "Seeing Daria made me realize something else. Something infinitely more important." She brushed a few loose strands of hair out of Reagan's face.

Reagan couldn't help the whimper that fell out between parted lips.

"Daria was just as I remembered her. But *I'm* not that same girl anymore. I'm a different Allison Hoge. And this new version of Allison Hoge, the woman who's standing in front of you," she said, lightly brushing her thumb along Reagan's right cheekbone, "is falling in love with Reagan Murphy." She smiled softly. "No, I take that back. I *am* in love with you."

Reagan blinked once.

Allison quirked an eyebrow. "Now it's your turn to say something, Murphy."

Reagan could count the moments in her life where she'd been rendered speechless on one hand. And this was one of those moments. So instead of scrambling for something eloquent to say to Allison, she kissed her instead.

+++++

EPILOGUE

Allison Hoge removed her reading glasses and rubbed at the bridge of her nose. She kept telling herself that if grad school was supposed to be easy, more people would have their PhD. But that didn't make the stack of books she needed to read and master before the end of the semester any less formidable.

She blew out a long sigh and looked at the wall clock nearest her. It was nearly 10pm on a Friday night, and she was cooped up in the stacks of the university library. She was close to finishing her minor field selections on contemporary tragedy literature, and had promised herself that as long as she completed her reading by the end of the week, she'd actually allow herself to have guilt-free fun with Reagan over the weekend.

They hadn't made any concrete plans, knowing the chance of her needing to read over the weekend was still high. She hated disappointing her girlfriend, so when self-appointed deadlines like this loomed, she felt it better to surprise Reagan with free time rather than unnecessarily get her hopes up.

Shortly after graduating from Brown, Allison had moved to New York City, where she'd been accepted into the graduate program in English at Columbia University. Reagan had graduated from NYU and was currently not making any money at a small art gallery. She thought she might go back to school for a degree in art restoration, but for now she was satisfied getting experience assisting at the contemporary gallery.

They'd recently moved into an apartment together in Brooklyn; at the time, Allison hadn't been convinced they were ready to take the big step of living together, but it was economically smart. She was making a small stipend through her grad program teaching English 101 to snot-nosed Freshman and Reagan wasn't making much at her own job, but she was proud that she hadn't used Rodger Hoge's credit card since relocating to New York. In fact, she hadn't talked much at all with her parents, especially her dad, upon moving to New York.

She sighed again. She'd have to do something about that soon.

"Uh oh," came a familiar voice. "That doesn't sound good."

Allison looked up from the page she'd been reading and re-reading for the past 15 minutes without success.

"Rea? What are you doing here?"

Reagan beamed at her studious girlfriend and marveled at how she managed to look uncommonly sexy even in a worn Brown sweatshirt and jeans. Her hair was hastily pulled back away from her face and she wore her rectangular black frames rather than her usual contacts.

"I love it when you look like a librarian."

"And I love it when you wear skirts," Allison countered. "I never realized how much I missed these skirts." Her nostrils flared as she raked her hazel eyes down Reagan's figure. She must have come straight from work; she wore a sinfully short, pleated skirt paired with an Oxford shirt under a v-neck sweater.

"Missed my skirts or missed my *legs*?" Reagan playfully teased.

Allison licked her lips. "Maybe a little bit of both," she admitted, unabashedly still staring at Reagan's legs.

Reagan bit her bottom lip. "Are you sure you have to keep studying?" she slightly pouted.

Allison hesitated. "I-I guess I could take a quick study break."

A grin broke over Reagan's face.

Allison stood up. "Sit on the edge of the table."

Reagan quirked an eyebrow in confusion, which was met by one of Allison's in challenge. She complied and sat on the table edge. The wood felt cool against the back of her legs.

Allison positioned herself between Reagan's parted thighs. Reagan looked anxiously around the space, worried that someone might see them.

"You'll have to be quiet," Allison husked into her girlfriend's ear. Her breath tickled against Reagan's earlobe. "I know how you like to be *loud* though." Her fingers traced along the sensitive inner flesh of Reagan's naked thighs. When she reached the edge of lacy underwear, she toyed with the hem, threatening to dip beneath the material. "So maybe I shouldn't do this."

Reagan whimpered and clung to the front of Allison's oversized sweatshirt. "Please."

Allison slowly wet her lips. She brought her palm in full contact with Reagan's mound, cupping her girlfriend's panty-covered pussy. Reagan's eyes snapped shut and a shuddered breath stumbled out of her mouth. Allison, her hand still firmly lodged between parted thighs, began to grind her heel in a small circle, manipulating Reagan's clit.

Reagan bit down hard on her full, lower lip to keep another whimper at bay. Allison released the delicious pressure on her clit, only to transfer her attention elsewhere. She pressed two firm fingers against Reagan's entrance.

Reagan shifted on the study table and spread her legs further apart. She knew the length of her skirt, along with Allison's body, would shield her most intimate parts from any casual observers, but anyone who stared at them for too long would certainly know what they were up to.

Allison ducked her head and captured Reagan's full bottom lip with her mouth. She sucked her lower lip into her mouth and lightly bit down. Her free hand cupped Reagan's left breast over the material of her sweater. She gently squeezed, feeling all the more like a teenager, feeling up her girlfriend over the confines of her top and bra.

Needing to feel more, she slid her hand under the bottom hem of Reagan's shirt and beneath the confining underwire cup of her bra. Reagan quietly sighed when Allison's hand made contact with her firm flesh. Allison palmed the fullness of Reagan's pert breast in her hand and felt her sensitive nipple immediately respond. She pulled back just a little in order to pinch the fleshy nub between her thumb and forefinger. She knew from experience how sensitive Reagan's nipples were and she fully intended to tease her and test how quiet she could remain when she had to.

She flicked Reagan's nipple back and forth with the tip of her finger, forcing it to harden, but then she abruptly yanked her hand out from beneath Reagan's top. The brunette gave her a pained, questioning look that immediately glazed over when Allison's tongue darted out and licked at the tips of two fingers. Her hand was back beneath Reagan's top before any other thoughts could filter their way to her brain. Wet fingers met sensitive skin, causing Reagan to squirm even more on the wooden library table.

Allison yanked the crotch of Reagan's underwear to the side and immediately slid one firm, long, feminine finger inside of her girlfriend. Reagan gasped at the sudden intrusion as Allison bottomed out on the first stroke. Allison pulled all the way out and then shoved back into her partner. Reagan's breath hitched on the down stroke. But just as she thought Allison was going to continue fucking her to oblivion, her girlfriend's finger was suddenly gone, leaving Reagan's pussy aroused, yet empty.

Allison collected some of Reagan's arousal on her fingers and spread the wetness to the rest of her sex. She slid her fingers along the outside of Reagan's shaved pussy lips, dipping between the folds every now and again to gather more juices. She paused long enough to give Reagan's clit a few firm swirls.

Allison wrapped her arm around Reagan's waist. She pressed her hand in the small of her back and pulled her closer, forcing Reagan deeper onto her fingers. The table made a squeaking noise of protest from the movement. Reagan's eyes were squeezed shut and her breath sounded erratic.

Allison moved the crotch material even further to the side. Reagan could swear she heard a slight tearing noise, but she was too far gone to care, particularly when Allison used the extra room to pinch at her clit.

Her eyes snapped open when she heard Allison's voice, low and raspy in her ear: "I wish you were on the table, on your hands and knees. I'd slowly pull your underwear down to your knees, keeping it there so you could only spread apart your legs so far. I'd have your thighs apart as far as they could go, straining the limits of your underwear." She paused and licked her lips. "Then I'd lick you from behind. Your back would arch when my tongue hit your pussy lips. You'd be so wet and ready for me. I'd grab onto your ass and pull your pussy into my face so I could fuck you properly with my tongue."

Reagan's nails bit into Allison's forearm, leaving little red half-moons in their wake. Her legs thrashed and she choked back a particularly desperate whine. Who knew you could have so much fun in a library?

As Reagan rearranged her undergarments and smoothed out the fixed the pleats on her skirt, Allison couldn't meet her eyes. "I-I'm sorry if that was too much," she stammered. She looked down at her hands. She could see Reagan's arousal drying between her fingers. "I don't know what happened."

Reagan placed a hand on her girlfriend's shoulder. "You have nothing to apologize for, Allie. That was *amazing*."

Allison finally looked up and searched Reagan's face. "Are you sure you liked it?" Her voice was heavy with trepidation.

"God," Reagan lowly moaned. Her eyes rolled back. "Those things you said to me…"

Allison felt her cheeks flush. "That's unlike me. I'm sorry."

"No, baby. It was so *hot*. You made me feel incredible." Reagan paused and licked her lips. "Would you like that kind of thing?"

"Hmm?"

"You know. Take me from behind? Dominate me?"

Allison cleared her throat. "I don't know. Maybe?" Her normally confident voice cracked on the final syllables, giving her away.

Reagan couldn't help the grin on her face. Allison's embarrassment and hesitance was endearing and so unlike her. "Well, I don't want to do anything that's going to make you uncomfortable, but just know that if the mood ever strikes again, and you want to Top me, know that I'm totally down."

Allison's jaw went lax. She nodded dumbly, unable to find her voice.

Reagan gave her girlfriend one final, lingering kiss. "Don't stay away too long, okay?" she smiled playfully. "I've still got a scratch that could use your expert touch."

Allison watched her girlfriend walk away, hips and backside exaggeratingly swishing from one side to the next just for her. When Reagan was out of sight, Allison sat back down and stared at the page of the book open in front of her. She shook her head. None of the words made any sense to her. They seemed to move around on the page and reshape themselves into the curved hips of her girlfriend and the soft swell of breasts that resided beneath her sweater.

She resignedly sighed and snapped the book shut. There was no way she was going to get any more studying done tonight while distracted by the promise of what and who waited for her when she got home. She stood up and started to gather her things from the study table. Her initial response was annoyance that she hadn't completed her self-imposed deadline, but that soon melted away to be replaced with a smile. She was going home to Reagan, and that wasn't a tragedy at all.

+++++

ABOUT THE AUTHOR

Eliza Lentzski is the author of lesbian fiction, romance, and erotica novels including *Date Night, Diary of a Human, Love, Lust and Other Mistakes,* as well as the forthcoming *Winter Jacket* (May 2013). Although a historian by day, Eliza has a passion for fiction. She calls the Midwest home along with her partner and their cat and turtle.

Follow her on Twitter, @ElizaLentzski, for updates and exclusive previews of future original releases.

Printed in Great Britain
by Amazon.co.uk, Ltd.,
Marston Gate.